MEANT TO BE

A DIRTY LOVE NOVEL

R.L. KENDERSON

For Kierra

PROLOGUE

Piper Stevens watched the casket being lowered into the ground and felt her legs begin to crumble beneath her. "I can't do this," she whispered as she started to hyperventilate.

"Piper," her mother said, her voice laced with concern. She grabbed on to Piper's hand to keep her from falling, but it didn't do much to help. Her mother was tiny compared to her daughter, and Piper feared she was going to collapse to the ground. She wasn't supposed to be a widow at twenty-eight years old.

A strong arm wrapped around her waist and pulled her close to his side. Piper breathed in the familiarity of Nate Hall's masculine scent, and she took comfort in it. She didn't know what she would do without him. Since her husband's accident and death, Nate had been the rock that Piper relied on.

As a Minnesota transplant, she'd moved to the area when her now-late husband, Jordan, got a job with the help and recommendation of his college friend, Nate, four months earlier. Jordan had been out of work for a few months, and they had barely been making ends meet, so Jordan had reached out to friends and old colleagues. When Nate had called with a job opportunity, Jordan had jumped at the chance. Two months later, she had moved to the Minneapolis-St. Paul area with Jordan.

As Jordan and she'd had no family or friends in the area, Nate had been the only one they knew. Nate had become one of Jordan's best friends and even one of hers. Especially now. She couldn't imagine life without him.

As the pastor prayed over Jordan's grave, Piper buried her face in Nate's chest and cried. He didn't seem to care that she was probably getting him wet with her tears and covering his suit with snot. He just held her tighter and let her bawl.

Piper heard the pastor finish, and she found the courage to look over once again at the place where her husband would reside forever.

Good-bye, my love. I will miss you always.

She had loved—still loved—Jordan with all her heart, and no one—*no one*—would ever take his place.

CHAPTER ONE

ONE YEAR LATER

Piper closed the lid of her laptop and rubbed her temples. The pounding in her head matched the pounding of the hammer outside. She reached for the bottle of ibuprofen that had taken up permanent residence on her desk and shook out four tablets.

After Jordan's death, she had thrown herself into her work, but lately, it hadn't been bringing the same fulfillment. She still loved her job. She was a women's advocate at a women's and children's abuse shelter, and she would always find satisfaction in helping women or children get away from their abusive spouses or parents.

But she had slowly begun to realize that it couldn't be her only source of happiness like it had been for the last thirteen months. She'd been exploring jobs for one of her clients today, despite it being Saturday, and even though she enjoyed doing research, a headache hadn't taken too long to make its appearance.

Piper heard shouting coming from her backyard and pushed her feet into the carpet so that her desk chair rolled back and she could look out the back window. She couldn't make out the words, but it was obvious that Nate was arguing with Luke about something. He shook his bald head along with the hammer in his hand, as if trying to make a point, and Piper found herself smiling. The two of them were both alphas and often butted heads about what should and what should not be done.

She scanned the backyard. The veranda was coming along somewhat slowly but nicely, and it would be done before fall. She was excited to see the conclusion, but it also brought a deep longing to the surface.

Jordan should have been the one outside, working with Nate. It had been Jordan's idea in the first place. When they had purchased the house, everything had been perfect, except for the backyard. Jordan had promised her he was going to make it the best yard on the block for their future children, and all the neighborhood kids would want to come over to their house to play.

They'd moved into their home in January, and it had been too cold to start a big project. But, four months later, Jordan was dead, the supplies he had purchased to start on the project a reminder that he was gone.

They'd sat in the garage for almost a year when Piper decided they needed to go. When she'd asked Nate if he wanted any of it, he had proposed to finish what Jordan had barely started. She'd tried to tell him not to bother. After all, there wouldn't be any children to play back there now, but Nate had insisted.

She didn't know what had transpired between Nate and Jordan while they sat in the wrecked car, waiting for the first responders to show before Jordan passed, but she suspected that her late husband had made Nate promise to take care of her.

Nate was always available when she needed him. He'd fixed her broken sink and helped her winterize her car and other things like that. She honestly didn't know what she'd do without him. In a way, he'd become her new husband—if you could count someone who lived in a different house and slept with other women while you were abstinent your husband. So, he might not have become her replacement spouse, but he had definitely become her best friend.

He'd been there for her as no one else had when Jordan passed. Not just fixing stuff but letting her literally cry on his shoulder. She knew he was a womanizer and a commitment-phobe, but to her, he was simply Nate.

Piper continued to watch the two men outside as their argument heated up. One might be worried they would hurt each other, but even though they were trying to act tough, both of them were smiling. Nate swiped his shirt off over his head, and Luke did the same. They looked like they were getting ready to brawl.

Both men were tall and nicely built. Very nicely built. Luke Long was half-Asian and already had a tan that she wouldn't get if she sunbathed every day of summer. His dark hair was wet with sweat, and she could almost see laughter gleaming in his brown eyes. But that wasn't the only thing gleaming on him. The sun shone off the ring he wore on the third finger of his left hand, telling all single women that this man was taken.

And Nate...well, Nate was pure sex on a stick. She might have been married when she met him, but she hadn't been blind. Nate was a mix of African American, Mexican, and Caucasian. He wasn't extremely dark, but his beautiful, bronzed skin definitely showed his mixed heritage. And thanks to his recessive genes, he had the lightest crystal-blue eyes that stood out from his tan complexion. He was just over six feet, and on his left arm, he sported a collection of tattoos. He kept his head clean-shaven, yet his face wore a sexy layer of stubble.

As a woman, she'd never understand why a man would shave one part of his head but not the other. She wasn't complaining though. It looked good on the man. And, if her libido hadn't died along with Jordan, she'd probably be drooling.

Actually, no *probably*. She would have been. Piper had always loved sex, and if she were single, she'd be hitting on Nate daily. But she was a widow with a dead sex drive and now only appreciated attractive men from a more objective point of view.

There was a knock at her front door just as Nate crouched down, put his shoulder into Luke's abdomen, and lifted the other man off the ground.

"Hello? Piper?"

"Back here," she called out to Elise Long, Luke's wife. "Hurry. You have to come see this."

Piper's office was directly off the dining room, so she had

a view straight through to the kitchen. She watched as Elise set down a couple of bags from the local fast food place and then scrambled in to join Piper at the window.

Elise's belly bumped against the window as she practically pressed her nose to the glass. "Oh my God, what are they doing?" she asked with a laugh.

Piper shrugged. "Fighting."

"Put me down, motherfucker," Luke shouted loud enough for the two women to hear.

"I swear, those two act like children when they're together," Elise said. "I think it's because they've known each other since they were kids. It's like part of them can't grow up."

Nate set Luke down. He wasn't rough, but he wasn't gentle either. He dropped Luke on his ass, but Luke must have been ready for Nate because, before Nate could straighten, Luke pulled him to the ground and put some sort of wrestling move on him.

Elise was still chuckling, but she sighed. "We'd better go out there."

"Were they like this when they fixed up your house?" Piper asked as the two of them went to the dining room and then out the sliding glass door.

She curled her lip. "Yes. I'm pretty sure it took months longer than it should have to finish. I'd complain, but they worked for free, and it's obvious they love fighting with each other. Who am I to deny them their fun?"

They stepped down from the deck.

When their feet hit the grass, Elise shouted out, "Food's here, boys."

Piper snickered at the other woman's use of the word *boys* when the two were obviously more than men.

Both guys froze at Elise's announcement and looked over at the women.

"Hi, honey." Luke grinned. He threw Nate's leg off of him and rolled up onto his knees. He was about to stand when Nate wrapped his arm around Luke's neck and pulled him back to the ground.

Elise made a sigh of annoyance, but she smiled. She approached the two men and raised her brow. "Nate?"

Nate looked up at Elise, smiling as he used his other hand to pull his arm around Luke tighter. "Hi, Elise. How can I help you?"

"Can you let go of my husband?"

"Yeah, asshole. Your dick is rubbing on my ass," Luke complained.

"No can do, sweetie," he said to Elise while he lifted his hips and brushed himself against Luke even more.

Piper put her hand over her mouth to stifle a laugh.

"Gross, dude," Luke shouted and tried to get away while simultaneously reaching back to punch his friend.

"That's what you get for calling me a pussy," Nate told Luke. He looked to Elise again. "I'll let him go when he learns his lesson."

Elise rolled her eyes. "Luke, will you please apologize to your friend before I give birth to our firstborn? I really don't want our child to grow up without a father."

Piper knew Elise was joking; the woman hadn't said anything that anybody else wouldn't say, and part of Piper did think it was funny. There was also a small portion of her, deep inside, that was stung by the words. Because, if she'd had a child, it would now be fatherless.

"Elise," Luke said, trying to pull Nate's arm off of him, "I can't let our child think I'm a total wuss."

Elise raised her brow again, this time without a smile, and she saw Luke's body relax as he stopped fighting.

"Fine," he muttered. "I'm sorry I called you a pussy..."

Nate immediately released Luke.

Luke jumped up and finished his sentence. "Loud enough for you to hear. Next time, I'll whisper it behind your back."

"Fucker," Nate said and made a swipe for Luke.

Luke took off and ran around to the front of the house, and Nate followed.

Elise turned and looked at Piper as she shrugged. "I give up. If they want cold food, that's their fault. Let's go eat."

Piper led the way back into her house and pulled the food out of the bags. She separated her order from the rest, and Elise did the same. The two pulled out the stools at the counter and sat.

"Would you be more comfortable at the table?" Piper asked her.

"Nah, I'm fine here," Elise said with a wave of her hand. "I have a while left before I'm really big." She tilted her head. "At least, I hope I do. I'm only twenty-two weeks."

Luke and Elise had been married for a few months, and Elise had told Piper that she was pregnant before they'd gotten married. Elise's father had cancer, and they had hoped to have at least one child before he passed away. Piper hadn't gone to their wedding because it was a small ceremony, and she hadn't known the couple that well yet.

Piper and Jordan had moved to the area in January the previous year, and when they had first moved, it had been all about getting situated. Jordan had settled into his new job while Piper had to search for her own. Then, before she had known it, it had been May, and she was a widow.

After that had come his funeral and sorting out all the paperwork after someone passed, all while trying to deal with grief. For a while, the only people Piper had seen outside of work were her mom and Nate. She had just wanted to be left alone. Socializing took too much energy.

But she'd slowly started coming back to life a few months ago, and that was when Nate had really started bringing his friends around. She knew he'd been afraid that she'd be lonely with no family in the area. She felt like she was almost back to normal. Well, her *new* normal because she was never going to be the same person she had been before Jordan passed away.

And, now, she was grateful that Nate had introduced her to Elise. The two of them got along great, and while Nate was her best friend, sometimes, a lady just needed some girl time. They still didn't know each other that well, but Piper hoped that could change.

Nate and Luke burst through the front door, shirtless, sweaty, and laughing. They went straight to the food without a word to either of the women and dug in like they hadn't eaten for a week. Neither of them bothered to sit either; both stood on the other side of the counter.

"I apologize for my husband's table manners—or lack thereof," Elise said.

Luke looked up from stuffing his face. "*Wha—*" he said around a mouthful of food, his brown eyes gleaming with humor.

"You're a pig," Elise said.

Nate nestled in the corner of the counter and laughed.

Luke swallowed and smiled. "But I'm your pig."

Elise shook her head and rolled her eyes, but Piper saw she was hiding a smile.

"Apologies, Piper," Luke said. "I'm hungry."

Elise turned to Piper. "Do you care if I get a glass of water?"

Piper jumped from the stool, feeling like a terrible hostess. "Oh my God, I'm sorry."

"No, you don't have to get up," Elise protested, also rising from her seat.

"Yes, I do. My mother would pass out from shame if I didn't take care of my company."

Elise sat back down and laughed. "I understand."

She looked around to the two guys. "Water okay with you guys, too?" she asked as she walked around to Nate and Luke's side.

"I can get my own, you know," Nate said.

It was true. He wasn't really a guest in her home anymore. He raided her fridge whenever he was hungry and helped himself to whatever he needed without asking anymore.

"That's okay," she said as she opened the cupboard and reached up for the glasses.

But Nate went for them at the same time she did. As he reached from behind her, she felt his naked chest against her back. A tingle went down her spine, straight to her belly, and she dropped her hands to the counter as she tried to fight a slight tremor.

Apparently, her libido hadn't died with Jordan. It had just gone dormant. And she didn't know what to do with it if it was coming back.

CHAPTER TWO

Several hours later, Nate Hall walked from the backyard into Piper's house. He locked the sliding glass door as he called out to her, "Piper, I'm going to head out."

She came out of her study as he reached the front door. "Oh. Okay," she said from just inside the room.

Nate studied his one and only girl friend. That was girl, space, friend. Two words. Because Nate didn't normally have girl friends. Or girlfriends for that matter. Too messy. But Piper was special. And, even if he didn't like her so much, he owed her. More than she'd ever know.

She'd been acting weird all afternoon. At lunch, she'd been reaching for some glasses when she suddenly stiffened and dropped her hands to the counter. When he'd asked her if she was okay, she'd looked up at him, and the series of expressions that had crossed her face passed so quickly that he'd almost missed them. She'd looked panicked, in awe, and then guilty. But, before he could comment, she'd muttered something about being fine, grabbed the plastic cups from his hand, and walked over to the fridge to fill them with water. He hadn't pressed her. It had been obvious she didn't want to talk about it, and he hadn't wanted to put her on the spot in front of Luke and Elise.

And, now, she was as far away from him as possible while still in the same room. She ran her hands through her black hair while her green eyes wouldn't meet his.

He walked forward. She stepped back and ran into the doorway. He replayed the day in his head, trying to figure out if he'd done anything, but the fact was, they'd hardly even seen each other. She'd been in the house while he was working outside.

"What's wrong?" Nate asked her.

Her eyes widened. "Wrong? Nothing's wrong."

"You're a terrible liar. Don't ever go to Vegas. Now, spit it out. What did I do?" Nate hated beating around the bush and playing games. It was one of the reasons he didn't do girlfriends.

She moved toward him, and her body visibly relaxed. "You didn't do anything."

At least she was telling the truth about that.

"Then, what's bothering you?"

"I'm..." She sighed. "It's not something I want to talk about."

He gritted his teeth. Not because he wanted to know all her secrets, but because he couldn't help her if he didn't know what was wrong.

"Is there anything I can do to help?"

She barked out a laugh as if his suggestion were ridiculous.

He didn't laugh.

She stepped closer. "I'm sorry. That was rude. No, there's nothing you can do. I simply realized something today since Jordan's...passing. It's something I need to figure out myself. But I appreciate it." She put her arms around him and laid her head on his chest.

He squeezed her tight, wishing there were something he could do, but he was glad that she was acting normal again. "All right. I'll see you tomorrow." He kissed her on the head and let her go.

Piper told him good-bye, and Nate headed to his truck and drove home. He took a quick shower, put on clean clothes, and was in his truck again.

Nate pulled into the driveway of a 1950s Rambler that had been a staple from his childhood. He went to the front door, knocked once, and pushed open the door.

"Geepa," he called out a couple of times before he got an answer.

"Down here."

Nate walked down to the basement and into his grandfather's workshop. Geepa was bent over his sander and held a two-by-four.

"Whatcha building?" Nate asked.

Geepa shut off the sander and blew on the wood to clear it off. "Don't know yet." He set the two-by-four down and removed his goggles. His light-blue eyes, an exact replica of Nate's, shone with a smile.

But that was where the similarities ended. His grandpa's

face was pale and weathered. He'd worked outside most of his life, and his alabaster skin had suffered from it. Another chunk of skin had been taken out of his nose, which had probably been the beginning of skin cancer. Unfortunately, his grandfather had worked back before sunblock was a thing.

Nate pointed to his own face and asked, "Everything okay?"

Geepa waved off Nate's concern. "Yeah. That pesky doctor just likes to cut into me. I think she likes to see me suffer."

Somehow, Nate doubted that, but as long as his grandfather let the doctor do her thing, Nate wasn't going to argue.

"You ready to go to dinner?" he asked, changing the subject.

"Yep. Just let me grab my cap."

Nate followed Geepa upstairs to the kitchen where his favorite Minnesota Twins baseball hat sat on the counter. His grandfather smoothed down his ever-thinning blond combover and shoved his cap on his head.

"Geepa, someday soon, we're going to share eye color and hairstyles," Nate told him.

"Keep laughing, young man. You know male-pattern baldness is inherited from your mother's side of the family."

"But I don't have hair."

"Now. You'll change your mind when you get older."

"We'll see," Nate said as the two of them walked outside to his truck. "How do you know that anyway?"

Geepa narrowed his eyes at Nate. "I read. I watch the news. I've gotta keep up with you youngins."

"You do realize I'm thirty-three, right?"

"And I'm seventy-six." He pointed to Nate. "Young." Then, he turned his finger on himself. "Old."

They each opened their door and got inside the vehicle.

"In that case, why don't you just shave your head like me?"

His grandfather sniffled. "Your grandmother liked my hair. I'm not getting rid of what little I have."

Nate's grandmother probably wouldn't have cared for his grandfather's current hairstyle, but Nate kept his mouth shut. He would have been one lost little boy if it hadn't been for his grandparents.

When Nate was four years old, his mother had passed away from a brain aneurysm. Nate had been an only child, and his father had struggled with his own grief, never understanding how much Nate needed him. But his mom had been his grandparents' only child, and they had taken him under their wings. There was a time, after his mother had died, when Nate had practically lived with *Abuelita* and Geepa.

A few years later, when Nate was seven, his father had remarried, but Nate had never gotten along with his stepmom. Not until he'd moved out of the house, and even then, there were no warm fuzzies between the two of them. The only good thing about his father's remarriage was that Nate had gained a little sister out of it. Tiana was one of the few women, besides his mom and grandma, whom Nate loved.

Nate backed out of the driveway and headed to their usual restaurant. "Do you miss her?" he asked Geepa.

"Every day, son. Every single day. Her and your mother both."

"Me, too," Nate admitted.

17

His grandparents had met when his grandpa was in the military and stationed in Texas. His grandma's parents had been immigrants from Mexico, and even though her whole family had lived in Texas, she had married his grandfather and moved to Minnesota. They'd lived happily ever after until his *abuelita* passed away when Nate was seventeen. But, unlike his father, Nate's grandfather hadn't pushed Nate away despite how much his grandparents loved each other.

And, now, the two of them were closer than ever. They would go out to eat together almost every week while Nate wouldn't go to his dad and stepmom's more than once a month for dinner. And Nate was more likely to ask his Geepa for advice than his dad. It made Nate proud that he had been named after his grandfather, although Geepa was Nathan to his Nathaniel. Nate's mom had wanted him to have his own identity.

Once at the restaurant, the two of them were surprised at how busy it was. It was a Saturday night, but it was still early in the evening.

"You can wait at the bar for a seat, or you can eat there, too, if you prefer not to wait," the hostess offered.

Nate looked at his grandpa, letting him decide.

"Let's go sit at the bar."

"Works for me."

They took their seats and each ordered a beer while they looked over their menus. After a few minutes, their server came over. She was a cute little redhead, and the smile she gave Nate told him he could have her phone number before their dinner was over. But then she had to go and ruin it.

"Can I ask, what are you?" she asked after their food was ordered.

And, just like that, any attraction he'd felt toward the lady vanished. "I'm a human being," he said dryly.

Oh, Nate knew what she meant. She wanted to know his race, his ethnicity. She was confused by his blue eyes and bronzed skin, his aquiline nose and thinner lips, and she wanted to put him in a nice little group in her brain. But Nate's ancestors were from Africa, Mexico, Germany, Poland, Ireland, Scotland, and probably a couple of other places he didn't know about. Nate was an *Other* on the forms he had to fill out. There was no one category for him.

He used to hate it. It was why he'd worn brown contact lenses in college and started shaving his straight light-brown hair. He'd come to embrace his features since then though. He'd ditched the contact lenses, and the only reason he still shaved his head was because it was easy to take care of, and he noticed the ladies liked it.

But he would love it if he could go more than a week without someone asking him this question. Why did it matter so much? It didn't change who he was on the inside.

His grandfather slammed his menu closed on the bar. "He's my grandson; that's who he is, young lady."

Her mouth parted in surprise.

That's right; this old white dude is my grandfather.

Nate held in his laugh because, now, Geepa was putting the waitress on the spot.

"I'm-I'm sorry, sir," she stammered.

"Apology accepted, although you should be apologizing to my grandson."

"I'm sorry," she said to Nate.

Nate shrugged. He wasn't mad, but he hoped she had learned a lesson.

The rest of their dinner was uneventful. Despite the server's questions, she'd done a good job, and Nate tipped her well.

When she returned his final credit card receipt with her phone number on it, Nate threw it in the trash on the way out the door.

CHAPTER THREE

Early Wednesday evening, Piper knocked once on Nate's front door before pushing it open. "Nate," she called out.

"I'll be down in a minute," he answered from upstairs.

As she stepped over the threshold, she was immediately greeted by a loud meow and a large, hairy beast twisting himself around her legs.

"Hello, Fred."

Meow.

It was a meow that clearly meant, *Pet me.*

Piper had never met a cat that wanted love more than Fred. It was a good thing her hands were full with dinner, so she didn't have to pet him. Instead of being satisfied when he got attention, he always wanted more.

Piper toed off her flats and attempted to step toward the kitchen, but she tripped as Fred wove around her feet again.

She screeched when she almost dropped the food as Nate

came from upstairs, wearing a T-shirt and jeans with bare feet.

He quickly scooped the bags out of her hands. "You okay?" he asked as he tried not to laugh at her.

"Besides your cat trying to kill me, I'm fine."

Nate turned and took the food into his kitchen. "Fred wasn't trying to kill you. He just wanted you to fall to the floor, so he could get closer to you."

Piper snorted as she followed Nate. "This is why I'm a dog person."

Fred, who had been trailing behind his owner, spun around and meowed at Piper. He then turned his back and walked away.

"I think you pissed him off," Nate joked.

There was no way the cat had understood her, but she found herself calling out, "I'm sorry, Fred. You're my favorite cat."

Nate set the bags on the counter and looked inside. "Davanni's. What did you bring tonight?"

After Jordan had passed away, Piper and Nate had discovered that they were both big fans of *Law & Order: SVU*. They'd started watching it together frequently. Soon after, it'd turned into having dinner every Wednesday. Now that it was summer and only reruns were on, the two of them were making their way through the many seasons of *NCIS*.

"I tried calling to see if you wanted your usual pizza or a hoagie, but you didn't answer, so I got both. I figured you could always take leftovers to work."

"Sorry. I didn't realize you'd called. Thanks for getting both. What do I owe you?"

Piper narrowed her eyes at him.

Nate laughed. "I know. I'll get dinner next time. Still, *Abuelita* would come down here and kick my ass if I didn't offer. You bought me more than one meal this time." He pulled out his food. "What did you get?"

She reached for the other bag. "I got pasta," she admitted.

"Good for you."

Piper felt her face warm even though she really didn't have anything to be embarrassed about.

She was not one of those people who lost her appetite under stress, and after Jordan died, food had been her go-to source of comfort. After a while, her hips and ass had begun to show it, and she'd even gone up a bra size.

It wouldn't have been a big deal, except she hadn't been a small girl to begin with. Piper had always been proud of her curves and loved that Jordan had loved her just the way she was. But, after the new wardrobe she'd bought began to feel tight, she had known she had to do something. One, her bank account couldn't afford another splurge in clothes shopping, and two, she was already predisposed to type 2 diabetes on her dad's side and high cholesterol on her mom's side. If anything, she needed to focus on her health.

And, while she had done a good job of eating well, she couldn't help being disappointed that she still couldn't fit into the clothes she'd worn before Jordan's death.

Nate, who was pretty much her best friend in Minnesota, knew all this, but he didn't agree with her. Yes, he thought being healthy was a good thing, but he'd told her she had nothing to worry about in the weight depart-ment. He'd told her she worried too much about what society thought and that she was beautiful just the way she was.

She supposed he was right. And it wasn't like she was looking for a new man. But, as a woman, it had been pounded in her head since she was little that she needed to be thin to be beautiful. Logic did not always factor into conditioning.

Still, she couldn't deny that she appreciated his praise in her choice of meals. Nate might have some faults, but he wouldn't tell her she looked good if she didn't.

"Thanks," she told him as she lifted off the lid of her chicken Florentine. "Where are we eating tonight? Kitchen or in front of the TV?"

"I'm eating my pizza, so let's go in the den." He picked up his food, and she did the same. "Have you heard of the show *Mindhunter*?"

"Is that on Netflix?"

They set their food on the coffee table, and Piper sat.

"Yes," Nate answered. "I'll be right back." He went back to the kitchen and returned with two bottles of water. Handing her one, he said, "I've heard really good things about it."

"Me, too."

"It's only ten episodes. I thought maybe *NCIS* could wait."

"Let's do it," she told him.

Nate brought up Netflix on his TV and started the show while they dug into their dinner.

After the first episode, Piper was hooked. She picked up her empty pasta container to take it to the garbage. They both had been so into the show that they didn't want to pause to clean up.

"I'm warning you," she told Nate. "I don't think I can wait until next week to finish watching this. I see a binge-watch feast in my future."

He laughed. "It's early. We can watch another one."

"But we're not watching all ten tonight."

Nate paused. "How about we watch as many as we can tonight, and then we'll meet up again tomorrow and watch some more?"

She smiled. "Okay. For now," she teased.

It was in the middle of episode three that Piper began to feel sleepy. She'd worked late the last two days, and now, it was catching up with her.

Nate put his arm around her when he noticed her yawn and pulled her down onto his chest.

She still remembered the first time Nate had done this very same thing to her. She'd been so tense and nervous. She hadn't known him that well at that point, and she hadn't known if he was hitting on her, thinking she would be an easy lay now that she was a lonely widow. But he hadn't tried anything. He'd simply held her close while they watched a movie. He'd been a perfect gentleman.

And, now that she knew she could trust him one hundred percent, Piper snuggled into his chest. He always smelled so good. Like a man.

Part of her felt guilty for lying on Nate's chest when it should be Jordan's chest she was lying on, but there was nothing she could do to bring her husband back. And, sometimes, she ached to feel the touch of another person. That was one of the hardest things to deal with after Jordan's death.

Nate might not be her husband or her lover, but he was her friend, and she no longer felt guilty for seeking comfort from him.

Piper rested her hand on Nate's chest, took in a soothing, deep breath, and settled in to finish their show.

The sound of a satisfied moan woke Piper from her nap. At first, she'd forgotten where she was until she recognized the hard muscles under her head as she moved up and down from Nate's breathing.

She heard another moan coming from him, and then she opened her eyes and craned her neck to look up at him. Piper had slid down in her sleep until her head was pretty much on Nate's stomach, but he had his head turned down and toward her. She could see he had fallen asleep, too.

"Mmm..." Nate gasped.

The next words out of his mouth didn't make any sense, but she could tell by his tone that he was enjoying himself and whoever was in his dream with him.

Afraid of waking him if she suddenly got up, she slowly rotated her head, so she was no longer looking at him in case he woke up. She moved until she was comfortable, and her nose was pointed at his feet, but when she realized what was right in front of her face, she sucked in a breath and froze.

Nate was hard.

And big.

Good God.

He moaned again, and Piper licked her lips.

That feeling she'd had on Saturday when Nate pressed his sweaty chest against her was back. Only this time, it didn't end at her belly. It kept going until the tingle stopped right between her legs.

She hadn't seen or touched a dick in over a year. And she hadn't realized how much she missed it until now.

Mesmerized by the hard-on straining against Nate's zipper, she gradually reached a finger out to touch it.

She was saved from doing anything inappropriate when Nate began to stir. Not knowing what else to do, Piper closed her eyes and pretended to sleep.

CHAPTER FOUR

When Nate had first met Piper, he'd noticed she was pretty and had a rocking body, but he'd immediately put her in the *wife of a friend* category.

Then, when Jordan had died, Nate had felt guilty about his friend's death. It wasn't every day that a person was in a car accident with someone they cared about, watching the life leave their friend's eyes before they went home from the hospital the next day. And, when Jordan had used the last of his strength to grasp Nate's wrist and make Nate promise to take care of Piper, Nate had seen her as an obligation.

But it hadn't been long before Nate realized how cool Piper was, and even though he knew she was his buddy's widow, he couldn't help but start to see her as a woman.

Piper was the type of female who always caught his eye. She was thick, just the way Nate liked woman to be. Piper would probably hate hearing him use that term because she had been brainwashed by the media into thinking that anything more than a size zero was a bad thing. But he liked his women to have meat on them. Skinny didn't do it for him. Of course, a part of him thought all women were beautiful and all body types should be appreciated. But, if Nate had to pick, he'd pick someone just like Piper. Big booty and big breasts.

And her breasts had been the bane of his existence for a while. He'd noticed them the moment he met her, and then after Jordan was gone, they had actually gotten bigger. The first time Piper had fallen asleep on the couch with him, he'd thought he might actually come in his pants. Something he hadn't done since middle school.

And then the dreams had come. For a long time, it seemed like he dreamed about her almost every night. And they definitely weren't playing cards in his dreams.

Thankfully, over time, he'd started to see her more and more as just a friend and less and less like a woman he would give his left nut to bang. He'd even gotten used to her body touching his without there being a sexual aspect.

But, sometimes, like tonight, he would dream about her. She'd come to his house, wearing a sheer white blouse that only magnified her impressive rack. Sure, she had a tank top under it, but it didn't stop her nipples from poking out just enough to get a man's mouth to water. The sexiest thing about it was, she had no clue. He knew Piper well enough now to know that, if he pointed out her shirt to her, she'd be mortified. No, she wasn't trying to dress provocatively at all.

He'd done his best to ignore her body, like he always did, and when they'd lain back on the couch, he'd commanded his own body to concentrate on the the show.

But then he'd started falling asleep; all he could think about was her pillowy breasts pressed against his side, and it wasn't long before she showed up in his dream. Naked.

So, when he managed to shake off the effects of sleep, he wasn't surprised in the least to see his fucking boner. Inches from her face.

He groaned out loud with embarrassment, and Piper moved.

"Shit," he whispered as he frantically looked around. For what, he had no clue, but he couldn't let her see his hard dick.

He spotted movement out of the corner of his eye.

"Fred," he called out as loud as he dared.

His cat stopped and looked at him.

Nate patted his hip. "Come here, Fred."

It was times like these that Nate was grateful his cat was an attention whore and willing to do anything to have someone pet him.

Fred jumped up onto Nate's chest, and he nudged his cat down until he was lying down on his lap. Nate pushed Fred down and gave his head a couple of pets to get him to stay.

Just in the nick of time, too, because Piper opened her eyes.

"Hello, Fred," she said and reached out a hand to stroke him.

His cat immediately began to purr, but Nate didn't miss the look Fred gave him, as if to say, *You dirty dog, using me to cover up your hard-on from the lady.*

Nate wanted to remind Fred that the lady didn't even like cats that much.

"Did I fall asleep?"

"Yeah. I did, too. I think we missed almost the whole episode."

Piper moved off him, giving Nate the opportunity to sit up and swiftly reposition himself before she turned to him.

Fred jumped off his lap, turning to give him one last dirty look before sauntering away. Nate quickly grabbed the pillow that had been on his head and set it over his crotch.

Piper finger-combed her long, dark hair with her fingers. She had once described herself as Black Irish, but he thought of her as more of a Snow White. She had black hair, pale skin, and red lips. Lips he had just dreamed were wrapped around—

"I should get going," Piper said with a yawn. "What episode were we on? I can go home and finish it."

Nate waved her off. "I fell asleep, too. We can finish it together tomorrow."

Piper grabbed her phone from the coffee table and looked at the time. "Probably a good idea. It's late, and I have to be at work early." She stood up and stretched her arms over her head.

Nate, finally ready to move the pillow off his lap, got up from the couch to follow her to the door. But, before either of them moved, his phone rang.

He looked at the display and groaned.

"Who is it?"

"My dad."

Piper put her hand on his arm. "You don't have to answer that. You can always say you were already sleeping when he called."

Nate and Piper had been spending a lot of time together

since Jordan's death. Not only had she cried on his shoulder many a time, but he had confided in her about his mom's death, his dad's mental absence from Nate's life, and his stepmom. She knew that he most likely didn't want to take this phone call.

"Might as well get it over with." He swiped the green button on his phone. "Yeah?" he said by way of a greeting.

"Nate, your dad here."

Nate rolled his eyes. "I do recognize your voice, you know. Plus, there is this new thing called caller ID."

Jerome Hall laughed nervously. Nate didn't think the situation was funny in the least. It was sad that a father couldn't talk to his son with ease. Sometimes, they felt like they were strangers despite the fact that they had lived together in the same house for eighteen years.

"Say, your mother would like you to come to dinner with the family on Saturday."

Nate scoffed. *His mother.* What a joke. The woman who had married his father would never be his mother—and not because Nate had rejected her. Sure, things were a lot better now between them than when his dad had married her, but it was too late for her to be any kind of a mom toward him.

Opening his mouth to let his dad know how he felt about *dinner with the family,* he was stopped by the feeling of Piper taking his hand in hers. She was standing close enough to hear his dad through the phone, and it didn't take a genius to read the look on his face.

Nate closed his eyes and sighed. He opened them again and squeezed her hand.

"Dad, I'm supposed to go to dinner with Geepa."

"Oh," his father said. "Well...invite him along. We haven't seen you in a while."

No way would he make his grandfather be his buffer. "I'll talk to Geepa." Instead, Nate would suck it up and go by himself.

"Great," his father said, his voice a little lighter. "See you at six."

Nate hit End on his phone and threw it on the couch.

"You're going to go to dinner, aren't you?"

"You know I am."

Piper let go of his hand, slipped her arms around him, and pulled him close. "You're a good son," she said against his chest.

Nate hugged her back. "I don't know about that. I just don't want Dad bugging me. Plus, I haven't seen Tiana in a while."

She tilted her head up and rested her chin on his sternum. "Well, at the very least, you're a good brother."

He raised his brow. "Better than yours?"

"Considering he tried to sell me automotive parts the last time I talked to him, yes."

Nate chuckled, and she laughed along with him. He looked into her eyes as she licked her lips, and suddenly, he realized she was in the perfect position for him to kiss her.

Just like that, his dream returned to him, and he was very aware of her perfect breasts pushed against him.

And he wasn't the only one who was becoming aware.

Nate dropped his hands from Piper and stepped back. "I'd better call Geepa and head to bed."

Piper tilted her head and smiled. "Okay."

Nate walked her to the door and said good-bye. He waited to make sure she got into her car before he went back to the den for his phone. He made a quick call to his grandfather about the change of plans. He, of course, understood.

After hanging up, Nate lay back on the couch again to watch some television and settle his mind before going to bed. But, after thirty minutes, he gave up. He was still horny from his earlier dream and irritated from his previous discussion with his dad.

He picked up his phone again and scrolled to the Vs. Vanessa picked up on the first ring.

"Damn, that was fast."

She gave a throaty chuckle. "Maybe I was lying in my bed, touching myself, just hoping you'd call."

And this was why he'd called Vanessa. "I suppose that means you don't feel like coming over."

"Baby, I always feel like coming for you."

Nate didn't miss the double entendre. "Get your sexy ass over here then."

"I'll be there in fifteen."

Fifteen minutes on the dot, Nate's doorbell rang. He opened the door to find Vanessa standing there in an overcoat, high heels—she pulled the coat open—and her birthday suit.

Dear Penthouse...

Nate pulled her inside, pushed off her coat, and led her to the couch. He never took girls to his room. Even the ones like Vanessa, who knew they were nothing but occasional fuck buddies, still got the wrong idea sometimes.

Vanessa pulled off his jeans, pushed him onto the couch,

and rode him like a rodeo queen. She got off. Nate got off. Both were happy. When it was over, Nate ditched the condom, and Vanessa pulled on her overcoat.

Nate told her good-bye and shut the door. He went upstairs, took a shower, crawled into bed, and went to sleep.

The best part was that there were no dreams of Piper.

CHAPTER FIVE

I t was almost six o'clock on Friday evening, and Piper was finishing up some work before she left for the weekend.

"Hey, Piper."

She looked up to see her coworker, Lainey, at her desk. She was surprised she hadn't noticed Lainey sooner. Lainey was almost six feet tall, sporting a pixie cut of bleach-blonde hair. Put that together with her eccentric dressing, just this side of professional, and she was a hard person to miss.

"Hey, Lainey. What's up?"

Piper considered Lainey and a couple of the other girls her work friends. She had a great time working with them, but she didn't hang out with them much outside of work.

Lainey sat on the edge of Piper's desk. "Kayla, Simone, and I are going to see this awesome cover band on Saturday night. Do you want to come with?" The eyebrows over her green eyes wiggled.

Piper didn't know what to say. She hadn't really gone out

and done something like see a band play since before Jordan passed away. And this was the first time a coworker had asked her to do something like this.

"Are you sure?"

Lainey laughed as if the question was ridiculous. "Of course. Remember how much fun we had at the company picnic last month?"

They'd had a lot of fun, but a picnic was a lot different than, say, going to a bar, having drinks, and listening to loud music. And, truth be told, Piper just wasn't sure she was ready to get out there again. Sure, it was hanging out with the girls; it wasn't a date. But it was the potential to meet someone new, and she felt like she would be betraying her husband.

"Can I think about it?" Piper asked.

"Yes." Lainey looked down at her shoes and back at Piper but didn't say anything.

"Go ahead and say it," Piper said with a smile.

Lainey could be blunt at times, and Piper could only imagine what her coworker was thinking.

"I know you loved your husband, and still probably do, but you're how old? Thirty?"

"Twenty-nine."

"You still have a lot of life to live, and if the situation were reversed, would you want Jordan to sit around for the rest of his life, mourning you?"

Piper swallowed, her heart heavy and her mind full.

"Listen," Lainey said, "just think about it, okay?"

Piper nodded.

Lainey smiled and rapped her knuckles on Piper's desk before walking away.

Lainey's words resonated with Piper as she finished up her work and drove home. If the situation were reversed, there was no way she would want Jordan to spend the rest of his life alone, pining for his dead wife.

Has enough time passed?

Piper had looked up grief on the internet on a few occasions, but of course, the answer was that there was no set amount of time that one had to grieve and that everybody was different.

But am I ready?

When Piper got home, Nate's truck was already in her driveway, and Luke's SUV was parked on the street in front of her house. She'd almost forgotten they were going to finish up a part of the backyard project tonight.

Piper didn't know if she was happy for the distraction from her thoughts or if she was wishing they weren't there so that she could be alone. Maybe she shouldn't have given Nate free access to her house to come and go as he pleased.

Her garage door was already open, so she pulled right in. When she got out of her car, she could hear banging and other noises coming from the backyard, telling her that the guys were already hard at work. Piper decided she would go in and change clothes and maybe collect her thoughts before she went to say hi to them.

The evening was surprisingly pleasant for a Minnesota summer. Either Nate or Luke had left her back door open for the cool breeze to travel through her screen door.

Piper entered through her screen door and made sure to

carefully close it, so it didn't bang against the doorframe, just in case the guys could hear in the back. Her garage door opened into her kitchen, but before that, off to the right, was a mudroom and laundry room combo. That door was closed, which was weird because Piper only closed that door if the washer was running. She supposed that maybe Nate or Luke was using her laundry facilities, but they never had before.

Taking a step closer, Piper listened for the sound of the washing machine or dryer and was just about to reach up and push the door open when she heard giggling.

"Come on, Luke. Please."

"Elise, don't look at me like that. You know it's hard for me to tell you no."

"Good. Now, take your pants off and fuck me."

"*Elise.*"

Elise didn't respond right away, and Piper couldn't be sure, but it sounded like clothing was being shuffled around. And then...

"*Ohhhhh. Yes.*"

That was Elise.

"Damn, I think I like you pregnant."

Elise chuckled, but the laughter turned into a moan. "Harder, Luke. Please, I need it."

A grunt came from the other side of the door and then the sound of squeaking from either the washer or the dryer.

Piper took a step closer just as she heard Nate shout, "Luke," from the backyard.

She jumped a foot in the air and quickly stepped away from the laundry room.

Holy hell.

Had she just been listening to two of her friends having sex? And she was pretty sure that, if Nate hadn't said anything, she would have put her damn ear to the door to listen for more. When had she become such a voyeur?

When Nate walked in from the backyard through the sliding glass door Piper was pretty sure her face was the color of a tomato, going by the fact that she felt like it was on fire.

"Long, I—oh, hey, Piper. Have you seen Luke?"

Nate and Luke often called each other by their last names. Probably because they'd known each other since elementary school.

Piper opened her eyes wide, hoping she looked innocent, and shook her head. It was the truth. She hadn't *seen* Luke.

Nate scrunched up his nose. "Are you okay? You look..."

Guilty, like a creeper, embarrassed...turned on?

"I-I—"

Nate raised his eyebrows at her stammering.

Piper cleared her throat and tried to compose herself. "What did you need Luke for? Maybe I can help. I just have to get changed first."

Nate frowned. "I don't know. It's pretty heavy. You really don't know where he went?"

Just then, the door to the laundry room slid open, and Luke and Elise walked out. They tried to look casual, but it was pretty obvious what they'd been doing.

"Really, dude?" Nate said. "What is it with you two and laundry rooms?"

Luke walked past Piper and punched Nate in the arm. "Shut up, man. You weren't supposed to say anything."

It was obvious the two of them were talking about something that Piper wasn't privy to. She glanced over at Elise to see if she knew what the guys were talking about, and this time, it was her face that was a deep crimson.

"Way to go. Now, you've embarrassed my wife."

Nate shrugged. "She shouldn't be. Now, will you come and help me?"

"Yeah."

The two guys walked into the backyard, leaving Piper alone with Elise. The air was heavy with awkwardness.

Up until Jordan died, Piper had always been sexual and pretty open on the subject. But it had been a while since she was physical or even talked about sex with another person. And Piper and Elise's friendship was still on the newer side.

"I'm going to—"

"I'm sorry we were doing it in your laundry room," Elise blurted out as she looked at the floor.

"Oh, well..." Piper didn't know what to say.

"At first, I was sick," Elise said, rubbing her belly, "and tired all the time. I just wasn't in the mood much. And, now, I'm the opposite." She swiped her hand out. "But that's no excuse for me commandeering your laundry room just so I can get laid." She finally looked up at Piper. "I'm sorry."

Piper smiled. "It was a little...unexpected, but all is forgiven. I was married once, so I get it."

Elise smiled sadly. "I bet you miss him, huh?"

"Every day."

Elise leaned closer and whispered, "Do you miss sex?"

"Up until recently, no. It was like that part of me was shut off. But..."

"But what?"

Piper thought about the last week. Her reaction to Nate's innocent touch last weekend, her interest in Nate's hard-on after they'd fallen asleep, and now, her newfound voyeurism. Piper shrugged. "I don't know honestly, but I think that part of me is waking up again."

Elise's eyes brightened. "That's good, right?"

Piper wasn't sure. "I'm going to go change my clothes. I'll be right back." She didn't answer Elise's question because she didn't know how to.

"Oh. Okay. I'll be in the backyard if you need me."

"Thanks," Piper said as she headed down the hall to her room.

As she changed her clothes, she contemplated her sexuality and the return of it. She'd always had a healthy libido, and while she wasn't the girl she had once been, she wasn't the girl she had been a year ago, right after Jordan's death, either.

Being a widow was something she had never thought she'd have to worry about in her twenties. She'd assumed that, when they married, the two of them would grow old together. But, obviously, life had had other plans.

She tried to think of it from another angle. What would she do if this had been a breakup? She'd take the time to get over her ex, and then she'd get back out there. So, maybe that was what she needed to do.

Piper tried to picture herself with another man, a faceless stranger, and she cringed.

Okay, so she needed to take things slowly. She didn't have to date someone right away, but she should at least put herself in a position to meet someone.

Piper brushed her hair and pulled it back into a ponytail. She then picked up her phone and pulled up her Contacts. She went to the Ls and opened a new message.

> Piper: I thought about it. Count me in for Saturday.

Less than a minute later, her phone pinged.

> Lainey: *Squeal* Really?

> Piper: Really. ☺

> Lainey: I already texted Kayla and Simone. We're all very excited.

> Piper: LOL. That was fast. I'm excited, too. Just be gentle with me. It's been a while since I had a night out.

> Lainey: Ha-ha-ha-ha! You got it. It'll just be drinks and a band. No pressure.

> Piper: Thanks. Text me the details.

> Lainey: I'll check with the other two and get back to you.

> Piper: Sounds good. Talk to you later.

> Lainey: Later.

With a smile, Piper turned the screen off her phone and made her way to the backyard. For the first time in a long time, Piper was looking forward to a Saturday night.

CHAPTER SIX

Ten minutes to six on Saturday, Nate knocked once and pushed open the door to his parents' house. Not surprisingly, no one greeted him at the door. He walked to the back of the house where the kitchen was and was greeted by his stepmother.

"Oh, hi, Nate," Tricia said. She smiled at him, but it was hesitant.

"Hey." He nodded in greeting. "Where's Dad?"

"He's not home yet."

Nice.

His father had guilted him into coming and wasn't even here.

"Is Tiana here?" Nate looked around for his sister since his dad had said it was going to be a family dinner.

"No, she's not here yet. You know her. She shows up right on time or five minutes late."

Great.

That meant it was just him and Tricia.

The two of them had come a long way, but a part of Nate —the seven-year-old in him—just couldn't seem to forgive her. They had a pleasant relationship now, but she wasn't a doting mother. At least, not to him. She was a good mother to his sister—her birth child—and he was thankful for that.

"So, how's work?" Tricia asked as she started taking plates out of the cupboard.

Nate shrugged. "Good. I got a promotion about a month ago, which put me in charge of about six people, and that's going well."

Tricia, who'd had her back to him, swung around, her dark eyes wide and her mouth parted in surprise. "Nate, congratulations. Your father never said anything."

Nate took the plates from her. "I never told him."

Nate saw the look of disappointment on Tricia's face, but he ignored it as he went to set the table.

It wasn't that he was trying to keep his dad out of his life. It was just that he and his dad weren't close, and Nate hardly ever talked to him. The only memories Nate had of hanging out with his dad when he was growing up was when the two of them would fix up houses, which was where Nate had learned everything he knew in the trade. If he'd called his dad up just to tell him about the promotion, it would have felt too much like bragging.

"I haven't seen you guys since before then, so I haven't had a chance to bring it up." He didn't know why he felt like he needed to explain the situation more. Maybe it was to wipe away the look of distress on his stepmother's face.

Nate walked around her and went to the silverware drawer. "What are we having for dinner?"

"Pot roast with potatoes and carrots."

Nate grabbed the appropriate silverware for four people and took it to the table. He just finished setting the table when his father walked in from the garage door and into the kitchen.

Jerome kissed his wife on the cheek and then came over to Nate. "Hello, son." His dad tried to give him a hug, and it was all kinds of awkward. It ended up being a half-embrace, half-pat on the back.

"Jerome, did you know that Nate got a promotion at work?"

His father's brown eyes opened wide and filled with pride. "No. Congratulations, son."

Nate rubbed the back of his neck. "Yeah, thanks."

The look of satisfaction in his father's eyes pissed him off. His father didn't really have a right to feel that way, as if he were responsible for Nate growing up the way he had. His grandparents were the ones who had pushed him to do well in school and go to college.

This was why Nate hated coming to his parents' house. Overall, he was a happy, easygoing person. But, when he was here, in the house he had grown up in, surrounded by his parents, it made him bitter. He didn't like thinking of himself as a resentful person. He didn't want to be that type of person.

The front door opened and slammed closed.

"Where is everyone?" Tiana called out.

The second she walked into the room, their father asked, "Did you know that Nate got a raise at work?"

"Of course." Tiana put her arm around Nate's waist. "I'm surprised you're not running the place already."

Nate put his own arm around her shoulders and pulled her close. "You're just biased because you're my little sister," he said with a grin. He drew himself away to get a good look at her. "Why did you go blonde?"

She pretended to fluff her hair. "Why? Do you like it?"

Nate studied her. He thought his sister was beautiful, of course. She had her mother's dark brown, almost black, eyes, but her skin tone was closer to their father's. Her smooth skin was a warm brown, compared to his sandy-beige complexion.

When he had been young, it was another thing that had made him feel like an outsider. His father was half-black, his stepmom was full, and his sister was three-fourths while Nate was only a quarter-black. His skin and his light-blue eyes stood out among their sea of brown.

When he had been little and they went out in public, people would actually ask questions ranging from if he was adopted to why his stepmother always brought the neighbor kid to the park with her.

As a man, he was proud of his heritage, but as a kid, it had been awkward.

"Your hair looks great," he told Tiana.

She narrowed her eyes at him.

"What? I'm telling the truth."

She smiled. "Okay, I believe you."

Tricia clapped her hands together. "All right then, let's eat."

Tiana left his side as she said, "I can help. What do you need me to do?"

Soon, they were all seated around the table, plates full, and they dug into their food.

"Your grandfather didn't want to come tonight?" Nate's father asked him.

The truth was, he never even asked Geepa if he wanted to come. "Nah, he decided to go down to the American Legion tonight."

"Speaking of grandfathers," Tiana said, "when are Grandma and Grandpa coming again to visit?"

Their father finished chewing the bite of food in his mouth and said, "Next month. They're looking forward to it." He looked at Nate. "Are you going to be around?"

"No big plans so far. You know I always make time for Grandma and Grandpa."

Nate's father's parents were older and had retired when Nate was a baby. They'd promptly moved to Florida to get away from the cold Minnesota winters. Due to their living so far away, Nate wasn't as close to them as he was with his mother's parents, but he still loved them and always looked forward to them visiting. Nate had even gone down there a time or two to see them.

"It's been a couple of years since I've been to Florida. I should look into going there this winter. I could take Piper with me."

She could use the time away and a nice vacation. He bet they would have a lot of fun. He knew they had talked about Florida before, but he couldn't remember if she'd ever been there. It would be exciting to show her around.

Nate set his fork down and picked up his glass of water.

He took a sip, and when he set the glass back down, he realized everyone was staring at him. "What?"

Tiana raised her brow at him. "You want to go on a vacation with a girl?"

"Woman, not girl." He shrugged. "What's the big deal about that?"

"That just doesn't seem like you."

He could play dumb and pretend like he didn't know what his sister was talking about, but he knew she wasn't happy about his lack of commitment to any one particular female. "Piper's different. She's my friend. You've met her. You know there's nothing romantic going on between us."

His sister burst out laughing.

"What's so funny?"

"You just used the word *romantic*. I'd have thought that word was struck from your vocabulary."

"Ha. You're hilarious. I could be romantic if I wanted. I just choose not to be."

Tiana's eyes widened with incredulity. "Whatever you say."

Nate threw his napkin at her.

"Hey, hey, hey. No fighting at the table," their father told them.

Tiana stuck her tongue out at Nate, and he grinned.

"That's real mature for a twenty-four-year-old," he teased her.

She shrugged and smiled at him.

The four of them finished up dinner, and as Nate was cleaning up his dishes, he got a text. It was from his friend Ty.

Ty: Busy?

Nate: Not really.

Ty: Ethan and I are going to head downtown
tonight. You in?

"Do you guys mind if I head out soon?" he asked his sister
and parents.

"I was hoping you would stay for a while," his dad said.

"Well, I was going to leave, too," his sister said. "I have a
date tonight."

"Are you still seeing that Craig guy?" Nate asked her.

"Yes, I am. Do you have a problem with that?" she asked
defiantly.

Other than the fact that the dude was dating his sister, he
was an okay guy.

"Nah, I met him. He seems nice." When their parents
turned their backs, Nate mouthed, *Thank you*, to her.

She blew him a kiss, and Nate picked up his phone.

Nate: Count me in.

Ty: I'll text you the details. See ya soon.

The next text Ty sent included the place to meet him,
and Nate put his phone in his pocket. He helped finish
cleaning up from dinner and sat around for another half an
hour to be polite.

But, as soon as he closed the front door behind him, he
breathed a sigh of relief. Ty couldn't have picked a better
night to go out for drinks.

CHAPTER SEVEN

Piper pumped her fist in the air and jumped up and down as the live cover band played Nirvana's "Smells Like Teen Spirit." She had to admit, she was having more fun than she'd thought she would. She had consumed just enough alcohol to loosen her up, to forget about being a twenty-nine-year-old widow for a while, and to just have a good time.

She looked over at her friends who were having just as much fun. Lainey had spiked her blonde hair up and was wearing a miniskirt with fishnet stockings and a black leather jacket. Add in the smoky eyes, and she looked rocker chick all the way.

Simone's dark blonde hair was piled on the top of her head in a stylish updo. In her little black dress, she was dressed a little more traditionally than Lainey. She always looked trendy and sexy. Piper was convinced that Simone could get dressed in the dark, and she'd still manage to pull together a cute outfit.

Last was Kayla, who was wearing white capris, which seemed the most conservative. But add in the leopard print stilettos and crop top, and she looked hot as hell. Her long brown hair hung down to the middle of her back in waves, and her plump lips were painted red, which only added to her sensuality.

Piper had decided to wear an above-the-knee crimson A-line skirt with a sleeveless black top that showed off a nice amount of cleavage. She had large breasts, and her only options were to cover them up or show the girls off a little. It was a night out, and she hadn't felt attractive in a long time. She might as well use this opportunity to see how comfortable she was with showing off some skin.

So far, she had no regrets. She'd gotten some appreciative looks, but no one had approached her, which was a relief. She wasn't ready for male attention quite yet.

She glanced at her left hand. Of course, she still wore her wedding ring, and she didn't know if she could take it off yet. Most guys would stay far away from a married woman.

The song finished, and Piper and the others cupped their mouths and screamed their appreciation for the band. They had two lead singers, one male and one female, and they had played everything from country to hard rock, from sixties music to today's top forty music. They were one of the best bands she'd seen.

The female singer pulled the microphone close to her. "Thank you all for coming tonight."

Whoops and hollers from the crowd followed.

"This next song is dedicated to Dolores O'Riordan.

There is no way I will do this next song justice, but I'm sure going to try. May she rest in peace."

The beginning chords for "Zombie" by The Cranberries started up, and the crowd went crazy, Piper included. Her mother was a huge Cranberries fan, and Piper had grown up, listening to the band. She made a mental note to call tomorrow and tell her all about it.

Piper took a big sip of her drink and closed her eyes to let the music take over her body. Despite the haunting lyrics, the song reminded her of when she was young and didn't have a care in the world. It felt good to reminisce on what it had been like not to worry about paying bills, go to work every day, or wonder what life would have been like if your husband hadn't died.

Toward the end of the song, someone nudged her arm with an elbow, and Piper opened her eyes. Simone was grinning at her.

Since the music was so loud, Piper shrugged, as if to say, *What are you smiling for?*

Simone pulled Piper close and shouted in her ear, "There is a hot guy who's been watching you." She stepped back and nodded her head, her eyes wide.

Immediately curious, Piper looked around but didn't see anyone. Simone took her arm and spun her around just as the hot guy approached her. He wore dark jeans and a black V-neck tee that showed off a hint of a muscular chest. No wonder Simone had noticed him.

Piper threw her arms around Nate's neck and jumped on him, wrapping her legs around his waist. Nate made an *oomph* sound and caught her under her butt. Sober her would never have done something like that, fearing she'd be too heavy. But drunk Piper was super excited to see her friend.

The song ended, and one of the band members said, "We'll be back in about half an hour."

Piper hopped off of Nate and smoothed her skirt down. "What are you doing here?"

"I'm here with my buddies." Now that the band wasn't playing, it was a lot easier for them to talk to each other. "They're sitting over there." Nate pointed to a table behind him. "Why don't you come sit with us?"

Somebody cleared their throat behind Piper.

She stepped back, so Nate could see her friends. "Nate, these are my coworkers—Simone, Lainey, and Kayla. Do you have room for all of us?"

"Sure." Nate led them to a table where two guys sat.

One was a handsome, pale redhead. The other guy was a good-looking black man. Piper had never met either of them before.

Simone grabbed Piper's arm and held her back from the group. "That's Nate?"

"Yeah...so?"

"Damn, girl, you never said he was hot."

Piper looked to Nate and then back at Simone and shrugged. "Sorry."

"Please tell me he's single."

"He is." Something peculiar pulled tight at Piper's chest. "But he doesn't do girlfriends. He's sort of a one-night kind of guy." That was stretching the truth because she knew Nate had a couple of women he regularly had sex with.

Simone fanned her face as she looked at Nate. "That's too bad."

"Come on," Piper said.

"Do you know his friends?" Simone asked as they kept walking.

"Never met either of them."

When they reached the table, Nate asked, "What were you two talking about?"

"Girl stuff," Piper said while Simone said, "Wouldn't you like to know?"

Everyone chuckled.

Nate introduced them. "Piper, Simone, these are my friends Ty"—Nate gestured to the black guy first—"and Ethan." Nate pointed to the redheaded guy. "Ty, Ethan, this is Simone, and my friend Piper."

Piper's ears had perked up when she heard Ty's name. "You're Nate's friend from France, aren't you?" she asked him.

Ty picked up her right hand and placed a kiss on it. "*Chère Piper, j'ai beaucoup entendu parlé de vous. Nate a parle beaucoup. Mais il ne m'a jamais à quel point vous êtes ravissante. J'aimerais vous emmener chez moi; cependant, je pense que Nate me couperez les couilles puisqu'il est déjà sous votre charme, mais il ne le sait pas encore.*"

The collective sound of female sighs surrounded the table. Even Piper's. There was just something about the romantic languages.

"What did you just say?" Piper asked him in awe.

Ty dropped her hand. "That I've heard a lot about you." His English had a Midwestern accent, which made sense since Nate had told her Ty had been living in the United States since he was little. "But Nate has never said how beautiful you are."

Piper blushed as she saw Nate scowl out of the corner of her eye.

"Me next," Lainey said. "And make it dirty."

Ty laughed and grabbed Lainey's hand. While he said something in French to her friend, Piper turned to Nate.

"You okay?"

Nate furrowed his brows. "Yeah. Why do you ask?"

"Because you don't look happy. Did something happen at dinner tonight?"

"Oh, no, that went okay."

"Oh, good." She pushed her hip into him. "I didn't know you'd be here tonight."

"It was a last-minute thing. Ty texted me, and my sister helped me leave early."

"And that's why dinner went okay. Because you got to leave?" she joked.

Nate grinned. "Pretty much."

"So, how do you all know each other?" Kayla asked the guys.

"We work together," Ethan answered.

"Are you all engineers?" Piper asked.

Ty shook his head. "Nope. I'm a programmer, and Ethan's a planner."

"Huh," Kayla said.

"I know," Ty said. "Everyone thinks Ethan should be a programmer since he looks like a nerd."

Ethan gave Ty the finger, and everyone laughed.

Ty leaned forward and pretended to whisper. "He's sensitive about the red hair. I tell him all the time that he should adopt Nate's hairstyle, but he doesn't listen," Ty teased his friend.

Kayla slid closer to Ethan. "I disagree." She reached up and ran her fingers through his hair. "I love red hair on guys."

Ty glanced at Nate and raised his eyebrows with a smile.

Piper looked at Simone and Lainey, and the three grinned at one another. Kayla had been unhappy with her single life lately, and Piper was sure the other two were thinking the same thing she was, which was, *Go, Kayla*.

Nate grinned back. "Hey, don't be fooled," he said as he swiped his hand over his bald head. "Not everyone can pull this off."

Piper had to agree. She had never been attracted to bald guys before Nate.

She frowned. *That didn't come out right.*

She meant, she'd never thought bald guys were attractive before she met Nate.

Being attracted to someone wasn't the same as finding someone attractive. She thought her three coworkers were attractive, but she wasn't attracted *to* them.

And I'm not attracted to Nate.

She looked over at her best guy friend as he threw his head back and laughed. The golden skin on his neck and upper chest looked good enough to eat, and for a moment, she wondered what he tasted like.

Am I?

She groaned. "I need another drink."

CHAPTER EIGHT

Piper and Simone went to get another drink at the bar, and everyone else grabbed a stool to sit at the table. There weren't enough to go around, so Nate chose to stand. When the two ladies came back, Piper took the seat next to him, which was what he'd wanted. He didn't know what Ty had said to Piper, but Nate was sure it was something he wouldn't like.

Ty was an attractive man, going by the amount of female attention he received, but Nate didn't think Piper was ready for someone like Ty, and it was Nate's job to watch out for her.

Lainey's cell phone vibrated on the table. She picked it up and groaned.

"What's wrong?" Kayla asked.

"Ugh. Mike has been texting me all evening. I told him I was out with the girls, but he keeps insisting he wants to see me tonight."

"Well, these guys are here now. Why don't you invite him?"

Lainey shrugged. "I don't really want to."

"I thought you liked him. How long have you been seeing each other?"

"For about three weeks. He is..." She paused, as if searching for the right word. "He is kinda meh."

"So, why haven't you gotten rid of him yet?" Ty asked.

"Because...do you know how hard it is to find a guy who is at least six feet tall, a decent human being, and good in bed? I will tell you. Since only about fifteen percent of guys are over six feet tall and a lot of guys couldn't care less whether a woman got off, it's really hard. There aren't many of them out there. I'll either need to start dating guys shorter than me or settle for blandness."

"Have you slept with him yet?" Simone asked.

"Once." Lainey wrinkled her nose. "It was okay. I'm hoping it was first-time jitters on his part, and the next time will be better. He at least put some effort into trying to make me feel good."

Nate was surprised by what he was hearing. "Life is too short to fuck someone who is bad in bed."

"Amen," Ty said, and Ethan nodded his head in agreement.

Piper took a sip of her drink and set it on the table. She put her hand on her hip. "That's easy for you to say when men have an orgasm almost every time they have sex." She pointed to herself and her friends. "Us women? We're not so lucky."

"She's right, you know," Simone said. "Porn has given you men unrealistic expectations."

Nate raised an eyebrow. "No, life has given me real experiences."

"Ladies," Ty said, "we aren't stupid. We know that porn is fantasy. We know that women don't have sex with the mailman or keep their high heels on while in bed."

Piper leaned in, a serious look on her face. "That's good and all, but what about the orgasm part?"

Ty shrugged. "What about it?"

Piper laughed like she couldn't believe Ty's question. "That the woman hardly ever gets off, yet the man orgasms every time."

"And usually on the woman's face or breasts," Lainey added.

Nate held up a hand. "Okay, yes, you have a point. But you have to remember that porn is targeted toward men, and that's why the orgasms are unevenly matched." It was his turn to point to his friends. "We all know that most women do not want us to come on their faces or boobs."

Ethan pointed a thumb at Nate. "He's right. We know that. Like Ty said, we're not stupid."

Piper met Nate's eyes. "What did you mean by, most women?"

Nate smirked and lifted his beer to his lips. He took a sip and set it on the table. "A gentleman doesn't kiss and tell, Piper."

There was something in her eyes. He'd never seen it before, but it almost looked like desire, and Nate suddenly had an image of Piper kneeling before him as he unloaded himself all over her perfect tits.

He almost groaned out loud, and it was a good thing he was standing up with the table in front of him. He used his free hand to reach underneath and adjust his erection.

She shook her head, as if she were in a daze, and held up her hand. She was addressing the whole group of them. "Regardless, did you know that only fifty to seventy percent of women orgasm during sex, whereas, like, ninety-five percent of men do? And seventy-five percent of women can't climax from sex alone, and ten to fifteen percent haven't had an orgasm ever."

Lainey practically slammed her glass on the table. "Are you serious? No orgasm? Like, ever?"

Piper shrugged. "That's what I read."

"Wow. Maybe Mike isn't so bad after all," Kayla said.

Piper spread her arms out wide. "*See?* This is what I'm talking about." She dropped her hands as a look of satisfaction settled on her face. "You guys are telling Lainey she needs to find someone new because he's not great in bed, but Kayla is telling Lainey it could be worse. You men don't realize how lucky you are."

Nate studied Piper while she looked at everyone as she drove her point home. He had to wonder if Jordan had given her the type of loving she deserved. Had her boyfriends before she met her husband been selfish lovers? He hated to see her so negative about sex because, if anyone was entitled to a good fucking, it was Piper.

He pictured her on her back, dark hair spread out on white sheets as she clutched them in her fists, while she orgasmed the way a woman should. And his dick was the one that was giving it to her.

Nate knew Piper had a point, but he was tired of talking about it. Besides his first few sexual encounters back when he had been a teenager, his partners didn't have anything to complain about. Except for him not sticking around, but that was a separate complaint.

Ty held up his hand and raised his eyebrows. "I get your point. I really do. But I'm going to go back to needing to find a man who takes care of you. There might be less of us out there, but we are out there."

Simone and Lainey leaned forward.

"So, you're saying you're one of those guys?" Lainey asked.

"Damn right I am."

Simone cocked her head to the side. "How do you know she wasn't faking it?"

Of course this topic would be brought up.

Nate rolled his eyes. "Because men—at least men who know what they're doing in bed—can tell."

Ty nodded, but the women looked doubtful.

Nate sighed.

"Look"—he held up two fingers—"when a woman is turned on, she gets wet and slick. Her face flushes, her nipples pucker and darken, and her pussy gets swollen. Then, as she starts to come, her pussy starts to contract." He placed his other hand around his fingers to demonstrate. "It's almost like little mini orgasms. Not only that, but her breathing also changes, and her eyes either become glazed or squeezed shut. And her arms"—he flailed his hands around him—"start to grab on to whatever they can find. Bedding, a piece of clothing, skin. They grab hold and don't let go." He had their attention, and he met each pair of eyes. "This stuff is all physiological and can't be faked. In fact, most women don't realize a lot of this is happening. Then, when she does come"—he held up his fingers with his other fist wrapped around them again—"she squeezes your dick so fucking tight, you feel like it's going to be amputated." He pointed a finger at them. "And that's how you know a woman isn't faking it. And, if she tries, you need a new woman. Nobody likes a liar."

Everyone stared at him in silence.

"In conclusion, if your man isn't getting you off, you need a new man."

The ladies didn't agree with him, but at least they stopped arguing.

"I'll be right back," he told them. He had spotted an old acquaintance, and he wanted to go say hi before they were drowned out by music.

He was about five steps away when he heard one of the ladies say, "Holy shit. Now, I'm the one who needs another drink."

CHAPTER NINE

"**A**re my panties on fire? I feel like my panties are on fire," Lainey said.

Simone fanned a hand in front of her face. "I need a shower. Preferably a cold one."

"Piper, why did you never tell us how hot Nate was?" Kayla asked.

Piper shrugged.

After Nate had left the table, her friends had dragged her to the ladies' room.

"The way you talked about him, I pictured some homely nerd who kissed your ass because he was grateful you gave him some attention," Simone said.

Piper frowned. "Nate doesn't kiss my ass."

Lainey raised a brow, but Simone kept talking, "First, we found out he was gorgeous, and then when he was describing what he could do to a woman's body and his attention to detail...holy shit, I was ready to lie down on the floor and tell him to use me as a demonstration."

"Yeah," Kayla said, staring off into space. "The way he said it too, like he was so matter-of-fact about the whole thing, you just *know* he knows what he's doing in the bedroom." She looked at Piper. "Does he have a girlfriend?"

"No, he doesn't do girlfriends. Besides, I thought you liked Ethan?"

Kayla shrugged. "I do. But can he make me come like Nate would be able to?"

Simone shook her head. "You might as well give it up. Piper already told me Nate doesn't date. He's a one-night-stand kind of guy. And Kayla, you are not a one-night-stand kind of girl."

"I might be for him."

Piper tried to laugh at Kayla's joke, but she was starting to get irritated.

Lainey stared into the mirror and touched up her lipstick. "Well, I definitely am a one-night-stand kind of girl."

"What about Mike?" Piper asked.

Lainey shrugged. "What about him? We're not exclusive. Besides, you heard Nate. If Mike doesn't get the job done, I need to find someone who does."

"So, does that mean you're going to give him another chance?" Kayla asked.

"I think so. I might just tell him to come here. Tonight can be his final test." Lainey laughed.

"I think you should, so then we can meet him," Kayla said.

"I agree," Piper said.

"Are you bitches ready to go back out there?" Simone asked. "It sounds like the band is back."

The four of them left the restroom, and on their way back to the table, Piper saw Nate talking with someone. She had planned to walk by, but he snagged an arm around her waist.

"Hey," she said.

"Hey," he replied. "This is an old high school buddy, Conner. Conner, this is Piper."

Piper held out her hand. "Hello."

"Nice to meet you," Conner said as he shook her hand.

Nate motioned toward the band with his head. "We're going to go dance. It was nice catching up with you, man."

"You, too. Tell Luke hi from me."

"Will do."

The two men bumped fists, and Nate steered Piper toward the dance floor.

"You don't have to dance with me, you know," Piper told Nate.

"Why? Are you really bad?"

She scoffed. "No. I'm an awesome dancer." She might be exaggerating a little. "But I'm probably a little rusty."

"You didn't look rusty earlier."

Her face heated. She hadn't realized he'd been watching her earlier until the song ended, and she might not have danced the way she had if she had known. "Thanks." Although why she would be embarrassed about dancing in front of her friend, she didn't know.

The band welcomed the crowd back and then began to play Christina Perri's "A Thousand Years." Nate pulled Piper close, and she wrapped her arms around his neck.

He smelled wonderful.

It was weird, some of the things she missed about her

husband or being in a relationship. Sometimes, it was the little things, like how good and different men smelled from women. She missed breathing in Jordan's masculine scent.

This wasn't the first time she'd been close to Nate. She'd just fallen asleep on his chest the other night, but this was the first time she hadn't been sober. She didn't hold herself back from rubbing her nose across his collarbone.

She tilted her head up to put her mouth next to his ear. "You know all the girls want to fuck you now."

Nate squeezed her hips where his hands held her. "Oh, really?"

"Yep. We were in the restroom, talking about you. You could have your pick of any of my friends."

Nate chuckled. "What if I don't want them?"

For some reason, this made Piper grin like crazy. "Then, you'd better let them down easy."

"I'll try."

Piper closed her eyes and let herself enjoy being in Nate's arms. Maybe she should drink more often. It helped her get out of her head a little and let her relax and appreciate some of life's simpler things.

The two of them finished their dance, and as the next song started with an upbeat tempo, the rest of their friends came out to join them.

Their group spent almost the whole night on the dance floor, dancing and drinking. When the band finished their set, the DJ took his spot in the booth, and the music continued.

At one point, Piper went to get a refill on her drink, and when she came back, she heard Simone ask Nate, "How would you like to come to my place after this for an *after-party*?"

Piper's breath seized as she waited to see what Nate would say. Simone had her back to Piper, which was good because she wanted to hurt her friend even if she had no right. Nate was a single guy who could sleep with anyone he wanted.

Nate, as if sensing she was there, looked at her over Simone's shoulder and smiled. His blue eyes sparkled. He looked back at Simone. "Thank you for the invitation, but I'm going to have to pass. I'm taking Piper home tonight."

She knew what Nate meant, but tingles still went up her spine at his words.

Nate reached around Simone and grabbed Piper's drink-less hand, tugging her toward him. He took the drink out of her hand and gave it to Simone. "Hold this, will you, please?" he asked her and drew Piper further onto the floor.

The DJ started playing Zayn's "Dusk Till Dawn" with Sia, and Nate dragged Piper's back toward his front. Her butt was right against his groin, but rather than pulling away, she let Nate wrap his arm around her waist.

Their bodies were in sync as they swayed to the music. Piper looked down at Nate's tattooed arm and wondered what it would look like against her naked skin. She pictured his hand sliding up her body and cupping her breast. Her pale skin against his beautiful, tawny complexion.

Overcome with desire and fantasies, she dropped her head back against Nate's chest, wishing the song would never stop playing.

Later that night, after Nate drove Piper home, she went straight to her bedroom. She stripped out of her clothes, and naked, she walked to her nightstand. She picked up her iPod and scrolled through until she found "Dusk Till Dawn," connected it to her alarm clock, and hit play.

Then, she walked over to her dresser and opened the bottom drawer. She moved her clothes out of the way and reached into the back. When her hand hit silicone, she knew she'd found what she wanted. She wrapped her fingers around the object and pulled it out.

Her purple dual-stimulating vibrator had been sitting in her bottom drawer for over a year, untouched. She closed her dresser drawer and went to her bed and drew back the covers. The sheets were cool against her overheated skin, and she closed her eyes as she spread her legs and brought her toy to her center.

First, she pictured Jordan but soon realized that thinking about him made her sad. So, she switched to a nameless, faceless man as she let the pleasure build in her body. But, soon, the nameless, faceless man turned into Nate. She imagined him over her, holding his body up on his tattooed arm and his chest glistening with sweat as he took her over and over.

When the song reached its crescendo, so did Piper. She cried out into her empty room as the first orgasm since her husband died crashed over her body.

She dropped her vibrator on her bed and waited for the guilt to take over her body, but instead, she curled up into a ball and fell asleep.

CHAPTER TEN

P iper kicked off the covers from her bed and used her
hand to shield her eyes from the sun streaming
through her bedroom windows. She'd forgotten to
close the shades last night in her drunken state.

She stumbled to the master bathroom and went pee. If
her stupid bladder hadn't woken her up, she could have still
been sleeping.

After washing her hands, she grabbed her robe from the
back of the door and slipped it on.

She padded her way to the kitchen, going straight for the
glasses and her medicine cupboard. She grabbed three
ibuprofen tablets and downed them with a large glass of
water.

She definitely couldn't drink like she had in college
anymore.

She opened the fridge to look for something to eat but
realized her stomach couldn't handle anything right now, so
she settled for making coffee at the moment.

She heard her phone ringing almost from a distance, and she had to think about where she had put it last night. She paused to listen.

Her purse.

She scrambled to the front door where she had dropped it last night and dug out her phone.

"Hello?"

"Hi, honey."

"Hi, Mom."

"You don't sound so good."

Piper walked back to the kitchen to finish making her coffee. "Yeah, I went out with my coworkers last night. I think I had a little too much to drink."

Her mom laughed. "I'm sorry you feel bad, but I am excited that you went out with friends last night."

Piper had really lucked out in the mom department. She was supportive, but she didn't smother Piper, and she knew that her mom worried about her.

Back at the end of 2016, Jordan had been laid off at his job where they lived in Nebraska. The company had filed for bankruptcy and closed their doors a month later. With a large number of engineers without work, the market had been flooded, and Jordan had struggled to get another job. Jordan had made more money than Piper, and the two of them had known they had to do something if they didn't want to file for bankruptcy, too.

Jordan, who had gone to college and graduate school in Iowa before moving back home, had reached out to his old college friends about possible jobs. More than one had come through, but Nate's job had paid the most, and being in the

Minneapolis-St. Paul area would give Piper a lot of opportunities to find work also.

So, with the help of Nate's good word, Jordan had applied, interviewed, and gotten the job in Minneapolis. Piper and Jordan had moved in January and been lucky enough to find a house about fifteen minutes from Nate's, so he and Jordan could commute to work together.

Four months later, they had been on their way home when the two of them were in a car accident. Jordan had died before EMS even arrived. Nate had only had to spend a couple of nights in the hospital to be monitored.

At first, she'd been mad that Nate survived, and Jordan hadn't. Nate was single and childless. Jordan had had a wife, and for a while there, Piper had thought she was pregnant. Piper had gone off birth control after she and Jordan got married, both of them wanting a big family.

Piper had never missed a period or even been late, so after Jordan had died, she'd thought she'd been left with one last present from him.

She'd been so angry that she almost didn't visit Nate in the hospital, but her mother had convinced her to go.

The second he had seen her in his doorway, he'd broken down in tears. It had been obvious that he felt guilty for surviving when Jordan hadn't even if Nate hadn't been driving. To see such a strong alpha male break down in tears had lessened her anger toward him.

Piper had gone to his bed and lain down beside him, and while they'd held each other, they'd cried. They hadn't been a man and a woman sharing a bed. They had been two people who'd lost someone they cared about.

That had been the beginning of their friendship.

Before that, Nate had been Jordan's friend, but now, he was hers, too. And, when she'd found out stress was the reason she'd missed her period, Nate had been the one to comfort her. She honestly didn't know what she'd do without him.

Piper's mom had tried to convince her to move back home, and she had gone to stay with her mom for a week after the funeral, but it held too many memories. She'd lived with her mom her last year of college while she did a forty-hour-a-week internship that paid nothing. That was the same year she'd met Jordan through mutual friends. Her mom's house felt like a shrine to her relationship with Jordan. Where he'd picked her up on their first date, where he'd kissed her good night the first time, where they'd had sex the first time while her mom was out of town.

She'd been very grateful to go home to Minnesota after that week. She'd only lived in her house with Jordan for a few months. It had way less memories, and she made more money in Minnesota than she had in Nebraska, so she stayed.

"So, did you have a good time?" her mom asked.

"Yeah, actually, I did."

"Thank heavens. I was afraid you would hole up in your house forever and never meet another man."

Piper chuckled at her mom's dramatics. "Mom, it's only been a little over a year."

"I know, honey. But you're still so young. I don't want to see you miss the opportunity to love again. You need to get back out there."

Piper raised her eyebrows. "Oh, really? Like you're one to talk."

Her father had passed away six years ago, and Piper had yet to see her mother go on a date.

Her mom cleared her throat. "Well, that's actually one of the reasons I'm calling."

Piper's ears perked.

"What are you doing the beginning of August? Can you get off of work?"

Now, Piper was very curious. "Yes, that shouldn't be a problem. What's going on?"

Her mother sucked in an audible breath. "I'm getting married."

"*What?*" Piper pulled out a chair at her counter and plopped into it.

"It's true." Her mother laughed. "I can't believe it myself."

"What—when—how?"

"Do you remember our old neighbors, the Gibsons?"

"Yes. Their dog used to poop in our yard, and their son used to drive that old car that would backfire every time he started it. Their daughter was nice though."

"Yes, that's them. I ran into Don a couple of months back, and we got to talking. Stella had passed about a year after your father, and we started hanging out, the two of us being widowed and all. And the rest, they say, is history."

"Wow."

"Are you mad?" her mom asked hesitantly.

"What? No, Mom. Why would I be mad?"

"Because I know how much you loved your father."

"Yes, I did, but I love you, too, and I want you to be happy."

"Oh, good, because I want you to be my matron of honor."

"Really?" Piper felt tears welling up in her eyes.

"Of course. You're my daughter, and I love you. There's no one else I'd rather have stand beside me."

Piper sniffled. "Thanks, Mom. I will be there. Let me know the final date as soon as you can, and I will put in my request at work."

"Thanks, baby. Maybe you can come home and visit before then, and then you can get to know Don a little better."

"I'll try to do that."

"Now, no more tears. This is a happy time."

"How did you know I was crying?"

Her mom laughed. "Piper, I've known you your whole life, and I raised you. You can't hide that stuff from me."

Piper rolled her eyes. "Okay, Mom."

"Well, I'd better go. Don is taking me to brunch. Just think about what I said, okay? It's okay to get back out there. Jordan wouldn't want you to be single for the rest of your life."

"You're the second person who's said something like that to me this week."

"Great minds think alike. But I'm serious."

"I know. I love you."

"Love you, too. Talk to you soon."

"Okay."

"Bye."

"Bye."

Piper hung up the phone and grabbed a cup of coffee. She sipped her favorite beverage on the way to her bedroom. When she got in the doorway, she saw a purple object lying on her white comforter, and she blushed.

She'd almost forgotten about coming home last night and pulling out her vibrator. She hadn't had an orgasm in over a year, and she admitted, it'd felt wonderful.

Maybe this was a sign that she was ready to start dating. She'd always had a healthy libido, sometimes wanting sex more than her past boyfriends, including Jordan. She knew that, if she was masturbating, it would only lead to wanting the real thing.

She didn't have to marry the first guy she went out with, but maybe she would like him enough to date and sleep with him. She honestly didn't know if she would ever get married again. Loving someone that much and losing them was like being eviscerated. But there was no harm in liking someone and seeing them occasionally.

Piper quickly downed her coffee, took a shower, put on some sweats, and made a beeline for her computer. She opened up two windows and went to Match.com and eHarmony.com.

As she began answering the questions on the first site, she knew it was going to be a long day. It was a good thing she didn't have any plans.

CHAPTER ELEVEN

The following Wednesday, Nate had just pulled the dinner from the oven when he heard Piper's garage door open and her car pull in. Two minutes later, she walked through the door and stuck her nose in the air.

"Smells delicious. What did you make?"

Nate always got off work before Piper, so oftentimes, he'd cook for her when it was his turn, and she'd often get takeout when it was her turn.

"Enchiladas."

"I'm so glad your grandmother taught you how to make those."

Nate laughed. "Me, too."

Not only were they delicious, but whenever he made them, he also felt closer to his *abuelita*.

Piper went to change out of her work clothes while Nate dished up the food and set the table.

Once they were seated, Nate asked her, "So, tell me

about your date last night. All you said in your text was that it didn't go well."

Piper finished chewing her bite of food and swallowed. "It wasn't that it was bad; it just wasn't good. He was very blah."

"What made you decide to accept in the first place?"

She shrugged. "He asked."

Nate set his fork on his plate, prongs first, and raised his eyebrows.

"I haven't dated for years. I figure I might as well get out there and see what it's like these days. And I also figure the more I weed out the bad ones, the more likely I am to find a good one."

While a part of Nate was happy that she hadn't enjoyed her date, he didn't want her saying yes to every single guy who asked her. "What's the rush? I mean, you just set up your dating profiles on Sunday, and you had a date on Tuesday."

"One, if the date didn't go well, I had the excuse all set up to leave early since I had to get up for work. Two, why wait until the weekend? It's not like I had anything I had to do last night. And, three, I miss sex," she said nonchalantly.

Nate coughed as he nearly choked on his food. He picked up his water and took a big gulp. "Excuse me?" he said after setting the glass down.

She looked up from her food and frowned. "I miss sex. When I got home on Saturday, I actually pulled out my vibrator."

"Holy shit, Piper. You can't just spring something like that on a guy. Warn me first."

She laughed. "Why? Because I said the word *vibrator*?"

"I don't know. Maybe."

"Well, we can't all have a harem of women on our speed dial, waiting for us to call them up for a booty call."

Nate shifted in his seat. "I don't have a harem," he protested.

"Let's agree to disagree. The point is, I miss sex. I haven't had sex for over a year. I have never gone that long, and I would like to have it again."

"This conversation is making me uncomfortable."

"Because we're talking about sex?"

He shrugged. "Yes."

Piper studied his face. "So, tell me this. If you were talking to one of your guy friends—let's say, Luke—and he lost his wife..."

Nate nodded to show her he was listening.

"So, one night, this friend told you he was gonna start dating again because he missed sex. Would your response be the same?"

"No." He hated to admit it.

She pointed her fork at him. "In fact, I bet you would have nagged him for months to go and get laid."

Nate actually thought about what she'd said. If a guy friend were still pining after a girl he'd broken up with, sure, he would tell him to go and get laid. But he didn't know if he would honestly do that if the guy were a widower.

"I don't think so."

"Well, you wouldn't choke on your food like you did when I said something."

"Yeah"—he rolled his eyes—"you're right."

"And you know why?"

"I have a feeling you're going to tell me, no matter what I say."

"It's because I'm a girl. You're being stereotypical."

No, it was because he didn't want to picture Piper having sex with some random guy. Just the thought of it made him uncomfortable. Not because he couldn't imagine Piper naked, but because he didn't want to even think about some guy sticking his dick in *his* Piper.

But he couldn't tell her that.

And what the hell was he thinking? *His* Piper?

She wasn't his. She was Jordan's.

Pretty sure when Jordan had said, "Take care of Piper," he didn't mean, *Fuck my wife.*

Yes, that had to be it. Nate was thinking about Jordan.

But he couldn't tell her that either.

Piper had cried on his shoulder about her husband many times. And, while it might be hard for Nate to see her with anyone else, Jordan would not want his wife to be lonely for the rest of her life.

"Actually," Nate told her, "you're a woman, and you're right. I would react differently if, say, Luke were sitting here with me rather than you."

She blinked a couple of times. "Wow, I didn't think you'd admit I was right so easily."

"Now, who's being stereotypical?"

She laughed.

"I'm glad you're moving on. But will you promise me one thing?"

She tilted her head to the side. "Maybe."

"Please be careful. There are some crazies out there."

She made an X in the middle of her chest. "Cross my heart."

He chuckled.

"If it makes you feel any better, I met my date at the restaurant. I didn't tell him where I lived or anything like that."

"Good." He nodded. "So, when is your next date?" he asked as Piper got up to put her plate in the sink.

"Saturday."

"*Saturday?*"

Piper spun on her heel and raised her brow.

Nate cleared his throat. "I mean, good for you."

She smiled sweetly. "That's what I thought you meant."

Nate got up from his seat, too, and the two of them cleaned up their dishes and put the food away.

"Let's go watch our show."

"Okay," Nate said as he followed Piper into her living room. They sat on the couch while she grabbed her remotes to turn on the television and Netflix. "What is the guy like, the one you're going out with on Saturday?"

"He's rich. He's a stockbroker."

Nate raised his brow. "Really?"

"Oh, yeah."

"Where?"

"On Wall Street."

"Wall Street? How in the hell are you—"

"I'm just kidding. He's actually a hit man," she tried to say with a straight face.

"Piper."

She laughed at her own joke and punched him in the arm. "Joking. He's an accountant."

"Oh."

She shook her head. "What's with the big-brother routine?"

Trust me, sweetheart, I feel anything but brotherly toward you.

He shrugged. "I'm just worried about you, I guess. I can't help it."

"Aw," she said and scooted closer to him. She wrapped her hand around his bicep and rested her head on his shoulder. "You're so sweet."

Inside, he cringed. He didn't feel sweet.

Piper hit play on their show, and he tried to concentrate on what they were watching, but she smelled and felt so damn good. The fucking hard-on in his pants didn't help. It was almost a relief when the episode ended, and Nate told her he needed to get home.

After saying good-bye, he got in his truck and thumbed through his Contacts. He went past the usual women he had sex with until he got to the end, and then he scrolled back up again. He picked a number and hit Send, only to immediately hit End.

He was hard and horny, but he just couldn't do the meaningless-sex thing tonight. He didn't know what had gotten into him because he couldn't remember ever feeling this way before.

Instead of calling someone over, he went home and used his fist. He imagined what Piper would look like naked. As she rode him. To her own climax. And that was what made Nate come.

After he cleaned himself up and dropped into bed, he couldn't help but wonder who Piper had thought about on Saturday when she did the very same thing.

Then, he laughed. Because he highly doubted she'd been thinking of him.

CHAPTER TWELVE

Piper pulled open the door to the restaurant and approached the hostess stand. "I'm meeting some-one. Carl Smith."

The hostess smiled. "Right this way, miss."

When Piper saw her date sitting at their table, she breathed a sigh of relief. He looked just like his picture. His hair was light brown, and he even reminded her of Jordan with his oval face and hazel eyes. Her date on Tuesday had looked like his profile picture, too, except she'd known instantly that it had to be at least ten years old.

Carl stood when he saw her, and a smile spread across his face.

"Here you are, miss. Your server will be over shortly."

"Thank you," Piper said.

The hostess left with a nod, and Piper held out her hand to Carl. "Hello."

He took her hand and kissed her knuckles. "Good evening, Piper."

She grinned. *What a gentleman.*

"Shall we sit?" Carl asked her.

"Oh, yes," she said and reached for her chair.

"Wait," he said and came around to pull her chair out for her.

Piper couldn't remember the last time she'd been treated like such a lady.

"Did you find the place okay?" Carl asked her.

"Yes. Nowadays, with Google Maps, directions are pretty easy."

Carl pulled open his menu. "This is very true."

Piper opened her own menu and perused the items.

Their server came over and took Piper's drink order. She decided to go with white wine because she didn't care for red much. After bringing Piper's wine, the server took their orders and menus and walked away.

The two of them sat together for a few minutes with neither of them saying anything.

Piper chuckled to herself. "I'm sorry. I'm bad at this. This is only my second date since..."

Carl leaned forward in his seat. "Hey, that's okay. It was hard for me, too, after my wife died. I felt like a fish out of water."

One of the reasons Piper had said yes to Carl was because he was a widower. Who better to understand her situation than someone who had been in her shoes?

She ran her thumb over the rim of her glass. "Can I ask, how many dates had you been on before it got easier?" She looked at Carl when he didn't respond. "I'm sorry. That was kind of personal." She rolled her eyes. "Lesson one: don't ask your date how many other dates they've been on. I told you I was bad at this."

Carl smiled. "It's okay. I know you're asking for future reference, not because you're quizzing me about how many women I've dated before you. Let's just say, it took about five to ten dates before I felt comfortable."

"Oh, great. You're only number two."

They both laughed.

"Well then," Carl said, "I guess it's my job to make you comfortable."

Piper blushed at his flirty words, but she was already starting to feel better about their date.

By the time dinner was over, Piper and Carl were talking like old friends. They had a lot in common from being Cornhusker fans to both not liking *Star Wars*. They also bonded over their widowed statuses and never getting to have kids. The more they talked, the more Piper felt like he was a really nice guy. And, when their check came, Carl paid for it even though Piper had tried to go Dutch.

"What are you doing tomorrow?" Carl asked her.

"Nothing exciting. I have some errands to run." She didn't mention Nate was coming over to work on her house. It didn't seem like the right time to tell Carl about Nate. "Why?"

"I was wondering if you'd want to have brunch with me tomorrow."

"I would love to. Would you like to pick me up?"

"Uh...no. How about we meet at the restaurant again?"

Piper thought it was kind of odd, but maybe he didn't

want to scare her away. "Okay. You tell me when and where, and I'll be there."

They made their brunch plans, and then Carl walked Piper to the front of the restaurant. Once they were outside, he leaned in close and gently kissed Piper on the mouth.

It was tender and sweet.

The next morning, Piper picked through her clothes, trying to decide what to wear to brunch. It didn't help that she was having mixed feelings about her second date.

At dinner the night before, she'd had a great time and really clicked with Carl. But, after she'd gotten home and lain in bed, she'd started to feel guilty. What if Jordan was up in heaven, watching her and feeling sad that she'd found someone so fast? Even though it wasn't like that and she hardly knew Carl yet, the remorse had weighed heavily on her shoulders.

She sat on her bed and took a deep breath. She fell back onto the comforter and stared up at the ceiling. "Jordan, I need your advice. Can you please tell me what to do? Or send me some sort of sign?"

There was no answer, of course.

Piper dragged her butt back up and finished finding an outfit. Since it was brunch, she chose a casual outfit of capris and a T-shirt. She looked cute but not sexy. She went to the bathroom where she put on her makeup and brushed her teeth.

When she left her bedroom and walked down the hall, she was surprised to see Nate in her kitchen.

"Oh," she said when she saw him. "When did you get here?"

"Just a few minutes ago." He looked her up and down. "Where are you going?"

Nate had been a little weird about her dating, so she lifted her chin. "I have a second date with Carl."

Nate curled his lip. "Carl? That's his name?"

"Yes, that's his name," she said as she stepped around Nate to grab a cup of coffee.

"He sounds...boring."

Piper set her mug down hard and spun around. "Why are you being like this?"

"Like what?" Nate asked, but he looked ashamed, so she knew that he knew what she was talking about.

"Like I'm doing something wrong." She sighed. "Is that it? You think it's too early? That I shouldn't be dating?" A horrible thought came to her. "Do you think I'm a bad wife?"

Nate's shoulders slumped, and all the defiance left his body. "No. Of course not."

"Then...why?"

He ran a hand down his face. "I don't know, Piper. But you're right. I shouldn't be putting whatever I'm feeling on you. You are not a bad wife. Jordan has been gone for a year, and I saw how his death devastated you. You deserve to be happy. I'm sorry if I'm standing in the way of that."

She wanted to ask him what he meant by whatever he was feeling, but her phone beeped in her pocket. It was a text from Carl, which told her he'd see her soon.

"I have to go," she told Nate.

"What about your coffee?"

"I'll get some at the restaurant."

Nate stopped her with a hand to her elbow. "I'm sorry, Piper."

She put her hand on his arm. "You're forgiven. But I really do have to go."

Nate opened his mouth but closed it again. "See you later," he said with a head nod.

Piper tried to shake off the effects of the morning before she met up with her brunch date, but it was hard. First, it had been her uncertainty and guilt, and then Nate's slight hostility had put her in a foul mood.

It was a good thing that, when she saw Carl waiting for her, he had a bouquet of flowers with him.

"Are these for me?" she asked.

"Yes. Beautiful flowers for a beautiful lady."

Piper blushed. His words were a little cheesy, but she needed them this morning. Maybe coming here for date two was the right thing to do.

"Thank you. They really are beautiful. I haven't gotten flowers in a long time."

Carl grinned. "Shall we go in?"

"Yes. I'm starved. And I haven't had any coffee yet."

"Why not?" Carl asked as he led her inside by the small of her back.

"Oh, I just ran out of time. I should have woken up earlier," she lied. She really didn't feel like her and Nate's argument was any of Carl's business.

They had to wait about ten minutes until a table opened

up. It seemed like Carl was getting antsy, waiting, because he looked at his watch every few minutes.

"Are you okay?" she asked him. "You seem impatient."

"What?" He looked at her. "Oh, no. I'm just hungry."

Once they were seated, the server came over with water for them.

"We'd like to order right away, please."

We would?

Nobody had told Piper that. Good thing she already knew what she wanted.

They had just put in their orders when someone yelled, "Carl Hughes! Where is that son of a bitch?"

Carl's eyes widened, and he sank down in his chair, but he couldn't escape the woman. She came charging for their table as fast as the busy restaurant would allow.

"So, this is why you didn't want to go to church with your family, huh? So you could take some hussy out on a date? Did you really think I wouldn't find out? Your wife wasn't born yesterday."

Piper sprang from her chair. "Whoa," she said in shock. "Ma'am, I am sorry. I didn't know he was married. He told me he was a widower."

The woman narrowed her eyes at Piper, and she was a little afraid of this woman's wrath.

"Let me guess. You're a widow, and you connected over the two of you losing your spouses?"

"Yes," Piper said hesitantly.

"Figures. That's kind of his thing now."

"His thing?"

"Yes, Carl likes to prey on vulnerable widows."

Piper looked at Carl, who wouldn't meet her eyes. "You're an asshole," she told him. "I'm sorry," Piper told Carl's very-much-alive wife. Piper wanted to ask the woman why she was still married to him.

"No, I'm sorry. I should have murdered him the last time I caught him cheating."

Piper grabbed her purse and her flowers. Before she walked away, she handed the bouquet to Carl's wife. "These are for you. You deserve them." Then, she escaped the restaurant as fast as she could.

Once she got in her car, she looked up at the bright summer sky.

"I got your sign, Jordan. You could have been a little subtler."

CHAPTER THIRTEEN

"**H**all."

Nate continued to hammer at the nail. *Pound, pound, pound.*

"*Hall.*"

He didn't understand why he was concerned so much with Piper's morning date.

"Nate!"

He stopped what he was doing and turned around to look at Luke. "What?"

Luke raised his brow. "I think you got the nail in."

Nate looked down at the wood that he had pounded so hard, there was now a large circle in the shape of the hammerhead. "Oh, I didn't mean to do that."

"What's wrong with you today? You've been off all morning."

Nate didn't want to admit to his friend that Piper's date bothered him. He put the ruined wood in the scrap pile and grabbed a new piece. He didn't answer Luke's question, but thankfully, his friend left him alone.

But, when it was time for a water and piss break, Luke cornered Nate before he could go back outside.

"Yes?" Nate said.

"You need to tell me what's bugging you. You've messed up five times now, and we're going to have to go back to the lumberyard. I'm sure Piper would love to pay more money than she already has."

"I didn't mess up five times."

Luke proceeded to list not five, but six mistakes that Nate had made.

Nate sighed in defeat and took a seat on one of the kitchen stools. "If I tell you this, you'd better keep your mouth shut."

Instead of being worried by Nate's threat, Luke chuckled, but at least he said, "I won't say anything."

"Not even to your wife?"

"Not even to Elise."

Nate ran a hand over his bald head. He had a tiny amount of stubble on there today because he hadn't shaved before coming over to Piper's. "Piper's dating."

Luke nodded in understanding. "Now, it makes sense."

Nate narrowed his eyes at him. "No. Nothing makes sense. What do you mean by that?"

Luke shrugged. "You like her."

"No. I mean, yes. She's my friend. I'm worried about her."

Luke chuckled.

"Why are you laughing? This isn't funny."

"It kind of is." Luke smirked. "If you were me, you would understand."

Nate stood up, ready to get back to work before Luke could say more, when there was a knock at the front door, and Elise walked through it.

Luke's attention immediately went to his wife, and he grinned.

"Remember, bros before hos," Nate hissed.

Luke laughed and punched Nate in the arm. "I'm not going to say anything."

Nate would have a better time believing Luke if the guy didn't have a silly smile on his face.

"Hey, guys," Elise said. "How's it going this morning? Have you gotten a lot of work done?"

"Not really," Luke said, and Nate shot him a stern look.

"That's too bad," Elise said. "I was hoping to steal you for lunch," she said to her husband.

Luke wrapped his arms around Elise and pulled them together. "As long as you don't mind me being sweaty."

Elise ran her hands along Luke's arms. "I love you sweaty."

Nate rolled his eyes. He was about to tell them to get a room when the door to the garage opened, and Piper came storming through.

She slammed the door behind her and stopped when she saw the three of them. "I am never going on a date again," she stated and took off down the hall.

"Uh-oh," Elise said. "I'd better take a rain check on our lunch date and go talk to Piper."

"Okay," Luke said and gave her a kiss. He let go of his wife and turned around. "I wonder what that's all about."

So did Nate.

♡

Piper threw her purse on her bed in frustration. She felt like such a fool.

A knock came from behind her. She really wasn't in the mood for Nate right now. She turned around to tell him to go away when she saw Elise standing there. "Hey."

"Can I come in?"

"Sure," Piper said and collapsed on her bed.

Elise closed the bedroom door as she entered the room. "I know we still don't know each other that well, but I thought maybe you needed someone to talk to."

"That would be nice."

Elise sat down next to Piper. "So, what happened today?"

Piper snorted. "I met this guy through one of the online dating sites I signed up with."

Elise nodded. "I remember you working on that last weekend."

"Well...the guy I met seemed really great. He was a widower, he had a good job, and we had things in common. We went out last night, and the only thing he did was kiss me outside the restaurant. No pressuring me to sleep with him or anything. He even asked me out on a second date today for brunch."

"Did you go and meet him this morning?"

Piper nodded slowly. "Yep."

"Then, what happened? Did he try something with you?"

"No, nothing like that." Piper shook her head. "We had to wait to be seated, and I noticed he was getting impatient. Then, when we got our table, he insisted on ordering right away."

"I'm thinking there's more to this than his impatience."

"Oh, yeah. His wife, who is alive and well, showed up at the restaurant."

Elise gasped. "*No way.*"

Piper laughed humorlessly. "That's not even the best part. While she was planning to go to church, he was taking another woman on a date."

"What an asshole."

Piper smiled. "Hey, that's what I called him. The worst part is that I think he might have kids, too. His wife said something about family. 'This is why you didn't want to go to church with your family,'" she quoted the woman. She dropped her head in her hands. "I feel so stupid."

Elise put her arm around Piper and hugged her. "You're not stupid. Some men are just douche canoes."

Piper whipped her head up. "Does this mean I'm a home-wrecker?"

Elise smiled kindly. "No, honey, you're not a home-wrecker. You didn't know he was married...or had kids. And it was a date and a half. He's the homewrecker."

"Yeah. Thanks. You're right. Thank you for making me feel better."

Elise dropped her arm. "You don't want to give up dating

just because of this one guy. He's not worth ruining all future dates."

Piper rubbed her hands together. "The only thing is that I have been feeling guilty about it anyway. I can't help feeling like I'm trying to replace Jordan, and that doesn't seem fair."

"Maybe you should wait a little while before your next date. What made you decide to start dating in the first place?"

Piper shrugged one shoulder. "I miss sex."

Elise's eyes rounded. "Okay. I was not expecting that answer."

Piper laughed. "Is that bad?"

"Not at all. I get it. Good sex is like chocolate. It's addictive as hell, and one can stay away for only so long."

"Right now, I'd settle for any sex. It's been a long time for me."

Elise smiled in sympathy. "I suppose it has." She patted Piper's leg. "If dating's not an option, there's always a one-night stand or a fuck buddy."

"What was that?" Piper asked, surprised. She needed Elise to repeat the words just to make sure she'd heard them correctly.

"You could have a one-night stand or find yourself a fuck buddy."

"Hmm...maybe you're right."

"Have you ever had either?"

"I had a couple of one-nighters in college." Piper tapped her chin. "You might be onto something here."

"It's an idea anyway."

"Thanks, Elise. I feel better."

"You're welcome." Elise stood. "Since you didn't get to eat, do you want to go grab lunch?"

"Yes." Piper got up from her bed, too.

The two of them headed for the bedroom door, but Piper stopped Elise with a hand to her arm.

"Please don't say anything to the guys. I'm still embarrassed, and Nate's been acting weird about me dating as it is."

"It'll be our secret."

Piper and Elise exited the bedroom and walked down the hall. The closer they got to the end, the louder Nate and Luke became.

"Remember, chicks before dicks," Piper reminded her.

Elise smiled. "I won't say a word."

CHAPTER FOURTEEN

The following Thursday, Piper sat at work with one of the shelter's newest residents. Tina was only twenty-three with four kids. She'd barely finished high school before she got married to her husband. He'd been abusive their whole relationship, but Tina had finally left him after he forced her to have sex with his dealer to pay for his drugs. To make matters worse, after he'd sobered up, he'd accused her of cheating. He'd beaten her so badly that her four-year-old ran to the neighbor's to call 911 because Tina had almost died.

One thing Piper would never understand was how men like Tina's husband lived life without any consequences while nice guys like Jordan were killed in a car accident.

"Are you sure you don't want to press charges against your husband?" Piper asked Tina.

She rapidly shook her head. "No. He'll get out and come after me for putting him in jail."

"Tina, you have a strong case. You have pictures from the

hospital, you have your neighbor as a witness, and you have the doctor's testimony. He won't get away with it this time."

Tina's lower lip quivered. "But I'm scared."

Piper's heart went out to the girl. "I know, but we will be with you every step of the way."

Tina didn't say anything.

"How about you think about it for a while? Will that make you feel better?"

Tina nodded.

Piper breathed a sigh of relief. Tina hadn't said yes, but she hadn't said no either. Piper would give her as much time as she could to show her that she and her children were safe at the shelter.

"Okay." Piper smiled. "Until then, do you want to talk about getting a job?"

"Yes, please." Tina blushed. "Tommy would never let me work. He said it'd give me too many ideas."

"The nice thing is, Tommy's not here. I have a list. Shall we go over it?"

Tina nodded timidly, but Piper could see excitement in her eyes.

Piper couldn't imagine a job—and probably a minimum wage job at that—would make her that happy. It made her realize how lucky she was. Yes, she'd lost her wonderful husband, and she'd gone on a date with a cheating loser, but at least she'd never lived in fear every day of her life. It made her realize she had a lot to be thankful for, and she shouldn't give up yet on finding a nice guy.

The rest of the morning passed swiftly as Piper helped Tina with her job search and with filling out applications.

Piper really hoped, one day, after Tina got on her feet, she could take some college classes at night to give her a chance at getting a better job to provide for her children.

On their hour lunch break, Lainey, Simone, Kayla, and Piper decided to go to a fast food restaurant.

"What are you ladies doing this weekend?" Piper asked once the four of them were seated.

She'd been thinking about what Elise had said about a one-night stand. Piper hadn't done the one-night thing in a while. The last time had been back in college before she met Jordan, but she was willing to give it a try.

It was better than watching porn on her computer every night.

Not that she did that or anything.

Kayla blushed. "I'm going on a date with Ethan."

"Way to go, girl," Simone said.

"I didn't know you were seeing each other," Piper said.

"We've only had one date so far. This will be our second."

"Good for you," Piper told her even if a tiny part of her was jealous.

Kayla hadn't even been looking for a man, and she'd found one. But that was kind of the way life worked.

"I have you to thank. If you didn't know Nate, then I probably wouldn't have been introduced to Ethan."

"You can thank me during your wedding toast," Piper joked.

Everyone laughed.

"What about you two?" Piper said to Lainey and Simone.

"What are you thinking?" Lainey asked.

"I want to go out. Dancing and drinking, somewhere fun."

Lainey's eyes widened. "Really?"

"Really." Going to see that live band had been fun, but that was a bar. If Piper was going to seek out a handsome man to take her home, she needed to go to a club.

"I'm in," Simone said.

"Me, too," said Lainey.

"What about Mike?" Kayla asked Lainey.

"I told him we'd be better off as friends."

"I'm sorry," Piper said, and the other two nodded.

Lainey shrugged. "I'm not. It's better this way."

"Hey, speaking of dates, didn't you go on one last weekend?" Simone asked Piper.

"Yes," she said regretfully. She'd been avoiding talking about the whole thing all week. She'd hoped they'd forgotten. "It didn't go so hot."

Piper told them all about the date on Saturday night and Sunday morning.

"What a dick," Simone said when Piper was finished.

"You're telling me," she agreed.

"Do you have any other dates lined up?" Kayla asked.

Piper shook her head. "No. I was already feeling guilty about going on a date. Part of me feels like I'm trying to replace Jordan. This past weekend didn't help. I think I need to wait a bit before I try dating again."

Simone grabbed Piper's hand. "I'm sorry."

Piper smiled. "Thanks."

"So, why do you want to go out this weekend?"

"I need to get laid."

Piper's three friends stared at her with mouths opened.

"Don't look at me like that. I miss sex."

"Hey," Lainey said, "I'm not judging. I'm just in shock, is all."

"I'm kind of surprised, too," Piper admitted. "I thought I was pretty much asexual now that Jordan's gone, but nope. My libido's back, and she's ready to party."

"Is this why you've been going on dates?" Simone asked.

"Yes. But, since that's not working for me, I figured I'd go another route."

"Have you ever had a one-nighter before?" Kayla asked.

"Years ago, yes."

"What about Nate?" Lainey asked.

"Nate? What about him?"

"Why don't you sleep with him?"

Piper was baffled. "I can't do that."

"Why not?" Lainey asked.

"Because...I just can't."

He was her friend. Besides, he had never given any indication he was interested in her sexually.

"That's a shame," Lainey said. "He seems to know what he's doing in the bedroom. If anyone should end your sexual hiatus, it should be him."

Piper laughed uncomfortably. "I don't think Nate would agree. He gets plenty. He doesn't need me. Plus, it would ruin his whole non-relationship thing he has going with his sexual partners because we're friends."

Lainey raised her eyebrows. "If you say so."

"What about Ty?" Kayla asked. "He sure seemed like he might be interested in you."

Simone cleared her throat. "I don't know if that's a good idea."

"Why?" Lainey asked as the three of them looked at Simone. Lainey gasped. "You had sex with him."

Simone turned red.

"How? When? You drove me home the night we went to see the band."

"I took my sister to the same bar on Saturday, and Ty was there again, too." She smiled coyly. "One thing led to another, and I went home with him."

"You bitch. You kept this from me all week," Lainey said. Her words were harsh, but she was smiling.

Simone shrugged.

Lainey leaned forward and whispered, "Was it good?"

Simone picked up her drink and took a sip.

"It was good," Lainey told Kayla and Piper. "She's just trying not to kiss and tell."

Piper was happy for Simone now, too, but again, she felt a little jealous. It seemed everyone was hooking up with someone.

Piper and the other three returned to work after making plans for Friday. She was excited and nervous at the same time. She hadn't gone out dancing in years. No matter what happened man-wise, she was sure she'd have fun with the girls.

What Piper hadn't told her friends was that, besides missing sex, she was kind of lonely. Yes, she had realized that she wasn't ready to date, and she couldn't imagine someone taking Jordan's place, but she still missed the physical closeness of being with a man.

Sure, she fell asleep on Nate's chest sometimes when they were watching television on the couch, but it wasn't the same as being close to someone after having sex. Maybe she was inviting trouble by sleeping with a stranger when she was lonely, and she would actually feel a little bad for using someone for that reason.

Although she wouldn't feel too guilty. There were plenty of men who wanted to have one-night stands who wouldn't be the least bit mad about being used and who would use her in return.

She just needed to find a guy like that on Friday.

CHAPTER FIFTEEN

"**D**o you want another drink?" Lainey shouted in Piper's ear.

The nightclub was packed, and the music blared on the dance floor.

She nodded yes. "I'll go with you," she yelled back.

Before following Lainey to the nearest bar, Piper looked for Simone. Her friend was still dancing with a guy she'd met at the club earlier. When Simone looked her way, Piper pointed to the bar to let her know where she and Lainey were going. Simone nodded and turned her attention back to her dance partner.

Piper hurried to catch up to Lainey, and the two took seats at the bar. The bartender took their orders, made their drinks, and moved on to the next customer.

"Are you having fun?" Lainey asked. It was a little quieter where they sat and therefore easier to hear each other.

"Yes. I haven't had a night out like this in a couple of years at least," Piper answered. "What about you?"

"Hell yeah. I'm so glad you had the idea to come out this weekend. I didn't know you were such a good dancer."

Piper blushed at the compliment. "Thanks. I think it was how I burned off all my empty alcohol calories in college."

"Same here." Lainey picked up her glass. "Cheers to us."

Piper laughed and knocked her drink against her friend's.

"So, talked to any cute guys yet?" Lainey asked.

Piper shrugged. "A few. None worth taking home though."

Lainey smiled coyly. "Well, don't look now, but there are two cute guys headed this way."

Piper slowly swiveled her seat around and reached for a napkin, just as two guys stopped next to her. One had dark hair and dark eyes, wearing jeans and a casual blue button-down shirt, and the other was a dark blond with lighter eyes, wearing jeans and a black henley. Lainey was right; they were both cute.

Piper looked over at her friend and fanned her face to let her know she felt the same way.

Lainey laughed as the two men looked at them, which made Piper laugh, too, and then Lainey laughed harder.

"What's so funny?" Dark Hair asked.

Shit. Piper didn't want them to think they were laughing at them. She scrambled to come up with something.

"Something that happened at work. We'd share it with you, but trust us, it's one of those stories that loses all humor once you say it out loud," Lainey told them.

Nice save, Lainey.

"That's good. For a minute there, we thought you were laughing at us," Blond Man said.

Piper shook her head and tried to look extra innocent. "Never."

Both guys laughed.

"I'm Bren," Dark Hair said. "And this is Travis."

Piper held out her hand. "I'm Piper. This is Lainey."

Both men shook their hands.

"What are you ladies doing tonight?" Travis asked.

"Having a girls' night," Lainey answered.

"Aw. Leave the men at home while you ladies party?" Travis said.

"Nah. No men to leave at home," Piper said with a smile while meeting Travis's eyes. She hoped he picked up on her message that they were single.

He raised his eyebrows. "Good to know."

Bren looked in both directions at the two bartenders. "What does a guy have to do to get a drink around here?"

The two male bartenders had been neglecting Bren and Travis in favor of serving the women who had walked up to the bar.

"It helps to have tits," Piper told them. And, since she came with a full package of them, she stood up from her seat and partway leaned over the bar. That evening, she'd chosen to wear a little white dress with a low-cut front, giving her plenty of cleavage to flaunt.

One of the bartenders noticed Piper and headed right for her. "What can I get you?"

Piper looked at the men.

"Whiskey sour," Travis said.

"Beer," Bren said.

She smiled at the bartender. "Whiskey sour and a beer, please."

She sat back down as Travis's and Bren's drinks were made, and the two men paid.

Lainey pulled Piper close. "I call dibs on Bren," she whispered.

"Deal," Piper whispered back. She'd already set her sights on Travis anyway.

After the bartender walked away, Lainey asked, "Do you two gentlemen dance?"

Bren held his hand out to her. "After you."

After Lainey and Bren walked away, Travis turned to Piper. "Shall we?"

She grinned at him. "We shall."

As they walked to the dance floor, Travis leaned over and asked, "I've never seen you here before. Are you new to the area?"

She didn't want to tell this sexy guy—and potential one-night stand—that she was a widow and that this was her first time at a nightclub since he'd passed away. So, she went with a shorter and easier answer. "Kind of. I've lived here awhile, but this is the first time I've come here with my friends."

They'd almost reached the dance floor when Travis turned around and started walking backward. "Well, in case I forget to tell you, I'm glad you came."

His smile was pure sex, and Piper blushed.

They reached a small table on the outside of the dance floor, and Travis took a long drink from his cup and set it down. Then, he picked up her drink and set it next to his. He grabbed her hand. "Let's go dance."

Piper laughed excitedly as he led her to the dance floor. The light hit his eyes just right, and she noticed they were blue. Darker than Nate's and definitely not as beautiful.

She mentally paused. *Why am I thinking about Nate? I should be thinking about Jordan.*

Piper met Travis's eyes, and he smiled at her again.

No, I should be thinking about the sexy guy in front of me.

And, with that thought, she wrapped her arms around Travis's neck and pulled him close. The song wasn't slow, but it had a good beat, giving them the right amount of rhythm to bump and grind with each other.

A couple of hours later, Piper was dancing with Simone when a strong set of arms went around her waist. The dusting of dark blond hair told her it was Travis, and she pushed her ass against his groin.

He pulled her tighter, and she tilted her head up and back and kissed Travis. She'd been waiting to kiss him, and now seemed like the perfect time. The man was a good kisser, without a doubt, and she imagined he'd be good in the sack, too.

Yet something was missing.

She pulled away and turned around in his arms; she studied him as if that would give her the answer she needed.

But then she realized it had to be that he wasn't her husband. She was simply used to her husband, and this guy was new. It was like a new house. At first, it felt like you were at a stranger's, but after some time, it would feel like your home.

She just needed to relax and remember that, while Travis wasn't Jordan, it didn't mean they couldn't have a good time together.

She moved closer and kissed him again. Shutting out all thoughts of her husband, she enjoyed the man standing in front of her. When she took a step back, she had to catch her breath.

"Whoa," he said.

Whoa was right.

He yanked her even closer and pushed his erection into her. "Do you want to get out of here?"

No, her immediate thought was.

Shut up, brain. This is what we want, remember?

"Yes," she said out loud, her heart racing but not necessarily in a good way.

Maybe, if she had another drink, she'd calm down some.

Travis picked up her hand and kissed the back of it. "Great," he said with a grin. He turned and led her to the door.

Suddenly, Piper felt like she couldn't breathe. The closer they got to the entrance, the more she felt like her chest was tightening. They were almost there when she jerked her hand out of Travis's.

He spun around. "What?" His eyes widened when he

saw her face. She could only imagine what she looked like at the moment. "Are you okay?"

Piper felt like crying. "No."

"What's wrong? Did I do something?"

"No, no, no." She rushed to reassure him. "It's not you; it's me."

His brow almost touched his hairline, and she had to giggle.

"This time, it's true." She grabbed his hand. "You are great. You're sexy, a good dancer, a great kisser..."

"But?"

"But I'm not ready," she admitted. She took a deep breath. "My husband died a little over a year ago, and I... haven't been with anyone since."

"Ah," Travis said, and she could see in his eyes the pity she hadn't wanted to see.

She dropped his hand. "Yeah. It's almost as bad as if I'd told you I was a virgin."

Travis laughed, and she felt better.

"I'm sorry. I feel like I led you on."

He put his hands on her shoulders. "Hey, do not be sorry. Shit happens. Sometimes to good people. So, we don't get laid tonight." He shrugged. "It's not the end of the world."

"Damn, you are going to make one woman very lucky someday."

He laughed again. "We'll see."

"You will," she said with conviction.

He nodded to the dance floor. "You want to go back out there?"

She thought about it and shook her head. "Nah. You go find your friend. I'm going to go get some water."

His hands fell to his sides. "Okay. It was nice meeting you, Piper."

"You, too, Travis."

Travis went to find his friend, and Piper headed to the bar.

CHAPTER SIXTEEN

Piper ordered a water and found an empty table to sit. She pulled up a stool and started nursing her drink.

A little while later, Simone ran up to her. "Oh my God, you're here. We didn't know where you went."

Piper winced. She was really off tonight. "I'm sorry. I've been sitting here, lost in my head."

Simone pulled up the only other stool and took a seat next to Piper. "What's going on? I saw the guy you were with all night come back alone."

Piper put her elbow on the table and propped her chin up on her fist. "I tried to go home with him."

Simone gasped. "Did he turn you down?"

Piper chuckled. "No. It was the other way around."

Simone wrinkled her nose. "I'm confused."

"I wanted to go home with him, but I couldn't. I think I almost had a panic attack, the closer we got to leaving."

Simone put her hand on Piper's arm. "I'm sorry."

Piper shrugged. "Me, too."

"Maybe you're just not ready yet."

"Yeah, my mind obviously isn't. Now, if someone could tell my vagina to get on board with waiting, that would be great."

Simone laughed. "Too bad you can't be with the guy who reawakened your sexuality."

Piper straightened. "What?"

"Oh, I assumed that a guy made you realize you wanted to have sex again. I'm sorry."

Piper shook her head, but her friend kept talking, "Well, it's too bad. Because whoever got your juices flowing again should be the one you have sex with." Simone leaned forward. "If I were in your position, I'm betting Chris Hemsworth or Henry Cavill would get my engine revving again." She fanned her face. "Those two get my senile grandmother in the mood." But then she stuck out her lip, exaggerating a sad face. "Not that I would ever get to meet either of those men." She tapped her lip in thought. "Hmm...maybe I would just need to find myself a foreigner since neither Chris nor Henry is American." She looked at Piper. "That's what we should do. Find you a handsome man from Australia or England."

Simone continued to make plans to find Piper a man, but she started to tune her out. In her head, she kept going over and over what Simone had said.

"Too bad you can't be with the guy who reawakened your sexuality."

"Too bad you can't be with the guy who reawakened your sexuality."

"Too bad you can't be with the guy who reawakened your sexuality."

And then a memory flashed of how Nate's naked chest had felt against her back that day in her house.

Piper jumped up from her seat so fast that Simone shrieked. "I have to go."

"What?" Simone asked, understandably baffled.

"I have to go," Piper said again as she dug around in her clutch for her keys. "Found 'em," she said more to herself than Simone.

"Are you okay to drive?"

Piper paused. She'd only had a couple of drinks and done plenty of dancing. Her last drink had been water, and her buzz had worn off hours ago. "I'm fine." She leaned down and hugged Simone. "Thank you."

The blonde looked very confused. "You're welcome?"

Piper laughed and started for the door. "I'll see you later," she yelled back at her friend and took off as fast as her heels would carry her.

Piper used her keys to unlock the door as quietly as she could. She shut the door behind her and relocked it just as silently. She was doing a good job of being stealthy when she tripped over the damn cat.

"*Fred*," she hissed. "You almost killed me," she scolded him as she slipped off her shoes and set them on the entrance rug.

Meow.

"*Shh*...you're going to wake up Nate."

Meow.

"Traitor."

Piper tiptoed up the stairs and headed for Nate's bedroom. She knew he'd had dinner with his grandfather earlier in the night. At one point, he had texted her, saying he was going to bed early for a Friday night, so she knew exactly where to find him.

As she had driven to his house, she'd considered waiting to approach Nate, but she had known, in the bright light of day, after sleeping on it, she'd lose all her nerve.

She crept into his room and saw that Nate was sleeping on his back. His torso was bare, and the sheet was pulled to his waist. She sat down next to him and hesitated for a second.

It was now or never.

She reached down and shook Nate awake.

♡

Nate was having another dream about Piper when someone pulled him from his sleep.

"Nate."

"Piper?" He lifted his head and shook it back and forth.

This was the most realistic dream he'd ever had. It felt like she was in his room with him. All he could see was her top half, but she was wearing white, and her beautiful breasts were on display. Tasteful yet not hiding. He was definitely still dreaming.

He dropped his head back to his pillow and closed his eyes again.

His body jerked again as he was shaken.

"No, Nate. You need to wake up."

That was enough for him to realize he wasn't dreaming anymore.

He quickly sat up. "What's wrong?" he asked on full alert.

Piper had never come to his house in the middle of the night while he was sleeping.

He began feeling her all over. He started with her head and worked his way down her arms. "Are you hurt?"

She laughed. "Kind of. But not in the way you're asking."

He stopped to meet her eyes. His room was bright from the streetlights outside and the fact that he never bothered to shut his shades. "Who the fuck hurt you?" Nate wanted to kill him.

She grabbed his hands. "No one hurt me."

He felt immediate relief. "Then, what's wrong?"

"I need you to fuck me."

Nate closed his eyes and opened them again. Maybe he was still dreaming because there was no way Piper had just said those words to him. He shook his head again to clear the cobwebs. "I didn't hear you."

She laughed again and cupped his face with both hands. "Nate Hall, I need you to fuck the ever-loving shit out of me."

CHAPTER SEVENTEEN

Nate almost jumped off the bed, but Piper was blocking his exit. That was probably a good thing since he was naked and at full mast. He'd been half-hard from his dream, but then her words had made his cock want to do exactly as she'd commanded.

But, while his dick was saying yes, his head was flashing a warning sign. This was his dead friend's wife. This was his friend. He didn't know if he could actually sleep with her, no matter how much he wanted to.

Plus, he knew she'd been out drinking with her friends. He did not want to be a drunken mistake that she regretted in the morning.

Speaking of drinking...

"Did you drive here?"

Piper tilted her head to the side and smiled as if she knew exactly what he was thinking. "I'm not drunk." She stood up and faced him. She held out her arms and touched each hand to her nose. Then, she went to his wall and turned and walked with one foot in front of the other.

She certainly didn't seem intoxicated.

"I think you know how to do that stuff a little too well. Is there something you'd like to share?"

She flipped him off as he swung his legs to the floor. He made sure his sheet and comforter still covered his goods though.

She stalked toward him and stopped only inches away. Then, in one fell swoop, she pulled off her little white dress.

And there she was.

Piper Stevens.

In only a white strapless bra and white underwear.

She did a three-sixty.

Correction. In a white *thong*.

Nate groaned. He was only so strong. "If we do this, nothing changes between us. You're not going to ignore me or act weird around me, okay?"

She leaned over and kissed him. She pulled away and whispered, "I knew you were perfect," before she kissed him again.

He had no idea what she meant by that, but at that point, he no longer cared.

Piper's tongue was in his mouth, and her almost-naked body was under his hands.

Nate gently nudged her back, so he had room to stand. He stood from the bed, no longer caring if she saw him naked. "Take off your bra and thong."

She didn't appear to even hear what he'd said, as she was

staring at his cock. She reached for him, and he grabbed her wrist.

Her eyes shot to his.

"Bra and panties, Piper. Take them off."

She looked down at his shaft. "But I want to touch it." Her gaze met his again. "Please."

Nate chuckled. "All in good time," he assured her.

If she touched him now, he wasn't sure how long he'd last. And he needed to last. There were so many things he wanted to do to her and her body before he could even think about coming.

He felt her arm relax, and he let her go.

She took a step back, and the anticipation of whether he would get to see her beautiful breasts or her pretty pussy first had him nearly seeing double.

She reached behind her back, and with a quick flick of her wrists, her bra fell to the floor.

She was perfect. Her large breasts were clearly natural by the way they lay on her chest.

She lifted her hands and cupped them. "They're real," she said in almost an apologetic way.

He hated that she was self-conscious because her boobs weren't fake.

He wished women could understand that there was no perfect woman and that one attractive thing did not make another thing unattractive. He'd been with some women with fake breasts, and he wasn't going to lie and say they hadn't looked amazing. But that didn't mean that Piper's were any less appealing. Small breasts, large breasts, real breasts, fake breasts. He loved them all.

"They're gorgeous," he told her. "I can't wait to taste them." He nodded once down toward her crotch. "Panties first."

She smiled, clearly pleased with his compliment. She pushed her thong off her hips and onto the floor. Using one foot, she flung them across the room.

He stepped off to the side and held out his hand. "On the bed. Face up. Legs open."

She made a humming noise and grinned as she did as he'd commanded.

And Nate about had a heart attack.

Piper's long, dark hair was fanned out around her, her eyes were filled with desire, and her pink nipples were puckered with her arousal. That was enough to stop any man in his tracks. But the part that nearly killed him was the tempting pussy that was completely bare.

"Damn." He couldn't wait to taste it.

She laughed.

He knelt on the bed and crawled closer to her. He put one leg between hers and looked her in the eye. "Are you sure you want to do this?"

"Without a doubt," she answered. "And you?"

"Abso-fucking-lutely." More than she knew.

Piper put her hands on his chest. "Touch me, Nate," she whispered.

She began trailing one hand down his stomach, but before she could reach his dick, he put his middle two fingers in his mouth and then inside her.

Piper's arms dropped to her sides, and she clutched his bedding in her fists. "Oh-oh," she stuttered. "*Oh my God.*"

Nate pulled his digits halfway out and noted how they glistened in the streetlight. He pushed them back in again, watching Piper's face when he discovered he'd hit pay dirt. "Ahh...there it is." Nate rubbed the tips of his fingers in a small circle. "Piper's G-spot."

Her back arched off the bed, lifting her butt in the air, as she tried to rotate her pelvis around his fingers. She was already clenching around him.

He pulled his hand away completely.

Her hips fell, and she swore at him, "You asshole."

Nate just laughed and tsked at her. "Now, now. We can't be letting you come already."

"Why not?" she half-moaned, half-whined.

"Because I'm not ready for that yet." At this point, he hadn't even touched her clit yet.

He put both legs in the middle of hers now and pushed her thighs open wide as he sat back on his haunches. He traced the outside of her lips with his fingers a couple of times before he flicked his thumb over her clit.

A long and low moan sprang from Piper's mouth.

It was always nice when he received positive feedback.

Nate gathered some of her wetness and brought it to her swollen nub. Soon, he had her panting and arching her back once more.

But he couldn't have that.

He pulled his hand away again.

Piper moaned, this time in frustration. "I hate you."

He chuckled. "Sorry, babe. I realized I hadn't tasted you yet."

Her eyes lit up at his words, and he was sure she thought he was going to go down on her.

But if she thought she'd hated him before...

Nate pushed his two fingers inside her pussy again, being careful not to touch her G-spot. He made sure he had plenty of her wetness on his hand before pulling out. He got up on his knees, leaning over her, and rubbed his finger over her right nipple. And the other finger over her left. He did this until they were both hard and begging.

Then, he dropped down to his elbows and sucked each one into his mouth. In between breasts, he made sure to tell her, "You taste even better than I thought you would."

Piper, clearly frustrated, began squirming underneath him. She grabbed on to the bed, on to his shoulders and his back, and lastly, on to his ass. She tried to push his cock toward her core as she lifted her lower body toward his own.

Man, did he want to sink into her sweet, wet heat. It would feel so good.

And, for a moment, Nate forgot what he was doing as he imagined doing just that.

But then he got his head together and got up on his hands again. "What's wrong?"

"I want to come."

"Well, why didn't you just say so?" Nate went straight for his nightstand, yanked the drawer open, and reached for his pile of Magnums. He'd win a record for fastest condom opening because he was already covering himself with the latex.

He looked up into Piper's green eyes. "I hope you're ready. Things are about to get real."

CHAPTER EIGHTEEN

For as long as she lived, Piper was never going to forget the moment when Nate pushed himself inside her.

There were no words to describe how it felt. How she felt.

Piper had never had sex with a friend before. Of course, Jordan had been her friend as well as her husband, but he'd been her boyfriend first. They'd been together for quite a while before she actually thought of him as her friend.

But Nate, he was just her friend. She trusted him completely.

The second he'd told her that she was gorgeous, she had known she had picked the right person to go to bed with. It seemed silly that she'd ever tried to find anyone else.

She looked up into Nate's amazing blue eyes and loved seeing the want, the need, that he showed there. There was no awkwardness between them as they made eye contact, like she'd had with some previous lovers. She knew he'd take care of her.

Nate pressed his cock inside her, slowly but steadily. She appreciated him giving her time to accommodate his size, but she also liked that he wasn't backing off. He trusted her to tell him if he was going too fast.

She would have thought it would be no problem with all the foreplay he'd given her, but he was bigger than Jordan had been. And the last time she'd had sex was over a year ago. And he was definitely bigger than her vibrator, so it was an adjustment to take all of Nate.

He leaned down and kissed her as he pushed deeper. She should have known he was a great kisser. He did everything with such confidence and finesse. As if his body had been made to do whatever it was he was doing.

From him lying on the couch to him working on her house, she could admit now that he was sexy. Everything he did was attractive. Even the time he'd gotten drunk and tripped over her rug. He'd landed on his back and laughed about it. It hadn't even mattered that he'd fallen because he looked delicious lying there with his jeans riding low on his hips and his T-shirt bunched up, his stomach showing.

And to know that, now, all that sexy maleness was over her and inside her ramped her up even more.

He tasted faintly like toothpaste as he licked his way into her mouth. His tongue was hot, and she momentarily sucked on it the way she hoped to suck on his dick sometime soon.

Nate groaned and slanted his mouth more over hers. She gripped his shoulders as he took complete control of their kiss. She was so into what he was doing with her mouth that she almost missed the fact that Nate had bottomed out and was beginning to thrust.

It was when his cock rubbed against her G-spot that she forgot about the kiss and had to gasp for air. "Oh God, oh God. Please, please, please don't stop," she said right against his mouth.

He briefly kissed her again and then pulled back. He arched his back over her, giving her a clear line of view to where their bodies met. She watched as his cock stretched her over and over again while he thrust in and out.

She was mesmerized by the sight.

His bronzed skin looked stunning next to her rather boring, pale complexion, and she touched him low on his abdomen, wanting to feel his slick skin.

He slowed slightly, and she quickly looked up to his face.

"No, don't stop. I just want to touch you."

Nate grinned at her. "Go for it, baby."

He probably called everyone baby in bed, but it didn't stop her from liking it.

Turning back to his body, she traced her fingers just above his V and over his treasure trail up to his belly button. She spread her fingers across his six-pack and up over his pectoral muscles. Everything on Nate was hot, but the best part about seeing him naked was his arm full of tattoos. He didn't have them anywhere else, and something about just that part of his body being covered in ink was sexy as fuck.

She brushed her hands up both his arms and over his shoulders. When she reached his neck, she outlined his jawline with her thumbs. She looked him in the eyes again.

"I want you to fuck me, Nate. Hard. No holding back. I want to still feel you inside me tomorrow."

"Fuck, Piper," he said as he leaned back on his haunches and grabbed her hands from his face.

He kissed one of her palms before he pushed both arms above her head and held them there with one hand. He slipped his other arm underneath her leg and pushed it toward her chest. And then he proceeded to do what she'd asked.

He'd held up a steady pace the whole time, but now, there was no holding back.

Nate ground his pelvis into hers and pushed even deeper now that her leg was up.

Piper threw her head back and cried out. She was suddenly overwhelmed by the stimulation.

Nate's chest brushed against her hard nipples, and his groin hit her swollen clit every time he drove hard into her. And, inside her, that was where his big, beautiful cock rubbed against her G-spot.

The sensations were almost overwhelming, and she wasn't sure what was going to send her over the edge first.

As Piper felt herself get closer to orgasm, an unusual fullness began to build up inside her. She had never felt it before, but something told her it was going to make her climax amazing.

Because of this, she tried to make herself come. But, instead of building up, it began to back off. Piper tried to free her arms from under Nate, although what she would do with them she didn't know. She didn't really want to be free. She just wanted to get off.

"Piper."

She continued to struggle.

"Piper."

She relaxed her body and looked up at Nate. She realized he had stopped moving as well, although their bodies were still connected.

"Hey, there you are."

Heat flooded her body. Something about Nate knowing that she had lost focus of their lovemaking was an incredible turn-on. She was surprised that he was in tune with her body, and she squeezed her vaginal muscles around him.

Nate grunted and looked away for a second. "Don't do that, or I'm going to come."

"Sorry."

"Liar."

She shrugged.

"Are you ready to go again?"

Squeeze.

"I'll take that as a yes." His face grew serious. "I want you to pay attention to me. To what I'm doing to you. To how I feel inside you."

She sucked in a breath. Even his words were hot.

"You need to get out of your head. You're not alone now. I'm here. And I'm going to take care of you."

It wasn't a question, but she nodded anyway.

Nate began thrusting again, and now, it felt like all the sensations she'd felt were amped up so much more.

The fullness returned, and soon, everything she felt all converged in one area below.

Piper could barely catch her breath as she hovered right on the edge.

She looked up into Nate's eyes, and it wasn't her breasts or her G-spot or even her clitoris that made her come.

It was knowing that Nate—her Nate—was inside her that sent her flying.

Her body clamped down on him so hard, she felt her body pushing him out of her. A warmth hit her legs and coated her thighs, and she could actually feel her pussy pulsing over and over.

"Holy fucking shit," she vaguely heard Nate say. He sounded far away, as her hearing seemed to dim.

As she started to come down, she became aware of how empty she felt.

"Nate," she cried out as she reached for him. She had no idea when he'd let go of her arms.

He slipped back inside her, and she groaned.

Nate wrapped his arms underneath her and held her close as he began to ride her. Even though she wasn't going to come again, he still felt incredible. When she knew he was close, she held him tighter and marveled at the feeling of him jerking inside her.

They lay together for a minute or two when Piper began to notice she was cold and wet between her legs.

She patted Nate on the shoulder, and he moved up to his elbows to look down at her.

"Are you okay?"

A part of her panicked, but she told herself it was going to be okay. "I think the condom broke."

Nate's face broke out into a grin, and he chuckled. He slipped from her body and rolled to her side.

The condom was fully intact on Nate's semi-hard penis.

"You squirted," he told her matter-of-factly, as if it were an everyday occurrence.

CHAPTER NINETEEN

Fred walked all around his house, looking for his human. His human had given Fred his yummy food this morning, but he'd forgotten Fred's new water. Fred didn't like old water, and he needed to find his human to fix it. Now.

Fred had looked in the room where his human sat and the room where his human ate, but he couldn't find him. Fred went up the stairs to look in the room where his human slept even though he'd already seen his human awake.

Fred nudged open the door.

"*Hooman. Hooman. Hooooomannnnn,*" Fred called out.

There was a noise from the big cat bed.

"Be quiet, Fred. Stop meowing."

Fred didn't understand stupid human words, but he knew it was not his human talking.

Fred jumped up onto the bed to see who had dared to lie in his human's cat bed.

There was a female human in his human's cat bed. Fred

had never seen a female human in his human's cat bed before. Fred padded closer and realized it was *his* female human.

His female human didn't live with him and his male human, but she was his all the same. His female human was trying to go back to sleep, and Fred yawned. He had slept on the couch this morning and on his favorite sunny spot on the floor, but he could go for another nap.

Fred circled the big, fluffy thing his human would lay his head on and curled around his female human's head.

Fred sniffed. She smelled like his human. She smelled like she was trying to make little humans. Fred liked this. He would have more humans to pet him.

To let his female human know he gave her his permission, Fred licked her face.

Piper had to admit that she liked it when she lay on Nate's couch, and Fred would curl around her head and snuggle in. Especially in winter when it was cold out. But she wasn't sure if she liked the licking. Although...she wondered if a cat tongue was a good exfoliator.

He'd woken her up from the best sex dream she'd had in a long time. It had felt so real. She hoped she hadn't been moaning in her sleep.

Piper reached up to pet Fred as he purred, and her hand smacked something, which was odd because there wasn't anything on the end of Nate's couch, except air.

She opened her eyes and looked around.

Oh shit. She let her head drop back to the pillow and pushed out a gigantic sigh.

It hadn't been a dream. She and Nate had boned last night.

She was bombarded with so many emotions that she rolled over, buried her face in the pillow, and laughed.

She was still laughing when she lay on her back again.

Holy shit. What was she supposed to do now?

She looked around the room again just to make sure she was alone even though she knew she was. Nate must have shut the shades because the room was semi-dark, so it didn't hurt to double-check.

She put a hand out and felt the other side of the bed. Cold.

Where's Nate?

"Where's Nate?" Piper asked Fred.

Meow.

She pushed off the covers, and for the first time, she realized she was naked. As she stood up, she felt a pinch between her legs and a residual soreness.

There was no doubt she'd done the nasty last night.

Piper walked around to the other side of the bed to look for her clothes, but the floor was empty. She did a quick scan and found them folded on the dresser.

She smiled. That was sweet of Nate to pick up her stuff.

She put on last night's underwear, bra, and dress and wished she had something more comfortable to wear home.

After opening the bedroom blinds, she went into the master bath and used Nate's toothpaste to brush her teeth and tongue with her fingers. She washed her face and used the toilet. When she exited the bathroom, she noticed a drawer slightly open with what looked like T-shirts inside.

Deciding Nate wouldn't mind, she slipped a plain white tee over her dress. At least she would look a little more modest when going home. Not that she planned to run into anyone, but now would be the time she'd get pulled over.

She went downstairs and found her clutch. She finger-combed her hair and pulled it back in a ponytail, using a hair tie she'd kept in her small purse. Next, she pulled out her phone.

There was a text from Nate.

> Nate: Come home when you get up. I told Luke I would meet him early. I'll have coffee waiting.

Piper looked at the time in the corner. It was after ten.

> Piper: I'm leaving now. Why didn't you wake me?

She slipped on her heels and stepped out the door. Just as she was locking it behind her, her phone beeped.

> Nate: You looked so peaceful sleeping, and I didn't want to wake you.

Several seconds passed, and then there was another text.

> Nate: Plus, I knew you had a hard night.

Piper felt her face heat, and she ran for her car. She should have known that Nate wouldn't beat around the sleeping-together bush. Meanwhile, she had no idea what to do when she saw him. She'd promised Nate that things wouldn't change between them.

But that was before he'd been *inside her*.

As she unlocked her car and got behind the wheel, she suddenly remembered the last words he'd said to her last night. Piper had never squirted with a guy before. She'd done it a few times when she had some one-on-one time but never with anyone else.

Her cheeks felt like they were on fire now.

She'd been so embarrassed last night that, after Nate got up to get rid of the condom, she had contemplated leaving. Knowing she wouldn't have enough time, she'd moved to one side of the bed and pulled up the covers to her nose. She had closed her eyes to pretend to sleep, but she had been so tired that she was halfway to dreamland by the time she heard Nate return.

She ran through some options in her head on where she could go besides home. She looked down at her current outfit. The answer was nowhere.

She groaned and started her car.

Maybe Nate would be outside in the backyard when she got to her house.

Almost twenty minutes later—because she had taken the longest route home while going the minimal speed—Piper realized she wasn't going to be that lucky.

Her garage door was closed, and of course, there was no way Nate wouldn't hear when it opened.

She could just park in the driveway and enter through

the front door, but Piper saw that her neighbor was outside on her porch.

Mrs. Grant was a sweet elderly lady who also happened to be a widow. She had tried to make friends with Piper after Jordan passed, but Mrs. Grant was in her eighties and had clearly come from a different generation than Piper. Being old-fashioned and a little sexist toward her own gender had made it hard for Piper to connect with the woman.

She could only imagine what Mrs. Grant would say about her not coming home all night. It was better to run into Nate than her neighbor, and Piper reached up and hit the button on her car to open the door.

Piper waved at Mrs. Grant and pulled into the garage. She quickly shut the door and got out of her car. Music came from the backyard, and Piper breathed a sigh of relief.

Nate and Luke usually had the music loud, so they probably hadn't heard her come home.

She walked in the door and kicked her shoes off in the mudroom. As she walked into the kitchen, she opened her clutch and grabbed her phone and money to empty it.

"About time you got home."

Piper screamed and threw her stuff in the air.

Nate stood, leaning against her counter, with an eyebrow in the air. His legs were crossed, and he looked as relaxed as ever. He took a sip of what she assumed was coffee and said, "My, aren't we jumpy this morning?"

Piper chuckled nervously and bent to retrieve her stuff. She set everything on the counter, and Nate handed her a mug.

"You scared me," she told him and took a long drink.

Nate laughed.

Piper heard the screen door open and close.

"Hey, Hall, I don't know what to do—" Luke stopped when he saw Piper. "Oh, hey, Squirt."

She frowned. "I'm not short."

Luke laughed, and Nate shot him a look.

"Oh my God," she said with realization.

Nate had told Luke about last night.

"Hey, don't sweat it. Nate thought it was awesome," Luke said. "Besides, I owe Nate. He called Elise FB for months."

"FB?"

"Fuck Buddy," Luke explained.

Piper narrowed her eyes at Nate. "I cannot believe you told Luke."

Nate shrugged. "Sorry, he's my person," he said in a clearly teasing tone.

Luke pointed his finger at Nate. "Don't you ever say some girlie shit like that again."

Nate grinned.

"And how dare you mention that sorry excuse for a 'medical'"—Luke used air quotes and practically spit out the word *medical*—"show in my presence." He turned and stomped back outside.

"Jeez. What's his problem?" Piper asked.

Nate shrugged. "Luke hates *Grey's Anatomy* and pretty much every other medical show. He can't watch it without listing everything they do wrong."

"Luke watches *Grey's Anatomy*?" she asked disbelievingly. *Grey's* was more of a chick show.

Nate laughed. "No. Elise watches it. Luke just bitches about it."

"That makes more sense."

Piper walked around Nate and filled up her coffee. "I'm going to go shower," she said as she left the kitchen.

"Okay...*Squirt*."

CHAPTER TWENTY

Nate was lying on Piper's couch while trying to keep his eyes open. Piper was in the kitchen, finishing up dishes from their dinner of homemade mac and cheese and grilled chicken. She'd pretty much kicked him out after he dropped a glass on the floor and then a plate in the sink. His only excuse was that he was tired.

Nate had met Luke pretty early in the morning to get a good day's work in. Luke and Elise had early dinner plans, so he'd known they'd have to quit early. It had been worth it though because they'd gotten a lot done. They only worked on weekends, so it was a slow process overall. Plus, Nate was going out of town the next weekend and didn't want to get behind.

The original project that he had planned out with Jordan was to tear down the old rotted deck and build a new one. Nothing fancy, just a basic structure that was big enough to hold a grill and a patio set. But, somewhere along the way, Nate had upped the design. The main deck was twice the original size with a pergola and secondary deck off the side that held a screened porch. He was also building a fire pit because who didn't like a nice fire pit in Minnesota? He was working with a landscape designer to put on the final touches.

Piper hadn't asked for any of the extra stuff and would probably insist on paying him and Luke, but he wanted the backyard to be perfect for her, and he refused to take her money. And he would pay Luke if it came down to it, not Piper. Nate knew he was doing it partly out of guilt for his role in her husband's death, but it didn't stop him from continuing on with the project.

Nate yawned and let his eyes drift shut for a couple of minutes.

But today's excursions were only part of the reason Nate was exhausted. He was also tired because he hadn't gotten much sleep last night.

After he and Piper had had sex—after they'd had *mind-blowing, amazing* sex—he hadn't been able to sleep. When he'd come out of the bathroom, he'd seen that Piper had already closed her eyes, and it had been only minutes later when her breathing deepened.

He wasn't used to being the one who stayed awake while his partner fell asleep. Nate rarely ever spent the night with someone, but it did happen every once in a while, and he always fell asleep without any problems.

Not last night. He would like to attribute the reason he had been awake was because he'd already been sleeping for an hour or two before Piper got to his house, and his body had thought a good nap was all it needed.

But he knew it was really because the two of them had actually done the deed. Never in Nate's wildest dreams would he have thought that Piper would wake him up and ask him to take her.

And then, when he'd pushed into her sweet, wet heat, it had nearly blown his head clean off. He'd gone slowly because he knew she hadn't had sex in a long time, but that wasn't the only thing that had factored into it. She had been so tight from not having sex in so long that he was afraid he would come before the show even officially started.

Thank God Piper had no idea. He had a reputation to uphold. And it wasn't one pump and dump. Nate would like to blame it on the fact that most of his sexual partners were as sexually active as he was, and their bodies were more used to having sex, but he knew that was only part of why he'd almost come so fast. The other part was that it was Piper he had been in bed with.

He had told her last night that he didn't want anything to change between them, and he'd been serious. But then, this morning, she had practically jumped five feet in the air when she realized that he was in the kitchen. And, aside from the little teasing he and Luke had given her, they hadn't discussed what had happened last night at all.

Piper had made sure they watched TV with the volume on high while they had dinner, so they couldn't talk about anything. But Nate knew she couldn't avoid it forever. They would have to have a conversation eventually. He wasn't about to lose their friendship over some sex. Even if it had been phenomenal.

Nate felt more than heard Piper come into the living

room. She paused when she reached the couch he was lying on, but she didn't say anything. He kept his eyes closed a little longer to see what she would do.

He heard her sigh, and he was afraid she'd leave the room again, so he opened his eyes and said, "I'm awake."

"Oh," she said.

Nate swung his legs off the sofa and sat up. He patted the cushion next to him. "Go ahead and sit."

Piper hesitated and then pointed behind her. "Well, I should—"

Nate cut her off, "Piper?"

"Yes?"

"You've been avoiding me all day. Don't you think we should talk about what happened last night?"

Her cheeks immediately flushed pink, and Nate had to try really hard to pretend he didn't notice, or he'd laugh.

She was just so damn cute.

A few more seconds passed, and it seemed like she wasn't going to say anything, whether out of embarrassment or other reasons. It was up to him to address the issue.

"Piper, sit down, please."

She sat.

"You're obviously feeling something about what happened last night."

This awkwardness and talking about feelings was why Nate didn't do relationships. It usually made him uncomfortable. One-night stands and occasional fuck buddies were much easier. Hello, have sex, shake hands, say good-bye. Done.

But, because this situation involved Piper and she was his

143

friend or because he knew she wouldn't want to get serious when she still loved her husband, Nate didn't feel all that uneasy.

"Well...I don't..." Piper started and failed.

Nate chuckled. "Do you regret what happened last night?" He decided to confront the whole thing head-on.

Piper's eyes widened, and then she looked confused. "No. Not at all."

The sense of relief that went through Nate surprised him. And it left him a little troubled. "Then, what's wrong? Are you afraid it will happen again?"

"No. That didn't even cross my mind as something to be worried about."

"Then, why have you been avoiding me?"

She held up a finger. "I would just like to point out that you were outside all day."

"And you were inside," he pointed out. She wouldn't spend all day in the backyard when he was working, but she normally came out several times during the day. "And then there was dinner and the incredibly loud television."

She winced. That was enough to confirm he was right.

"Spill it," he told her.

"I can't believe you're going to make me say it."

He had thought it was impossible, but she turned even redder.

He leaned closer and grabbed her hand. "Please don't feel like you can't talk to me about anything. I can tell you're embarrassed. I'm not going to tell you not to be because you get to feel how you feel, but know I won't judge you."

"Really? Are you sure?"

"I'm sure." He let go of her hand and sat back.

She sighed again and opened her mouth. "I'm embarrassed about what happened when I"—she sucked in a breath—"orgasmed last night," she quickly finished.

Nate had thought about that moment and how fucking amazing it was. He didn't know if he had ever made a woman come that hard before. A lesser man would have bragged about it to all his friends. That meant that Nate had no idea what she was struggling with.

"I'm sorry, Piper, but you're talking to a man. You have to spell it out for us guys. We don't pick up on beating around the bush well."

Piper closed her eyes and made an exaggerated crying face. She opened her eyes and said, "The part where I..." She used her hands to motion in between her legs, spreading them in a V shape several times, and then she flicked her fingers like there was water on the tips.

Nate burst out laughing.

Piper narrowed her eyes at him. "It's not funny."

"It kind of is," Nate barely said through his laughter. He held up a finger to indicate he needed a minute before he could fully speak. "Oh my God, Piper, what you did last night—"

"When I squirted. All over you," she cried out. At least her anger had made her less embarrassed.

"Yes, when you squirted. That was *fucking* amazing. That is something many guys strive for, yet few achieve."

"Really?" The anger had left her now.

"Well, at least any guy who wants to make a woman happy in bed."

Piper fell back against her seat. "Wow." She looked at him. "So, you're saying, I shouldn't be embarrassed."

"Hell no," he said kind of harshly. He didn't like it when she felt insecure. "I personally hope it happens again."

She raised her brow. "You hope it happens again?"

He shrugged. "Yeah. As long as you're up for it. I was a little disappointed in how you crashed on me." He looked up to the ceiling, as if he had a serious thought. "Oh gosh, maybe that means I wasn't any good."

She pushed him. "Shut up. You know it was good. I squirted, for heaven's sake."

Nate looked at her and grinned. "I know."

She shook her head, but she smiled back. "You're horrible."

"Yeah, I know that, too." He tilted his head. "So, does that mean you want me to go, or do you want me to stay?"

CHAPTER TWENTY-ONE

Monday morning, Piper stared out her front window while she sipped her coffee. The weekend had been great weather-wise, but today was promising to be hot and humid. The kind of day where your clothes stuck to your skin.

Yuck.

Thankfully, Piper worked in an air-conditioned office. She scanned the neighborhood. It was the sort of day where even the kids didn't want to go outside.

She was about to turn and finish getting ready for the day when her eyes landed on the mailbox. She'd forgotten to check the mail Friday and Saturday, and she'd promised her mom she'd watch for her wedding invitation.

Piper set her mug down on the table at the front entrance and braced herself to go outside. It was already muggy out, but at least the temperature hadn't risen to the high for the day. She probably shouldn't complain at all after the long winter they'd had.

When she reached the box on the street, she retrieved her mail and quickly flipped through it. No invitation. But she did get two credit card bills. *Yay.*

"Yoo-hoo."

Piper looked up from her mail.

"Oh, Piper, dear."

It was her neighbor, Mrs. Grant.

Piper walked toward the elderly woman to meet her on the lawn. "Hi, Mrs. Grant."

Mrs. Grant was a tiny woman. Piper guessed she couldn't be any taller than five feet, and she was skin and bones.

She put her hand on Piper's arm. "Dear, I was wondering if you would be willing to come with me to church on Sunday." The older woman looked so hopeful.

"Oh...um..."

Piper had grown up, going to church and Sunday school, but her parents hadn't raised her to be overly religious. As a result, she'd pretty much stopped attending church on a weekly basis after college. It hadn't helped that Jordan's family was a *church on Christmas and Easter* kind of family. Because of this, she liked to think of herself as more spiritual than religious.

After Jordan had passed away, Mrs. Grant had tried to get Piper to go to church with her. It had been hard though because Piper was mad at God for a long time for taking her husband away from her. Whether it was fair or not, God had received a large amount of her wrath.

Some of her anger had left her during the past few months, but that didn't mean she wanted to go to church with Mrs. Grant. The two of them had almost nothing in common, and Piper could only imagine the stiff, traditional service Mrs. Grant attended. She'd bet her car that almost everyone was similar in age to Mrs. Grant, too.

Mrs. Grant's face fell. "Oh. Well, after Saturday night, I thought maybe you'd changed your mind about church."

Piper ran through everything that had happened on Saturday. She could not come up with one single thing that her neighbor could be referring to. "I'm sorry, Mrs. Grant, I am not sure what you mean."

The elderly woman turned red. "I apologize, dear, but I was eavesdropping. I didn't mean to hear you praying, but your window was open, and so was mine."

"Praying?" Piper asked, having no idea what her neighbor was talking about. Maybe she should mention something to Mrs. Grant's daughter the next time she visited about getting her mom checked for dementia.

"Yes. I heard you say, 'Oh God, I'm coming.' You said this several times, each time louder than the last."

Piper might not be going to church, but she was praying pretty hard at the moment that the ground would open up and swallow her up.

She knew the exact moment the woman was referring to. Nate had been lying on his back, and she had been straddling him. She really liked Nate's take-charge attitude in bed, but she also liked that he was man enough to let her be on top and take the lead. It hadn't been long before she was coming all over him and, yes, crying out as she came. She hadn't even known what had spewed out of her mouth at the moment. Until now, that was.

The older woman kept talking, oblivious to Piper's mortification. "I thought you meant you were coming to church. But I didn't see you at church."

How in the hell was she supposed to tell her elderly neighbor that she hadn't heard Piper praying, but heard Piper having sex?

Is she really that clueless?

Piper looked the lady up and down. Yeah, she probably hadn't had sex since 1762 and had no idea what people did in their bedrooms nowadays.

But that didn't help her get out of this conversation. So, Piper did what any other trapped female would do.

She lied.

Piper put her hand to her ear. "Oh, I hear my phone ringing. I'm expecting an important call," she said as she walked backward toward her house. "We'll talk again."

Mrs. Grant put her hand in the air. "But, Piper, dear—"

"Sorry, gotta go." Piper turned around and ran. The second she was through the front door, she slammed it behind her.

She reached for her phone and pulled up Nate in her text messages.

Piper: We are never having sex AGAIN!

Nate: What happened?

She could almost hear the sigh in his voice. He knew her well enough to know that she wasn't mad at him or anything, and it warmed her heart. But she wasn't going to let it deter her from her current mission of telling Nate how embarrassed she was.

Piper: Mrs. Grant heard us having sex. Actually, she heard me orgasming. She thought I was praying!!!

Nate: Bwaha-haha-haha!

Piper: That's not funny!

Nate: Yes, it is.

Piper scowled at her phone.

Piper: That's it. Friendship over.

Nate: No, it's not.

Piper: Yes, it is. I don't want to see you anymore.

Nate: Yes, you do. I'll be there on Wednesday.

Piper: Maybe I just won't show up.

Nate: It's your house.

Piper stomped her foot.

Piper: Fine. I'll see you on Wednesday.

Nate: ☺

Piper: But we're not having sex.

Nate: We'll see. Gotta go.

Piper: No, we will not see.

She waited a few seconds and nothing, so she finished her coffee and put the mug in the dishwasher. She grabbed her things and got in her car to go to work.

Before she pulled out of her driveway, she looked at her messages again.

Nothing.

That turd. She was going to have to think of a way to get back at him for having the last word.

It didn't take long.

She'd noticed that Nate liked her breasts, which was good because she was blessed in that department.

She unbuttoned her blouse until she showed a lot of cleavage. She repositioned the girls in her bra, so her nipples peeked out. Then, she used her phone to take a picture.

She sent it off to Nate with a message.

> Piper: A pic to remind you of what you WON'T be seeing on Wednesday.

Two seconds later...

> Nate: We'll see.

"Grr!" she said out loud.

He was supposed to call her mean or something. *She* was supposed to be the one affecting *him.*

Her phone beeped.

> Nate: Tease.

Piper laughed, satisfied that she'd gotten what she wanted. And, with a grin, she threw her phone on her passenger seat, buttoned up her shirt, and went to work.

CHAPTER TWENTY-TWO

Nate sat back in his office chair with a smile on his face and scrolled back up to the picture that Piper had sent him.

"What are you doing?"

Nate threw his phone on his desk and sat up so fast, his seat snapped in place. He turned to see Ethan walking into his cubicle, laughing.

"You scared me, man," Nate told him.

"I saw that," Ethan said as he perched his butt on the edge of Nate's desk. "What were you looking at?" He wiggled his blond eyebrows and reached for Nate's phone.

Nate snatched it out of the way before his friend could see what was on there. Piper would kill him if anyone else saw her boob picture. "I don't think so."

Ethan sat back. "Wow, she must be special if you're not willing to share."

"No. I mean, it's not like that." He had no idea how to describe his relationship with Piper. Friends with benefits didn't sound right, and they'd only been intimate two nights. Despite his joking with her earlier, he didn't know if it was really going to happen again.

Ethan held up his hands. "Whatever you say, dude."

"That's right. Besides, aren't you dating Piper's coworker, Kayla?"

Ethan shrugged. "Yeah. I mostly wanted to see how you'd react to what was on your phone more than to actually see what was on your phone."

Nate narrowed his eyes. "Is there a reason you came in here in the first place?"

Ethan laughed and stood. "Nah. I just walked by and saw some drool hanging from your chin, so I thought I'd better get you a napkin before you were swimming in spit."

Nate motioned his head toward the exit. "Get out of here," he said with a smile.

Ethan rubbed his hand over his mouth. "Say, how did you know about Kayla and me?"

"Piper told me."

Ethan snapped his fingers. "Right. Of course. You two are pretty close, aren't you?"

"You could say that. She's one of my best friends."

Ethan nodded in understanding. But, out of nowhere, his eyes widened, and he said, "You dog."

"What are you talking about?" Nate asked, baffled.

Ethan shook his head and laughed. "Nothing. I gotta go." He slapped Nate on the back as he walked out of the cubicle.

Nate watched his friend walk away and shook his own head. He had no idea what that had been about.

Nate picked up his phone and opened his messages again. Piper had sent him a great photo of her breasts.

He couldn't wait to see her on Wednesday.

Piper stared off into space from her desk. She'd been trying to be as inconspicuous as possible. It was hard when they all worked in the same area. Thankfully, her three friends were off, doing other things, at the moment.

The second she'd walked through the door, Simone had asked her where she'd gone in such a hurry from the night-club. Piper had promised she would tell everyone at lunch.

And she would, but it didn't mean she was looking forward to it. It wasn't that she didn't want to tell her friends. She wasn't trying to keep it a secret or anything.

What she didn't want was for them to make a big deal out of it. But there was no way they were going to let the fact that she'd slept with Nate blow over without wanting to know every detail.

Piper saw movement out of the corner of her eye and looked to see Kayla practically running up to her desk with Simone and Lainey behind her. Kayla clutched her phone in her hand as she ran into Piper's desk.

Piper jumped from her chair. "Are you okay?"

Kayla waved a hand in front of her face. "Yeah, I'm fine."

Simone and Lainey had stopped behind Kayla with expectant looks on their faces.

"We want to know why you're sending nude pics to Nate," Kayla said.

"Is that why you told us to stay away from him?" Lainey asked.

Piper held up her hands. "Whoa, whoa, whoa. The picture was not a nude pic." She dropped her hands as something occurred to her. "How did you know?"

"Ha!" Lainey said. "I knew she'd admit it."

"You were right," Simone said.

Kayla waved her phone. "Ethan told me."

Piper gulped, and her eyes widened. "Nate showed Ethan?"

"If it wasn't a nudie, then why do you look like you're going to puke?" Lainey asked.

"No," Kayla said, "Nate didn't show anything to Ethan. Nate was looking at something on his phone, and when Ethan walked in, Nate threw his phone on the desk. The guys were talking, and your name came up. Ethan put two and two together."

Piper dropped into her seat with relief. Not only did she not want anyone to see the picture she'd messaged Nate, but she'd also been hurt for a brief moment when she thought Nate had been showing it around.

"So?" Kayla said.

Piper's eyes snapped to her friends. With her sudden worry, she'd almost forgotten they were there.

"So, what?" Piper asked. She'd forgotten what they'd even asked her.

"Why are you sending pics to Nate?" Simone said as if she thought Piper was crazy for forgetting the conversation.

Piper laughed. "What time is it? I was planning to tell you all at lunch."

Lainey looked at her watch. "It's barely after ten. We cannot wait that long."

Piper held her hands up in surrender. "Okay, okay. I'll give you the CliffsNotes version for now." That was probably a mistake since it would give her friends a couple of hours to come up with five hundred questions. "Something Simone said on Friday—"

"Me?" Simone interrupted, looking proud and in awe.

Piper chuckled. "Yes, you," she said to Simone. To everyone, she said, "Something Simone said made me realize that Nate was the person I should be sleeping with." She looked at Lainey. "It was not why I told you not to hook up with him." She looked at all of them again. "I honestly didn't know I was going to sleep with Nate until Friday."

"So, you had sex with him?" Simone asked.

"Yes."

All three of them started talking at once.

"Hey, hey," Piper said.

They went quiet.

"I *promise* I will tell you everything at lunch."

Simone stomped her foot. "But I don't wanna wait," she whined.

Piper nodded behind them. "I just saw Andrea walk in the door."

Andrea was the shelter's director. She was a good boss, but she made sure her employees were doing what they were supposed to be doing.

Lainey sighed. "I have a phone appointment in a few anyway." She started for her desk and pointed a finger at Piper. "Don't say anything without me."

Piper made a cross over her heart. "I promise."

Nate's phone buzzed. It was Piper. He leaned back in his seat and opened his messages.

> Piper: So, the cat's out of the bag. Everyone knows we did the nasty.

> Nate: What? How?

> Piper: Apparently, something you said to Ethan tipped him off. I got bombarded at work by Kayla, Simone, and Lainey.

So, that was why Ethan'd had that look on his face when he was in Nate's cubicle earlier.

> Nate: That fucking weasel.

> Piper: LOL. They were going to find out eventually.

> Nate: So, you're okay?

> Piper: Yes, except they wouldn't stop asking me how you were in bed.

Nate grinned.

> Nate: What did you say?

> Piper: Meh.

Nate sat up in his chair. *What the hell?*

> Nate: Meh? MEH?

Piper: Sorry. Should I have lied?

> Nate: Yes! No! I don't know! I'm not
> supposed to be meh!

Piper: Ha-haha-haha-haha!

Piper: I'm just kidding.

Piper: They didn't even ask.

He knew she'd purposely made the last bit of information into three messages to make him suffer.

> Nate: Paybacks are a bitch.

Piper: I know. That was for laughing when I told you about Mrs. Grant earlier.

Nate laughed.

> Nate: Truce?

Piper: Truce.

CHAPTER TWENTY-THREE

Nate looked out Piper's front window. His body told him it was going to rain, but it was sunny outside, although it had been humid all week.

"What are you looking for?" Piper asked from behind him. They'd had dinner and just finished cleaning up the kitchen, which was where she'd come from.

"Rain."

She came to stand beside him. "Was it in the forecast?"

He shrugged. He was horrible at watching the weather. He usually got his reports from other people talking about what they'd heard. "I don't know. I didn't check." He rubbed his right shoulder. "I can just tell by my body. It aches."

"It does?"

"Yeah, ever since the accident." Nate had dislocated his shoulder in the accident. It hadn't been the same since.

"You never told me that," she whispered.

He shrugged again. It was because he didn't like talking

about the accident or reminding her of that day. As if she could ever forget. "I don't talk about it much."

Nate looked over at Piper. Her eyes looked so sad, and even though he felt like an asshole, Nate put his arm around her. Jordan would have been home safe that night instead of driving in his car if only Nate hadn't insisted they go out for a beer after work.

She cuddled right into him and put her hand on his chest while she curved the other around his waist. They stood there for a few minutes, just staring out the window, holding each other. Soon, the blue sky began to cloud over.

Piper gasped. "Oh my God, I think you're right."

He chuckled. "You sound so amazed."

"I know it has to do with barometric pressure, but it still seems like magic sometimes. My dad used to predict storms, too, but he always felt it in his knees." She laughed. "When I was a kid, I really did think my dad was magical."

Nate looked down into her green eyes. They were lit up from her talking about her father. Nate couldn't imagine having a relationship with his own dad like she'd had with hers.

She met his gaze, and her face turned from laughter to heat.

Nate cupped her cheek and kissed her.

She turned in his arms, and the kiss turned urgent. She wrapped her arms around his neck. She jumped, and he grabbed her underneath her legs just in time to catch her.

He carried her into the living room and laid her on the couch.

Her chest heaved from her deep breathing, and he wanted to see her naked breasts.

He wanted to forget all about the accident and the day he'd ruined Piper's life. He wanted to make her forget, if even for a moment. He wanted to make her feel good. He *needed* to make her feel good.

He reached for her shorts and pulled them and her panties down and off her legs. He didn't even pay attention to where he threw them.

Her beautiful, bare pink pussy was open to him. He could practically hear it say, *Taste me, Nate.*

"Take off your shirt."

Piper whipped off her top without any hesitation. It always turned him on when a woman listened to him in bed.

Nate reached down and adjusted his cock under his boxers. He dropped to his knees on the floor and spread Piper's legs open wide. He watched her for a second before sliding his middle finger between her folds. When he reached her clit, he lightly swept his finger over it and then pushed down with a small amount of force.

Piper's ass lifted into the air, and she moaned.

He moved his hand away and replaced it with his mouth. He licked in between her folds, trying to taste as much of her as he possibly could. He loved how wet she was. He grabbed on to her thighs to make sure they stayed open while he felt her nails digging into his head.

He moved his mouth north until he reached her swollen nub. He circled the tender spot with his tongue and sucked it into his mouth. He hummed around her clit to see what she would do.

She screamed in pleasure, and Nate smiled.

He pulled away enough to say, "Shh...or Mrs. Grant is going to hear you."

She opened her eyes and gave him a dirty look.

Nate laughed and took her in his mouth again. He pushed his middle finger inside her and headed straight for the spongy spot. He rubbed his finger over and over on the area while he sucked on her nub. He had only been with her two nights, but he'd already learned she loved the combo of both areas being touched at once.

He could tell she was getting closer by how fast her hips pumped in the air and how tight her pussy was squeezing his finger, but all of a sudden, she seemed to plateau. It didn't take him long to figure out why.

"Piper, it's okay to let go. What happens, happens. There is nothing you can do to turn me away."

It seemed to be the right thing to say because, five seconds after he put his mouth back between her legs, she combusted. Turned out, she had nothing to worry about.

She cried out, "Oh God. I'm coming. I'm coming. Don't stop. I'm coming."

The police would have to come and drag him away before he stopped.

He waited until her orgasm finished before he crept up her body. She still had her eyes closed, and he smiled at what he had done to her. He gently pulled one of her bra cups out of the way, giving her plenty of time to stop him if she didn't want him to do it.

Her rosy nipple was erect and begging for his mouth. Again, he heard, *Taste me, Nate.*

He sucked the bud into his mouth, pushing it against the roof of his mouth with his tongue.

She grabbed on to his head with both hands. "God, Nate," she panted in his ear. "Your mouth is amazing."

"Thank you," he said as he switched to the other breast.

Piper's fingers dragged down his body and into his shorts. "I want to taste you now."

His cock jumped at that idea.

Nate kissed his way up her neck until he reached her ear. "Next time. Right now, I just want to be inside you."

"I want that, too," she said and kissed him again.

He sat up and stood from the couch. He stripped off his shirt and grabbed the condom from his pocket before pushing his shorts to the floor.

Piper stretched her arm out and grabbed him. She pumped him in her fist a couple of times, and since he was selfish, he closed his eyes and let her.

Piper sucked in a breath, and he looked at her face. Her eyes were big and wide.

"What's wrong?" he asked.

"You're uncircumcised."

"You didn't notice before?"

She shook her head. "It was dark."

He tried to remain relaxed. "Is that a problem?"

He held his breath, waiting for her answer but hoping she didn't notice how important her approval was to him.

"Not at all," Piper said, and Nate breathed again. "I've just never seen one. In real life, that is."

Nate grinned. "Why, Piper, are you telling me you watch porn?"

Her cheeks flushed. "Maybe."

He grabbed her hand and removed it from his dick. "You can explore later. Like I said, I want to be inside you."

She smiled and opened her arms and legs wide.

He pushed the condom down his length and settled himself between her legs. He rubbed the head of his cock between her labia to make sure she was still wet and ready for him. His dick glistened with her arousal, and Nate was satisfied she wasn't lying about her discovery.

He pushed inside, going faster and harder than he had their first time. Her body was already getting used to his.

Nate pumped his hips into hers, finding the best angle to give them both pleasure. Of course, being a guy, it didn't take much for him, so when he heard Piper suck in a breath, he knew he'd found what he was looking for.

He pulled her upper body close and moved his lower body in and out of her at a steady rhythm. "God, you feel good," he told her.

She clutched his back. "So do you. I think...oh God...I think I'm going to come again."

"Fuck yeah," he told her. "I want you to. I want to feel it. Come all over me, Piper."

And come all over him she did. It wasn't much longer before Piper orgasmed again. When he felt her get so tight that she almost pushed him out and the warmth of her orgasm hit his legs, Nate came, too.

Goddamn.

At least this time, he managed to stay inside her.

CHAPTER TWENTY-FOUR

Piper rested her head on Nate's chest while the two of them lay, cocooned under a blanket, on the couch, enjoying their post-coital bliss.

Nate was trailing his fingers up and down her arm, and his touch was making it hard for her to stay awake.

"Hey," Nate said, turning his head toward her. His chin rubbed the top of her head. "Can I ask you a question?"

She yawned. "You just did."

"Smart-ass. No, it's something you texted me the other day."

They messaged each other every day, so he could be talking about anything.

"What did I say?"

"It was when you said your friends asked how I was in bed."

She tilted her head back onto his shoulder to look into his eyes. "Really? You don't strike me as the insecure type."

He frowned. "I'm not, thank you very much. No, I was wondering if women really talked about that stuff."

Piper laughed. "You really don't have any friends who are female, do you?"

His frown deepened.

"Sorry, I meant no offense. You just surprise me sometimes. You have a sister, for heaven's sake."

He nodded. "I do. A much younger sister. Who will remain a virgin until her wedding day."

Piper raised her brow.

"It's true. At least in my mind. What I don't know can't hurt me in this situation."

She supposed he had a point. "Okay, I'll give you that one. We can't have you going around, intimidating all of Tiana's boyfriends."

"Exactly."

"So, to answer your question, yes, women really talk like that. I don't think men know that women can be just as nasty as guys. And just as sexual."

Nate shrugged. "Well, I knew that part."

She wrinkled up her nose. "But do you? I mean, I know you have women that you"—she didn't know if she should say *have* sex with or *had* sex with; she didn't want to insinuate anything, like she thought he was only sleeping with her now —"have sex with, and that's all you do, but do you realize that they are more than sexual beings?"

Nate didn't reply right away, and she had to give him points for honestly thinking about the question.

"Yes, but I didn't really think about it until you said something. I see what you're saying."

She smiled. "That's good. Because, sometimes, the sweetest girls can be the naughtiest."

"Like you?"

She mock gasped, putting a hand on her chest. "*Moi*? I do not think so."

Nate laughed. "So, you're telling me that your friends didn't ask any details about the two of us having sex?"

Piper moved her head back to his chest. "I plead the fifth."

Simone, Lainey, and Kayla had asked her every possible question about her Friday night with Nate.

"Does he look as good with clothes off as he does on?"

"Yes."

"Is he hung like a horse?"

"Yes."

"Is he amazing in bed?"

"Yes."

"Did he make you come?"

"Yes, yes, and yes."

She wasn't about to tell him all that though. It would go straight to his head, and Nate didn't need any help with his ego.

Thankfully, Nate laughed and didn't interrogate her on what had been said about him.

She moved her head to his shoulder again. "My turn for a question."

"Shoot."

"Your penis."

Nate chuckled. "Okay. What about it?"

169

"I noticed earlier that the uncircumcised topic might be a bit of an issue."

He sighed. "You noticed that, huh?"

She rubbed his smooth chest with her hand. "Yes. What's that about?"

He shrugged as if it were no big deal, but the seriousness of his face said otherwise. "Growing up, I was pretty much the only guy in the locker room who was uncut." Piper knew that Nate had played football all the way through high school. "When you're a kid, you know how any little difference can make you stick out."

Oh, Nate.

"Were kids horrible to you?"

"Some, but I learned to hide myself pretty quickly. Thankfully, by the time high school came around, I wasn't the only one, and nobody really cared anymore. But middle school was the worst. Middle schoolers are brutal."

"Hey, I always thought the same thing. At my middle school, everyone had to wear the right clothes and have the right hair. When I got to high school, no one cared as much, and it was much less cliquey." She rubbed her finger along his hard jaw. "I'm sorry they were so mean to you."

He took a deep breath. "Yeah, well, it's nothing like taking your clothes off in front of a girl and having her tell you that you're gross."

Piper sat up, furious for Nate. "Are you fucking kidding me?"

He laughed and squeezed her arm.

"What a bitch! Please tell me it only happened once."

"Yes, and no. I was only told by one girl I was gross. That

was in high school. But I did date a few who refused to go down on me because they said it made them uncomfortable."

"I'm sorry, Nate. No one should ever be told their body is gross. This is the way you were born. This is how God made you." Her heart hurt for Nate. Even though he was strong and confident, she couldn't imagine what it would be like to be in high school, naked in front of the opposite sex, and be told something like that. If it had happened to her, she probably would never have gotten naked again.

He squeezed her arm again. "You don't have to apologize. You didn't say it."

"I know. And, if it makes you feel better, there are more and more guys out there like you."

"There are?"

"Yes. More and more parents are choosing to leave their boys intact."

He raised his eyebrow. "How do you know all this?"

She laughed. "Coworkers. I have several who are part of Facebook groups where they talk about all this stuff."

"Wow."

An idea came to Piper, and she smiled.

"Why do you look like the Cheshire cat all of a sudden?"

She licked her lips and flipped the blanket off of them. She went straight for Nate's dick, wrapping her fingers around it. He was soft, which was understandable from the conversation they'd just had, but it didn't take long before he was hard and thick. A bead of pre-cum leaked from his tip.

She looked into his eyes. He looked like he was holding his breath, just waiting to see what she would do.

"What are you hoping will happen right now?" she asked him.

"I'm praying to every known god I can think of that you put me in your fucking mouth."

Piper threw her head back and laughed. But only for a second. Because then she swiftly moved down his body and enveloped his cock with her mouth.

"Mmm," she hummed around him. Piper loved giving head. She'd almost forgotten how much.

Apparently, Nate liked it, too, because he jerked in her mouth, and she tasted him at the back of her throat. She pushed him as far in as he could go, touching her nose to his belly and enjoying the noises he made above her.

She grabbed the base of him and pulled his shaft from her mouth. "Grab my hair," she told him. "Show me what you like."

"Damn, you are a walking wet dream, Piper," Nate said. He took her hair into a makeshift ponytail in his hand. "You sure?"

"Show me, Nate," she whispered.

He guided her head down to him. "Open."

She parted her lips.

"Take all of me. Like you did before."

She took him to the back of her throat, sucking and massaging him with her tongue as she went. He held her there until her eyes began to water, and then he pulled her away. She liked that he was paying attention to her and watching for any signs of her being uncomfortable. She didn't mind a few tears in her eyes though.

Nate did this a few more times and then gave her some of

the control back. She enjoyed doing her own thing, but she really liked it when Nate told her what to do.

She could tell he was getting closer to coming by the way his breathing quickened and his hips rotated on the couch.

He grasped her hair in his hand and said, "Put me in your mouth again. Just the head."

A tingle shot between her legs at his words, and she did as he'd said.

"Suck me."

Again, she did what he'd told her, gripping the base of him as she did so.

His eyes closed, and his head fell back. "I'm going to come. Don't stop. Please don't stop."

She wanted to tell him, *Never*, but that would require stopping.

When he climaxed, his cum hit the back of her mouth, and she swallowed him down. After several seconds, his grip loosened on her hair, and his body collapsed.

She sat up, kneeling between his legs. "Just to be clear, I find you anything but gross."

CHAPTER TWENTY-FIVE

One week later, Piper heard a knock at her front door just before Nate opened it and stepped inside.

"Hey, stranger," she said with a smile.

She hadn't seen Nate since last Wednesday when she sent him home with a smile on his face. He'd had to leave town from Friday to Tuesday for work, and even though they'd texted while he was gone, she'd been surprised by how much she missed him.

Only as a friend though. She'd missed him only as a friend.

"Hey," he said. "Are you ready to go?"

She looked at her kitchen counter. "I think so." She began ticking her items off her list. "Salad, dessert, plasticware, wine...I don't think I forgot anything."

Nate came to stand beside her. "I think you forgot the kitchen sink."

Piper turned to him. "I told Elise I would bring a couple of things. I wanted to do my share for the barbeque."

"I think you did more than your share. There's only going to be, like, eight of us at Luke and Elise's."

"I know. But my mother always says, 'It's better to have more food than not enough.'"

"Smart woman."

Piper chuckled. "I'll tell her you said that." She grabbed the pasta salad and the forks and knives. "Can you grab the other two?"

"Sure."

"What did you bring?" she asked Nate as they carried the stuff to his truck.

"I brought brats and beef for hamburgers. I got them from the local meat market, so you know it'll be good."

"Sounds delicious."

They loaded everything into the backseat of Nate's truck, and Piper went inside to get her purse and to lock up.

When she came back, he was leaning against the vehicle. When she reached him, he made no move to get in his vehicle.

"I'm ready if you are."

Nate grabbed the front of her summer dress and pulled her close to him. "In case I forget to tell you, you look very sexy today," he said against her mouth and kissed her.

Woo. She almost fanned herself.

The man could kiss. So much so that she momentarily forgot about her nosy neighbor.

Piper pulled back just enough to look him in the eye. "Thanks. I just threw my outfit together."

She was lying, of course, and Nate probably knew it, but he didn't call her out. She'd purposely picked her hottest summer dress, wanting to look appropriate for the Fourth of July barbecue with friends while also wanting Nate to know what he'd missed when he was away. She'd also thought of him when she put her hair up and makeup on.

She tugged on his form-fitting light-blue T-shirt. "You don't look too bad yourself."

His tee looked great against his skin, and it made his blue eyes pop. He paired it with gray shorts and sandals because it was way too hot to wear pants.

He grinned at her. "We'd better get going before we're late."

She stepped back and walked around to the passenger side. "You should've come over earlier."

"Hey, you wouldn't let me."

Piper laughed to herself. "I know." She had something else planned for later.

She opened the truck door and got in.

Piper and Nate pulled up to Luke and Elise's home. They unloaded all the food and brought it into the house. Elise greeted them at the door and gave Piper a hug. Piper embraced Elise back the best she could with items in her hands.

She had to admit that she was really starting to enjoy her new friendships with her coworkers and Elise. It felt nice to have some women friends again. After Jordan had passed away, she'd lost touch with most of her friends since they lived far away.

"You can bring everything out back unless it needs to go in the fridge," Elise told them. "Everyone is already here."

As they walked through the house, stopping in the kitchen to put away food, and out to the backyard, Piper wondered who everyone was. Outside, she only took a quick glance around while Nate said a few hellos, paying more attention to setting the food down and putting everything in a good place among the other items.

Once that was done, Elise pulled her close and first introduced her to a shorter couple. The guy had blond hair, and the woman had light-brown hair. They were both petite, and they looked very cute together.

"Piper, this is Sean and Rachel. Sean and Rachel, this is Piper. And you already know Nate."

Piper shook their hands, recognizing their names. She had heard Elise and Luke talk about them a few times. "It's nice to meet you."

Next, Elise brought her over to a redheaded couple. "Piper, this is Joe and Shelly. Shelly is a teacher with Rachel. Joe and Shelly, this is Piper. And you two have met Nate once or twice, right?"

"Nice to meet you, Piper," Shelly said. "Yes, we met Nate at your wedding."

"Duh." Elise smacked her palm against her forehead, and everyone laughed.

"I was forgetful about things like that when I was pregnant, too," Shelly said.

"Shelly and Joe have an eleven-month-old at home," Elise

told Piper.

"Yes, who just started sleeping through the night about a month ago. Elise, I'm so jealous that you're married to the baby whisperer."

"Baby whisperer?" Nate asked as he pointed to Luke with a look of skepticism on his face. "This guy?"

"Yes, he's the one who got Virginia to stop crying in the hospital," Joe said.

Nate looked at Luke like he was the one who was pregnant.

Luke shrugged. "What can I say? The ladies love me."

Nate snorted. "In your dreams."

Everyone laughed again.

Elise took their drink requests while Piper and Nate took a seat around the patio table. She looked at Rachel and Sean, then Shelly and Joe, and lastly, Elise and Luke. They were all married. And then it was her and Nate.

They weren't even dating.

Piper looked around again and stopped when she reached Nate. She wondered if he realized that everyone else here was a couple, except for them. Did he feel weird or feel any pressure about it now that they had slept together?

Nate smiled at something someone had said. He certainly didn't look uncomfortable, which was a relief.

Piper grabbed her wineglass and took a long drink. She didn't know why she was so worried about it anyway. She didn't want to be in a relationship either. That was why she had picked Nate. She shouldn't worry that Nate would feel unnecessary pressure to be an item—at least, not from her.

"I'd like to make a toast," Elise said, pulling Piper's

thoughts away. "Today is my and Luke's one-year anniversary." She tilted her head back and forth. "Kind of. It's a long story."

Luke laughed, and Elise swatted him in the chest.

"Anyway, I want to say, happy anniversary, Luke. I promise not to spill any drinks on your head this year."

Luke and Elise kissed, and then everyone clinked their glasses together and took a drink.

A round of congratulations made their way around the table, and that was when the words hit Piper. She knew they'd just gotten married in March, so Elise wasn't talking about their wedding anniversary.

"Wait, you two have been together only a year?" She swirled her finger around in a circle. "Like, together, *together*? But you just got married." After she said it, she realized how that sounded. "I'm sorry. I didn't mean to make that sound judgy or anything. I just had no idea."

Everyone was smiling, and Elise laughed, putting Piper at ease.

"No, that's a good question. We only really started hanging out recently, so it's understandable you didn't know," she said, setting her glass of water down. "Yes, Luke and I haven't been together very long. We wanted to get married and try to start a family as soon as possible due to my father's diminishing health."

Piper knew about Elise's father having cancer, but she hadn't known it was so serious. She immediately sympathized with Elise, having lost her own father. "I understand that." She was very grateful her dad had gotten to see her get married. "I'm sorry to hear about your dad. How is he doing?"

"He's doing okay. He got to walk me down the aisle, and he should still be around when this little one is born," she said, rubbing her belly. She grabbed Luke's hand. "Right now, I couldn't ask for more."

Piper could feel the beginnings of melancholy come over her at seeing how content Elise was with Luke. She hadn't felt that real deep sadness for a couple of weeks now, and she didn't want to start crying here of all places.

"Barf. You two make me sick," Rachel said teasingly.

Thankfully, it was enough to bring Piper back from the edge.

Elise rolled her eyes. "Please. I remember, last year, I had to leave the kitchen because you and Sean practically started dry-humping each other."

"*We did not.*"

"Ha," Luke said. "You did more than that. I caught the both of you coming out of the bedroom with messy hair. You're just as nasty as we are."

Elise swung her gaze to Luke. "We're not nasty."

Luke shrugged. "You know what I mean."

Rachel and Sean laughed at the two of them while Shelly and Joe clinked their glasses together.

"To being the old married couple and not gross newly-weds," Joe said.

Piper raised her glass to Nate. He tapped his to hers.

"To not being married at all," she told him. She leaned close to him and lowered her voice. "And to being the nastiest of them all."

Nate smiled. "I will drink to that."

CHAPTER TWENTY-SIX

Nate was relaxing in his seat, making small talk with Luke and Joe, when his phone buzzed in his pocket.

Piper: What are you doing?

He looked up and around the backyard. Everyone else was outside but no Piper.

Nate: Sitting here. What are you doing?

Piper: I'm in the house. I need your help.

Intrigued, Nate excused himself and walked into the house, making sure to close the door behind him.

"Piper," he called out.

"Psst. Over here," she yelled in a loud whisper.

He looked over to see Piper peeking from around the corner by the front door.

Because of her tone, he naturally searched his surroundings to see if anyone else was around, but they were alone.

When he reached the spot she'd talked to him from, she was gone.

Suddenly, an arm reached out from the coat closet and pulled him inside. Nate ran right into Piper, and she burst out laughing.

"Piper, what are you—"

She gasped. "Close the door." She pointed behind his head.

"What's going on?" He narrowed his eyes. "How much have you had to drink?" He'd seen her with at least two glasses of wine.

"Close the door," she said through her teeth. She was trying to sound stern, but it was hard to do when she was still giggling. "And I'm not drunk."

Nate rolled his eyes, turned around, and closed the closet door.

It was a small space, and Nate had to do some maneuvering to twist his body back around. It didn't help that it was dark with only a small patch of light coming in from underneath the door.

When he faced her again, Piper kissed him.

Nate pulled away. "What's going on?"

There was just enough light for him to see Piper wiggle her eyebrows. "We're going to have sex."

"What?"

"Sex. Right here, right now."

"We can't do that here."

She reached for his zipper, and before he could tell her to

wait, she had it open with her hand in his shorts and her fingers wrapped around his cock.

He made a noise like he was being strangled.

She snickered. "Someone's up for the adventure."

Nate circled her wrist with his own hand. "He's always up for anything. You can't count on him to be responsible." Like saying no to having sex in his friend's coat closet.

He had grabbed her with every intention of pulling her arm away, but the way she was stroking him felt incredible. He hadn't had sex in a week, and it wasn't going to be hard to convince him this was a good idea. He let his hand drop.

"Oh, Nate, don't be such a wiener."

This caught his attention. "Did you just call me a wiener?"

Piper started laughing so hard that her head fell against his chest. She looked up at him. "I meant, weenie."

He raised his brow. "I'm not sure how I feel about you calling me a weenie either. Especially with your hand down my pants."

She pulled her fingers back from his shorts and grabbed his shirt. "Don't be a stick in the mud. Let's do it."

"Do it?"

"Yeah."

"What's *it*?"

She laughed. "Have sex."

He took a step closer, causing her to take a step back, and her back hit the wall. "Hmm..."

She licked her lips. "What does that mean?"

He grabbed her sides, lifting her up, and she let out a squeak.

"God, I love your hips."

She grabbed on to his shoulders. "You do?"

"Fuck yeah." He rested her legs on his thighs, so he could move his hands out of the way. "Pull up your dress for me."

Piper smiled and pulled up the lower half of her dress.

He loved how she did whatever he asked when it came to them getting down and dirty. He hadn't realized he had a bossy streak until someone pointed it out to him. He'd been young and immediately tried to stop doing it. When she'd called him out on it, she'd explained she had told him for purely educational reasons, not because she wanted him to change.

"I also love your ass." He slipped his hands under her dress to cup her cheeks. "Well, well, well, Piper Stevens, are you wearing a thong?"

"Yes. Do you like it?"

"Is the Pope Catholic?"

He traced the seam of her panties toward her front until he found her center. He pushed a finger inside her. She was already wet.

She moaned from deep in her throat.

He kissed her on the side of the neck and sucked on her skin. "Shh...someone might hear you."

"You should know by now that I can't be quiet when you're inside me."

Fuck.

"Where have you been all my life?"

She knew it was a rhetorical question, so she just laughed. Until he rubbed her G-spot, and then she was moaning again.

"Reach into my front pocket," he told her.

Her hands went into his front pockets until they found what they needed.

"Undo my jeans, pull me out, and cover me, so I can be deep inside you, where I belong."

She pulsed around his middle digit and fumbled with the condom. Not only did she *not* mind being bossed around, but she also liked it.

She was amazing.

Piper quickly rolled the condom down Nate's remarkable length. It wasn't easy with her back resting against the wall and Nate holding her up, but she was bound and determined to get that sucker on.

As soon as she accomplished her goal, she quickly told him, "Now, now."

Nate slightly lifted her and set her around his girth. She almost couldn't wait.

"Please, please," she pleaded.

Funny how she'd gone for over a year without getting laid, and now, she was going crazy after one week.

Nate slowly pushed his cock inside her, and she felt herself stretch around him.

"Oh shit," rushed out of her mouth as she grabbed on to Nate's shoulders.

"You feel so good," Nate said against her ear.

"So do you," she cried out as his dick hit a particularly sensitive spot. "I feel so full. Yet I want you in further."

"I'm trying not to hurt you."

"Hurt me. Please," she panted. "I want it. All of it. All of you." She pulled him tighter. "More. I need more."

Nate made a sound that was half-grunt, half-groan and pulled her hips down.

Overwhelmed with his size, Piper bit down on his neck.

Nate began to pump inside her, and she let her jaw go.

"Oh God. I'm sorry," she said right next to his ear. "Please don't stop."

"I won't." He moved his face back and took her mouth. He tasted like beer and Nate, and his tongue stroked her mouth like his cock stroked her pussy.

She broke their kiss to get more air.

Nate continued to pound away inside her. "Fuck. I'm not going to be able to last long."

"That's okay," she said between breaths. She'd known going into this that it would have to be quick. "I'm almost there."

Nate slightly shifted their bodies.

"Oh shit." Breath. "Oh, damn." Breath. "I lied." Breath. "I'm there." The next thing out of her mouth sounded like a baby whale being taken from its mother, but she didn't care because the orgasm that crashed through her body made her see stars.

"Goddamn it, I love when you come," Nate said and pulled her hard against him. He pushed her down on his cock, holding her there as his own climax took over his body.

For a minute, it was just the two of them, their deep breathing, and the feeling of their bodies still connected. But that was all interrupted by the sounds of voices.

Crap. How long had they been in the house?

"You'd better let me down."

"Yeah," Nate agreed and set her on her feet.

Piper smoothed down her dress and quickly undid her hair to put it up again. She looked up to see Nate watching her. She couldn't read his face, but he looked so handsome, standing there, that she kissed him.

"I'll go out first and make sure the coast is clear, so you can go to the bathroom."

Nate kissed her again. "Thank you."

She grinned. "Um...no, thank you. The pleasure was all mine."

Nate laughed, and when Piper opened the door, he swatted her butt as she walked out.

Luckily, there wasn't anyone standing right outside the door, but as soon as Piper turned the corner into the kitchen, she ran into Elise and Rachel. "Oh, hey."

Rachel put her hand to her mouth to cover her laugh, causing Piper to laugh, too. She knew she'd been busted.

Elise wasn't laughing, but she didn't look mad either. "*Oh, hey?* That's it?"

Piper shrugged. "What else do you want me to say?"

Rachel pulled her hand away from her mouth. "Did you just have sex in Elise's closet?"

"Yep."

Elise's mouth dropped open. Piper didn't know if it was because Elise was surprised it was true or surprised that Piper had admitted it.

"That is *awesome*," Rachel said. "I think I like you, Piper."

"Don't look so shocked, Elise." Piper slipped her arm through her friend's. "You had sex in my laundry room, and now, I've had sex in your closet. We're even," she teased.

Elise turned red, and Rachel barked out a laugh so hard, she had to grab the counter to stay standing.

Elise narrowed her eyes at both of them. "You're both bitches, you know that?"

"Aw," Piper said. "We love you, too."

CHAPTER TWENTY-SEVEN

The sun was beginning its descent, which meant the fireworks were starting to go off around the neighborhood. Everyone had moved to the front of the house to watch the neighbors' fireworks and to set off their own.

"Hey, Nate, can you help me?" Luke asked him.

Nate set his beer down on the ground by his chair. "Sure." He got up and followed Luke into the garage.

His friend was pulling five or six bags off of the shelf in the corner.

"How many did you buy?"

Luke looked over his shoulder and smiled. "Hopefully enough that we don't run out anytime soon." He handed Nate several sacks that were all full. Luke had always liked fireworks.

Once the shelf was clear, Nate asked, "Is that everything?"

Luke turned, his own hands full. "Yep."

Nate turned to go back outside.

"Hey, Nate."

"Yeah?" Nate glanced over his shoulder.

Luke hadn't moved from his spot in the back of the garage.

Nate stopped and turned. "What is it?"

Luke took a deep breath. "It's Piper, man. Do you think it's smart to be sleeping with a widow?"

Nate stepped closer to Luke. "It's not like that."

Luke raised his brow. "Not like what?"

Nate sighed. "What exactly are you worried about?"

"Look, I don't know Piper well, but what I do know, I like. My wife likes her." Luke paused, as if searching for the right words. "You're not exactly...relationship material."

Nate scowled. Did Luke really think he'd hurt Piper?

Luke must have known what he was thinking because the next thing out of his mouth was, "I know you care about her. I admit, I've never seen you like this with a chick. And I would hate to see you push her away."

Nate shook his head. "That's not going to happen."

Luke looked sad. "I know that's what you think, but please just be careful. She's a widow, Nate. I know she's strong, but she's still been hurt before. She doesn't need to get hurt again. And I don't want to see you staying with her just because you don't want to hurt her. I don't know what you two have going on, but she's been married before. She might want more than just casual sex."

Nate knew Luke was just looking out for Piper and him, but it still grated on his nerves. "Why are you asking this now? You already knew we'd slept together."

"Yeah, but I thought that was going to be a one-time thing. You'd been out at the club, and some alcohol had been involved. But it's obviously happened more than once since then."

"How do you know?"

"Well, Elise told me about the closet."

Of course she had.

"But, even if she hadn't, you have a bite mark on your neck and fingernail cuts on your head that are about a week old." Luke smirked. "She must have really gotten you good."

Nate instinctively reached up with his hand to feel the back of his head and smacked himself in the chest with the bags full of fireworks. Nate dropped his hand and scowled at Luke. He should have known that Luke would notice Piper's fingernail imprints. She'd really dug her nails in when he went down on her last week.

"Do you have to be such a damn doctor all the time?"

Luke laughed. "I can't help but notice things like that." He walked toward the front yard. "Come on, I've said my piece."

"I appreciate your concern, but you don't have to worry." Something Luke had said came back to Nate. "Oh, and the first time we had sex, it was only Piper who had been out at the club, drinking. I was in bed when she came to my house."

Luke looked at him. "Oh. Really?" They stopped at the entrance to the garage. "Huh. Maybe I really don't have to worry."

"Why do you say that?"

"Well, if Piper came to your house after drinking, you

were basically a booty call. I was probably getting ahead of myself when I was thinking she might want more from you."

"See, I told you. Nothing to worry about." Nate had said the words, but a spot deep inside him didn't agree. He suddenly felt unsettled.

"Good." Luke smiled. "I'm glad." His smile turned into a grin, and he wiggled his eyebrows. "Let's go blow some shit up."

Nate laughed and followed Luke to where everyone was sitting, but his enthusiasm didn't quite reach his heart.

Hours later, Nate pulled up to Piper's house. They both silently got out of his truck and brought in the stuff she'd taken to the barbecue.

"You can just set everything in the kitchen," she told him. "I am beat. I wish we didn't have to go to work tomorrow."

Nate grunted in response. Normally, he'd agree, but right now, he welcomed the distraction of work. His stupid brain wouldn't stop racing with thoughts of him and Piper. He kept thinking about what Luke had said over and over again.

"*Hey.*"

Nate jumped. He'd been staring off into space.

Piper stepped toward him and put her hand on his chest. "What is going on with you? You've been acting distant the last couple of hours."

"It's something Luke said."

"What did he say?"

Nate lifted his shoulders and let them drop.

"Don't shrug like you don't know. If it's bothering you, obviously, you know."

He sighed. "I don't want to hurt you."

"Okay, now, you really have to tell me what was said."

Nate put his hands over Piper's. "He said I should be careful with you. That you want more than I can give you. He thinks that I'm going to hurt you. But then he turned around and said that I was just your booty call, so who knows?"

Her eyes filled with some kind of emotion he couldn't decipher. "Oh, Nate. I'm sorry Luke worried you. There was a reason I picked you."

"Picked me?" He frowned. "How many were in the running?"

Piper laughed, but Nate didn't think it was funny.

She shrugged. "No one. Not really. I went on that bad date, but I probably wouldn't have slept with him even if he hadn't been married."

He didn't know if that made him feel any better.

"I picked you because you turn me on." She blushed and looked down at their hands. "It's because of you that I realized I wanted to have sex again."

Nate's chest puffed as some of the tension left his body. "What can I say? I'm irresistible."

Piper laughed again. "I also picked you because you're my friend. I trust you."

He relaxed more. He really didn't have anything to worry about.

"Also, I know you don't do relationships, so I don't have to worry that you'll want something more." She quickly kissed him. "That's why you're perfect."

Nate tried to smile, but his sudden contentment was gone.

She wrapped her arms around his neck. "Do you want to stay the night? Or for a few more minutes at least?" She kissed his throat.

Nate reached back and pulled her hands from around him. "I'm going to have to take a rain check."

She lost her smile. "Oh. Okay."

He didn't want her to feel bad. "Hey," he said, pulling her into his arms. "I would love to stay. But I have an early meeting." Thank God it was the truth.

"The holiday is officially over, huh?"

"Yeah." Nate kissed her and said good-bye.

As he walked to his truck, he thought about what Piper had said. He didn't know why it bothered him. He *didn't* do relationships, so why did it trouble him to hear Piper say it?

By the time he got home, he still didn't have an answer.

CHAPTER TWENTY-EIGHT

I t was Friday night, and Piper and Nate had decided to go out for dinner. They were sitting by the hostess stand, waiting for a table, when an older black couple walked in. There was something about the man that struck Piper as familiar, yet she couldn't place where she'd seen him before.

She was about to nudge Nate, who was looking down at his phone, to see if he recognized the man when the couple walked over.

"Nate."

Nate's head shot up. "Dad."

Ahhh. That was why he looked familiar. Nate had some of his father's features.

It was a little strange to think that she and Nate were friends, but she'd never met his parents. She'd met his grand-father a couple of times and his sister once but never his parents. She knew that Nate was not close to them.

When nothing more was said, Piper elbowed Nate in the arm.

"Oh. Dad, Tricia, this is Piper. Piper, this is my father, Jerome, and my stepmother, Tricia."

Piper held out her hand. "Nice to meet you." Even though Nate didn't care for his parents, she felt like a kid in a candy store. She and Nate were close, but there was still this whole part of him that was a mystery.

Jerome shook her hand, as did Tricia.

Just then, the hostess came over with her clipboard. "Sir, we have you down for only two people. Did you want to change that to four?"

Piper noticed the look of hope in Jerome's eyes, even as Nate opened his mouth to probably say no.

"Yes, that would be wonderful," Piper told the hostess. She then turned to Nate's parents. "Oh gosh, I hope that's okay. You two didn't have a romantic date planned or anything, did you?"

Tricia laughed. "No, we just didn't feel like cooking tonight. We'd love to have dinner with you." She looked at her husband. Maybe Tricia had seen the same expression on Jerome's face that Piper had.

"Great," the hostess said. "We have a booth ready for the four of you."

As they were led to their table, Nate grabbed Piper's arm and pulled her back. "Why did you invite them to eat with us?"

Piper could either play dumb or tell him the truth. She went with part of the truth. "Because I want to get to know them better. It's only a couple of hours at most." She patted him on the arm. "I'm sure you'll survive."

"Don't be so sure about that," he muttered under his breath as they continued toward their seats.

The four of them got situated, and the hostess told them their server would be with them soon.

"So, how do you and Nate know each other?" Tricia asked.

For a second, Piper was surprised that they didn't recognize her name, but then she remembered that Nate had told her that he didn't share much with his family.

"Nate and my husband went to college together. Nate actually helped Jordan find a job here. That's how we moved from Nebraska."

Tricia and Jerome looked around, and Piper realized she'd forgotten to say her *late* husband.

"Oh, I'm sorry. Jordan passed away a year ago in a car accident."

Recognition dawned in both Tricia's and Jerome's eyes.

"This was the same accident as Nate?" Jerome asked.

So, maybe they had heard of her. They just hadn't known her name.

"Yes."

"I'm sorry to hear about your loss. I'm sorry we brought it up," Tricia said.

"Thank you. And it's okay. Really. It's my reality and a part of who I am. Yes, it makes me sad when I think about it, and I miss him every day, but it doesn't mean that I don't want to talk about him."

Nate flinched beside her, and for some odd reason, Tricia looked guilty.

"But I try to look at the positive things," Piper continued. "I wouldn't have become such good friends with Nate if things had been different." And she would never have known what it felt like to have Nate inside her. Since she couldn't control the situation, she might as well take what good she could get out of it.

Jerome smiled at the two of them with a slight sadness in his eyes, and Piper's heart went out to him. It was obvious he wanted a better relationship with his son.

Their server approached their table, and the previous conversation dropped. After taking their drink orders with a promise to be back, their server walked away.

"What is it you do?" Tricia asked.

"I work at a women's shelter."

"Piper's a women's advocate," Nate told his parents. "She won't admit it, but she's amazing at her job."

Piper blushed. She'd had no idea that Nate thought that way about her.

"Wow. That must be intense sometimes," Tricia said.

"Oh, yes," Piper agreed. "But, other times, it can be very mundane. What about you?"

"I'm an accountant," Tricia said. "And Jerome has his own contracting business," she said proudly.

"That's impressive. I wouldn't know where to start if I had my own business."

Jerome put up his hands in modesty. "It's a small business. I've been in construction most of my life. My body can't handle things the way it used to, but I'm too young to retire.

Something had to change, and now, I'm the boss. I step in when help is needed, but I don't do as much labor as I used to."

Piper smiled. "I think Nate once said that you taught him everything he knows, which I'm certainly grateful for because my backyard is coming along beautifully."

Jerome's brows furrowed. "Backyard?"

Nate really doesn't *tell his parents anything.*

"Yes, Nate has been working on my backyard all summer."

Nate shifted in his seat, as if he was uncomfortable, but it didn't seem like a big deal that he was doing work at her house.

Jerome cleared his throat. "Who's been helping you?"

When Nate didn't say anything, Piper offered the information. "Luke. He kind of owed Nate since Nate worked on Luke and Elise's house for free."

Nate kicked her under the table.

"*Ow.*"

What was that for?

Jerome's eyes widened, and he looked sad. "You worked on Luke's house, too?"

"It's not a big deal," Nate said.

"I would have helped, you know."

Nate sighed. "I know, Dad."

He shot Piper a look that said, *Now, look what you've done*, and she finally understood what all the tension was about.

I'm an idiot.

Jerome was obviously hurt that Nate hadn't asked for his

help, and she'd had to open her big mouth and add more fuel to the fire.

She put her hand on Nate's thigh and squeezed. When he looked at her, she mouthed an apology.

Once again, their server had excellent timing, and the subject was dropped. They spent the rest of the meal making small talk, and there were no more mentions of deceased spouses or odd jobs on the side.

"Here's the bill, whenever you're ready," their server said as she set the slip of paper on the table.

Nate went to reach for it, but his dad beat him to it.

"I've got this, son."

"Dad," Nate protested.

His father looked him in the eye. "I said, I have got this."

Nate knew when to push and when to back off. "Okay. Thank you."

Piper picked her napkin off her lap and set it next to her plate. "Yes, thank you very much. That is so kind of you to pay. It wasn't my intention when I asked you to eat with us."

His father laughed. "We know."

"Well, thanks again." She turned to Nate. "I'm going to go use the restroom. Should I meet you out front?"

"Sure."

"I'm going to go use the restroom, too," his father said. "Are you going to put this on the Visa?" he asked Tricia.

"Yes," she said and put her credit card on the table with the bill.

For as long as Nate could remember, Tricia had kept track of the finances, which made sense since she was the accountant in the family.

Both Piper and his dad got up and left as the waitress snagged the payment from the table, leaving him alone with Tricia. He watched Piper walk away, wishing they could be far away from here—preferably alone and naked.

"You care about her."

"Huh?" Nate turned his attention to his stepmom.

"You care about her. Piper," she explained.

"Oh...well...yeah. She's my friend."

Tricia didn't come out and call bullshit. It was written all over her face. "Can I say something?"

If I said no, would that stop you?

"Sure." He shrugged. "Why not?"

"I was very wrong to treat you the way I did when your father and I first got married."

Whoa. What? Where is this coming from?

"When I first met your dad, he was very much in mourning, and I knew that he loved your mother so incredibly deeply." Tricia looked down at her hands. "And, now, years later, I can admit, I was jealous. And part of that jealousy was taken out on you. It didn't help that you were a constant reminder of what your father and mother had together." She looked up and met Nate's eyes. "I should have treated you better, Nate. You were a young boy who had just lost his mom. All you wanted was to be loved, and I threw it back in your face."

Nate felt his eyes widen as Tricia's filled with tears.

"It wasn't until years later, when Tiana was born, that I

realized how awful I had been to you. If I thought about someone treating Tiana the way I'd treated you..." She took a deep breath. "Let's just say, I am very sorry. I'm sorry that I wasn't a better stepmom to you. I know I'm a huge reason that you and your father aren't close, and I'm sorry for that, too."

His dad and stepmom had been married for years, and this was just coming out now.

"Why are you telling me this now? After all this time?"

She shrugged. "Partly because I never knew how to tell you. Partly because I was embarrassed, and I didn't want to admit out loud how horrible I'd been. But I'm telling you now because I know something that I didn't know back then."

"And what is that?"

"That the heart has no limit to how much it can love. I learned that I had no reason to be jealous of Jerome's love for your mother because he loves me, too. And his love for you doesn't mean he loves Tiana any less. Your father can love your mother and me."

Nate didn't understand what she meant by all this. "What does this have to do with me?"

Tricia smiled, but her eyes were sad. "Just because Piper loved her husband doesn't mean she can't love anyone else."

Nate sat back in the booth. "Whoa, whoa, it's not like that."

"Whatever you say. I just wanted you to know and maybe learn from my mistakes."

"But—"

"Here comes Jerome," Tricia said, looking over Nate's shoulder. She met his eyes once more. "Also, please give your father a second chance. He knows he messed up when you were little. If you gave him a chance, he would like to apologize to you, too. He loves you very much, Nate."

Nate sat, stunned, as his dad walked up to the table.

"Are you ready to go?"

"Almost." Tricia smiled at his father, and for maybe the first time, Nate saw how much love was between them. "Here comes the waitress now."

The server returned the card, and Tricia quickly signed the receipt.

She stood and grabbed his father's hand. "Think about what I said, okay?"

"What did you say?" his dad asked.

Tricia kissed him. "Nothing for you to worry about. Let's go home."

Jerome smiled. "Okay, dear." He looked at Nate, and his smile turned tentative. "Thanks, son, for letting us have dinner with you."

Nate nodded, and thinking about what Tricia had talked about, he said, "Thanks for eating with us."

His father's smile no longer wavered, and he gave Nate a nod before leading his wife out the door.

A few seconds later, Piper appeared. "I thought I was meeting you at the front."

Nate stood. "Yeah, I got to talking to Tricia and my dad."

She winced. "I hope it's okay I asked them to eat with us. You're not mad, are you?"

Nate grabbed her hand. "No, I'm not mad."

She breathed a sigh of relief. "Oh, good."

Nate laughed and kissed her. "Let's go home."

CHAPTER TWENTY-NINE

The next morning, Piper was awakened by her cell phone ringing on the nightstand. She blindly reached out an arm from where she had buried herself underneath the covers in the middle of the night to grab her phone from the table.

She cleared her throat and swiped to answer. "Hello?" Her voice still sounded scratchy.

"Piper!"

"Hi, Mom."

"What are you doing today?"

It was kind of an odd question, but she was too sleepy to really think about it. "I have to run to the grocery store, but I think that's it."

"Do you have plans tonight?"

She and Nate had talked about going out, but they had also talked about staying home and watching a movie.

"Nothing firm." A little prick at the back of Piper's neck

began to tingle, and she pushed the covers off her face. "What's going on?"

Her first thought was her mother was in the hospital or something, and alarm bells began to go off.

"Can you text me your grocery list?"

Piper calmed somewhat. A woman in the hospital wouldn't ask for a grocery list.

"Yeah," she said hesitantly. "Why?"

"Well, I was going to surprise you, but Don insisted that I give you some warning first."

"Surprise me how?" A different sort of panic began to set in.

"Don and I decided to visit you!"

Piper sat up. "When?"

"Now! We've been driving all morning."

Piper looked at the clock. It was almost ten in the morning. "What time did you leave?"

"Four."

It was about a six-hour drive from Omaha to Minneapolis with pit stops, which meant—

"We're going to be in town in about twenty minutes! Text me your grocery list, and we'll go to the store before we come. Love you. Can't wait to see you." And then her mom was gone.

Piper pulled up her memo pad app in her phone where she kept a list of groceries and quickly sent it to her mom. She added a few items to hopefully stall her mother some. She was not prepared for a visit. She needed to shower. She needed to pick up her house. She needed to put sheets on the guest bed. She needed to clean the bathroom.

She rolled over.

"*Ah.*" She needed to get a naked Nate out of her bed.

He was sprawled on his back, sheet pulled down to his crotch, pillow over his face, with his tattooed arm slung over his pillow and a slight snore coming from his mouth. He obviously hadn't heard a single thing. And he looked like such a sexy Adonis, lying there, that she wanted to cry. It wasn't fair. She wanted to touch him, not push him out of her bed.

She put her hand on his stomach and shook him. "Nate, it's time to get up."

He shifted and made a humming noise. He grabbed her hand and pushed it under the sheet and over his hard length. He wrapped his fingers around hers and squeezed. "Hmm."

"Nate, you have to get up." Despite her words, she didn't remove her hand.

He pushed the pillow off his face. "I am up. Can't you tell?"

"Not your penis. All of you."

He reached up and thumbed her nipple.

"Please." She didn't know if she was saying, *Please get up,* or, *Please do more of that.*

Nate reached over to the nightstand on his side of the bed and opened the drawer. He pulled out a condom from the pile he had stocked there for them.

She knew she should stop him, but instead, she watched as he rolled the protection down his beautiful cock. As soon as he was sheathed, she swung a leg over his hips.

"We have to make this quick," she told him as she pushed him inside her.

"Damn," he gasped. "Are you even ready?"

She laughed. She was always ready for him. "Yes," she assured him and rotated her hips.

Nate pulled her down to him and cupped her breast, sucking her nipple into his mouth. He removed his palm from her breast and placed both hands on her hips, guiding her movements.

Piper sat up, pulling her tip from his mouth, and pushed two fingers between her legs. If they were going to get this done before her mom and her mom's fiancé got there, she was going to need a little extra help.

"Fuck, it is so hot, watching you touch yourself."

Piper bit her lip and ground her hips over Nate's.

"Keep doing just that," he said and slid his hands up to her breasts again, molding them in his palms, brushing his thumbs over her nipples.

She arched her chest toward him and rode him. His hands on her breasts, her fingers on her clit, and his cock on her G-spot were the perfect trifecta, and Piper exploded. She didn't stop until her orgasm waned and Nate bucked underneath her.

She collapsed on his chest, and he wrapped his arms around her. She wished she could lie like that all day, but her mom was coming.

Piper shot up, flinging Nate's arms off her. "Oh my God, we have to get up."

"What? Why?"

Piper climbed off him. "My mom's coming."

Nate put his arms under his head and yawned. "When?"

Piper looked at the clock again. "Oh, in probably fifteen minutes...unless she takes her sweet time at the store."

Nate's eyes widened, and he scrambled out of bed. "Why didn't you tell me?"

Twenty-three and a half minutes later, Piper and Nate had showered–separately—put clean sheets on her guest bed, and picked up things, like magazines and mail, from her living room and kitchen. She'd made sure to hang her mother's wedding invitation on the fridge.

They were sitting at her kitchen counter, drinking coffee, when her mom and Don, her mother's new fiancé, arrived. Piper opened the door, and her mother pulled her in for a hug. Her mom's dark blonde hair smelled like her favorite perfume, and Piper breathed in the familiar scent.

She squeezed her mom, not realizing how much she had missed her until now. Her mother pulled away and brushed her wet hair from her face. Piper saw that her mother had noticed her newly washed hair, but she didn't call her out on it. She simply smiled.

"How's my baby doing?"

Piper grinned. "Good. How are you?"

"So glad to see you." She looked up and over Piper's shoulder. "Nathaniel!"

Her mom walked around her and pulled Nate into her arms. Piper was grateful that Nate had shaved his head this morning, so her mother wouldn't see they were both freshly showered.

"Hi, Mrs. Donovan."

Piper's mom took a step back. "Now, now, you call me

Karen." She turned and looked at Piper. "I tell him this every time."

Piper rolled her eyes. "Mom, you've only met Nate, like, two times."

"Three, but who's counting?"

You are, Piper thought.

"Any man who is nice enough to drive my daughter home for her husband's funeral doesn't call me Mrs. Donovan."

When Jordan had passed away, at the request of his parents, she'd brought him back to Nebraska to be buried. They had no family ties in Minnesota, and it didn't make sense to keep him from those who loved him.

Nate smiled at Piper. "Okay, Karen it is," he said to her mom.

Piper's mom turned to the open door and waved her arm. "Don, get in here."

A man in his fifties with thick gray hair stood in her threshold. He held his hands up. "I was just waiting for my turn, dear." He stepped inside her entryway and closed the door behind him. "Hello, Piper. I don't know if you remember me—"

"Yes, of course I remember you. Your dog thought our yard was his yard. How is Percy, by the way?"

Mr. Gibson laughed. "Percy is long gone now, but he always did like your lawn." He turned to Nate and held out his hand. "I'm Don."

Nate shook it with a smile. "Nate."

"Come into the kitchen." Piper motioned them with her hands. "Would you like some coffee?"

"I would love some," Piper's mom said.

209

"I'll take one, too, please," Don said.

Piper led them into the kitchen with Nate bringing up the rear.

As Piper poured her two new guests cups of coffee, her mom looked around her house.

"I didn't get a chance to clean since no one had warned me you were coming," Piper told her mom in a half-joking, half-serious tone.

Her mother waved away her concern. "I don't care about that. I just wanted to see you. And I wanted you to get to know Don a little before the wedding." Her mom's gaze landed on the fridge. "Oh, you hung up the invitation."

Piper looked at Nate, who winked. "Of course I did, Mom."

"Did you get the time off of work?"

"Yep, Wednesday through Monday."

"What about Nate?"

"Excuse me?" Nate said.

"What do you mean, Mom?"

Her mother looked at her and Nate like they were children. "Did Nate get the time off work, too?" She put her hands on her hips and narrowed her eyes. "Nate is your plus-one, isn't he?"

Piper didn't know what to say. A wedding was always the big-date question. What if Nate panicked at the thought of her inviting him? What if his feelings were hurt if she didn't? She didn't know what exactly had happened on the Fourth of July, but something had been bothering him. What if this was one of those things?

Piper looked at Nate with an apologetic look. "I would, of

course, love to have Nate come." She turned to her mom. "But I can't ask him to take off work and drive six hours to a wedding—"

"I'll go."

Piper looked at Nate. "What?"

"I'll go," he repeated himself.

She hadn't known how much she wanted Nate to be there until he said those words. "Really?"

"Really."

She grinned and resisted the urge to throw herself in his arms.

"Well, now that that's all settled, show us how the backyard is coming along," her mom said. "I've been anxious to see the results in person."

CHAPTER THIRTY

On Sunday, Piper and her mom went shopping together for a little girl-on-girl time. Their mission was to find dresses for her mom and herself for the wedding.

Nate had plans to go to a sports bar with his grandpa for the afternoon to watch...whatever sports were playing in July, and he was sweet enough to take Don with him.

"What are you looking for in a dress, Mom?"

"Something simple, and I was thinking off-white since I'm not a virgin."

"*Mom.*"

Her mom laughed and shrugged. "Well, I'm not. You're proof of that."

Piper wrinkled up her nose. "No offense, but gross. I don't want to think about you and Dad. Or you and Don."

Her mom laughed harder and patted Piper's hand. "That's okay, dear. I don't want to think about my parents either."

"Ew. And, now, I'm picturing Grandma and Grandpa." Piper glanced away from the wheel and gave her mom a dirty look. "It's not funny."

"Oh, Piper, I didn't take you for a prude."

Piper gasped. "I'm not a prude." She just didn't want to picture old people doing it. "Although that's something I shouldn't protest in front of my mother, huh?"

Her mom leaned over and put her arm around Piper as best she could in the car. "Oh, baby, I've missed you."

Piper laid her head on her mom's. "I've missed you, too."

"I don't suppose you'll ever move home?"

"Well..."

Her mom pulled away and waved her hand, as if her question was silly. "Of course not. Especially now."

"Especially now?" What was her mom talking about?

"I'll just have to come and visit a lot," she said, totally ignoring Piper's question.

"Mom, what did you mean by—"

Her mom gasped. "Let's go there." She pointed to a store off to the right. "I've heard they have a great selection."

Piper concentrated on getting over into the far-right lane and getting into the parking lot. By the time she parked, she'd completely forgotten her mother's comment.

They walked into the national chain store and were immediately greeted by a salesperson. Piper's mom began to tell the lady what she wanted, and Piper wandered away to look at bridesmaid dresses.

Three hours later, her mom finally found what she was looking for, and she also found a dress for Piper to wear. Piper had only had to try on eleven dresses, but at least she was happy to note that there was no lace, no frill, and no bows. It was a simple light-blue dress. Some might not even guess it had been bought at a bridal store.

"Are you sure you don't want to go somewhere else to get a better feel of what's out there?" Piper asked.

The saleslady shot Piper a look, but she ignored the woman. She didn't want to go anywhere else either, but this was for her mom's wedding day.

"No, I'm good. You know me; I hate shopping. I just want to go to the store, find what I want, and leave. Quick and easy is what I say. I don't need to shop around." She put her hand on Piper's forearm. "Unless you want something else."

Piper held her hands up and smiled. "No, no, I'm good. I was making sure you didn't want to go somewhere else."

She was very glad to be done with this quick and easy shopping trip, and she wasn't going to offer to go to another store again.

Piper looked at the clock on the wall. "I need a drink."

She wondered if Nate was having more fun than she was.

Nate fingered the edges of his phone for what was probably the hundredth time.

"Son, whatever you're going to do, just do it."

"Huh?" Nate looked up at his Geepa, who raised his brow and looked at Nate's phone.

Nate threw it on the table.

"I've watched you pick that thing up multiple times with that look on your face."

"What look?"

"It's the same face you had before asking that Heather girl to the school dance in seventh grade."

Except, this time, Nate wasn't asking a girl to do anything.

"Just do it already. And before that Don guy comes back with our drinks. He probably thinks you're cheating on his woman's daughter."

Nate scowled but chose not to comment. He wasn't going to discuss his relationship with Piper with his grandfather. He picked up his cell again and unlocked it. He went to his messages, let his thumb hover over the Send icon for two seconds, and then hit the button.

It was too late to back out now.

Nate told himself not to expect anything and that he should set his phone down and forget about it, but the kid in him willed it to ding.

He mentally rolled his eyes at himself and placed the phone facedown on the table. He felt like a loser.

Ding.

Nate turned the phone over and lit the screen.

I'll be there in ten minutes.

He swallowed. He'd thought a no or no reply would be bad. He didn't know what to do with a positive response. *How awkward is this going to be?*

"It'll be okay, son," Geepa told him as Don walked back to the table with three beers.

"Did I miss anything?" Don asked, referring to the game. "I was in the corner and didn't have a good angle?"

His grandfather looked at Nate and back at Don. "Nah. It was mostly commercials."

Don sat. "Oh, good."

"So, you're a Twins fan?" Geepa asked Don.

"Yep. With no team of our own in Nebraska, there are a lot of Minnesota fans."

Geepa nodded in approval. "Good, good."

Ten minutes later, the door opened, and Nate's father walked in. Nate glanced at his grandfather, looking for the approval he shouldn't need as a man in his thirties.

He hadn't been able to get Tricia's words out of his head since two nights ago. He hadn't told Piper what his stepmom had said, instead choosing to take her home and make love to her. And, the next day, her mom had shown up at her house.

Could his dad really want more of a relationship with him? Part of Nate felt like his father should have been the one to reach out since he was the parent and all. But, sometimes, a person couldn't wait around for someone to give them what they wanted.

So, he'd sent his father a text, inviting him to watch the baseball game. And, less than a minute later, his dad had said he would come.

His grandfather smiled at Nate, as if he understood exactly what Nate was thinking. Hell, he probably did. He knew the things that Nate had gone through, growing up.

When Nate's dad reached the table, his grandfather stood and held out his hand. "Jerome, it's nice to see you."

His father looked a little uncomfortable, but he shook Geepa's hand. "Nathan, it's good to see you, too." His father looked at Nate. "Nate, thanks for inviting me."

Nate kicked out a chair. "Here. Sit."

His father sat.

"Dad, this is Don. Don is engaged to Piper's mom. Don, this is my father, Jerome."

Don held out his hand. "Nice to meet you."

"Likewise," his dad said as he took Don's hand.

"You like baseball?" Don asked his dad.

His father nodded. "Yeah. I played football in high school, like Nate, but if it's a sport, I like to watch."

Don looked at Nate. "You played football?"

"Yeah. Only in high school though. I wasn't good enough for college."

"Hey, football's football. I played myself in high school."

His grandfather raised his bottle. "To playing football in high school."

"You didn't play football in high school," Nate told him.

"And I don't have a drink," Nate's dad said.

"Well, what are you waiting for?" Geepa said, and everyone laughed.

Nate's dad got up to get a beer and another round for the table. Soon, the group of them were talking about all kinds of sports and bonding the way men bonded.

Nate looked over at his father. Maybe the afternoon wouldn't be so awkward after all.

CHAPTER THIRTY-ONE

Nate didn't know if it was because of the slightly emotional day he'd had or what, but that night, he dreamed of Jordan.

They are sitting at the same table in the same bar and grill where they sat the night of the car accident. Jordan's brown hair and green eyes look the same as always. There is no head wound in sight.

Part of Nate knew it was a dream, yet at the same time, it felt like they were really back in the restaurant.

Jordan brings his drink to his lips and takes a sip. As he sets the glass down, he says, "So, you're screwing my wife now."

Nate looks down at the table. "I'm sorry." Because what else is there to say? "I tried to resist her, but she came to me."

Jordan snorts. "That's supposed to make me feel better?"

Nate looks up. "Yes. No." He sighs. "I don't know, man. I don't know what to do here. I'm out of my element."

Jordan laughs. "I'm just messing with you, man."

Nate's skeptical. "You're okay with me fucking Piper?"

Jordan shrugs. "Someone has to."

"Dude."

Jordan scowls. "You know what I mean. She's young, and she has so much life ahead of her. I know she's not going to stay single forever." He picks up his drink and gestures toward Nate. "There was a reason I asked you to take care of her."

"I think you asked me because I was the only one in the car."

Jordan laughs. "Well, there was that." He leans in as his face grows serious. "But I do trust you, Nate. I know you don't do relationships, but it's not because you're not relationship material."

Nate watches as blood begins to roll down the side of Jordan's head. He points to his friend. "Jordan, you're bleeding."

Jordan picks up a napkin from the table and wipes his face. But it doesn't matter because the blood keeps coming. Jordan looks at the now-saturated napkin and frowns. "Ooh, that doesn't look good."

Nate wants to help his friend, but when he tries to get up to ask for a towel, he can't move. "Jordan, you have to stop the bleeding."

Jordan shrugs. "Nah, it's too late for me now." He puts his hand on Nate's.

Nate looks down to see that Jordan is getting blood all over him, but he can't pull away.

"Nate."

Nate looks up.

"It's not too late for you. Don't let your past ruin this."

Nate shakes his head and tries to free his hand. "Don't ruin what? I don't understand."

"It's not too late for you. It's not too late for you."

Nate bolted upright, heart pounding and sweat rolling down his temples. It made him think of the blood on Jordan, and he hastily swiped it from his face. The dream had felt so real.

Nate quickly looked around. He was in bed, alone. No sign of Jordan anywhere.

Nate flopped back onto his pillow. Not that he'd really expected to see his dead friend in his bedroom.

He took a couple of deep breaths to calm himself down. His heart was still racing, and at this rate, he wasn't going back to sleep tonight.

Nate tried to remember what Jordan had said in the dream, but it didn't make sense. *What did he mean by it wasn't too late for him?*

Nate snorted. It was such a stupid question. Jordan hadn't really said it. It was all in Nate's head.

It was probably best to forget about it since he'd never been able to decipher his dreams. He had no idea what he'd been trying to tell himself.

He closed his eyes, but all he saw was Jordan sitting at that table, laughing, with blood running down his head.

He should have never asked Jordan to go out after work that night. He'd noticed that Jordan had hesitated before saying yes. The two of them had carpooled to work since they lived only ten minutes away from each other, and it had been Jordan's day to drive.

What would have happened if he had just told Jordan to take him home? If they had never gone for a beer? A beer that had turned into two?

And, when Jordan had gotten a text from Piper asking where he was and why he wasn't home, he'd laughed. Not because he didn't love his wife, but because he was in trouble.

Piper had wanted Jordan home, and it was Nate's fault that he wouldn't be again.

He could still feel the wind in his hair as the two of them had driven with the windows down. It had been a beautiful May evening. They had come to an intersection. The light had been red, but he could have sworn that Jordan stopped and looked before making that right turn.

However, the next thing Nate remembered was the sound of crushing metal and being thrown against the window. There had been a big burst of powder as the front airbags deployed, and Nate remembered coughing as he tried to breathe.

He remembered assessing his injuries. He had felt sore all over, but he hadn't thought he'd broken anything. He had next turned his attention to Jordan. Jordan's head had been covered in blood, and he'd had a huge gash on the side.

He'd called his friend's name, and Jordan had miraculously opened his eyes. Nate had been so grateful in the moment because he'd thought his friend was dead.

But then Jordan had coughed, and blood had come with it.

That was when Nate had noticed the piece of metal from the door sticking out of Jordan's side.

"Jordan, hold on. The ambulance is coming." Nate couldn't *hear sirens, but someone had to have called 911.*

Jordan seized Nate's hand with surprising strength. "Please." Jordan coughed. "Please."

Nate shook his head. "Please what?"

Jordan met Nate's eyes. "Please take care of Piper. She doesn't have anyone here. I don't want her to be alone."

Nate shook his head. "No. I'm not going to promise that because you're going to go to the hospital and get stitched up, and you're going to take care of her yourself." Nate refused to think his friend wasn't going to make it.

Jordan's grip increased, and his eyes pleaded with Nate. "Please. Please. Promise you'll take care of her and help her."

Nate closed his eyes. If he made this promise, he felt like he was giving Jordan permission to give up. But, if something did happen, he didn't want his friend to worry.

Nate opened his eyes and met Jordan's. "You're going to be fine. You hear me? Fine. But, if something happens, I promise I will take care of Piper."

Jordan coughed up more blood. "Thank you."

· · ·

And that was the last thing Nate remembered before he'd heard more metal crunch, and everything had gone black.

When Nate had woken up in the hospital, he'd found out that the accident had caused the car to spin out into the middle of the intersection. While they'd been sitting there, waiting for help, they'd been hit. That part of the crash had knocked Nate out, resulting in a concussion. Jordan hadn't made it.

Nate was the reason Jordan hadn't gone home after work. Nate was the reason Jordan had been drinking before driving his car. Nate was the reason Jordan had died, and Piper had lost her husband.

He never wanted to feel like that again.

And, now, as he was lying in bed, that day was playing over and over in his head.

Kicking back the covers, Nate got out of bed. He put on sweats and a T-shirt and grabbed his phone before going downstairs in the dark.

He snagged his keys off the counter, slipped on the nearest shoes, and headed for his car.

When he got to his destination, he used his key to open the door. He dropped his stuff at the door and walked down the hall.

Once in the bedroom, he stripped to his boxers, got into bed, and put his arm around Piper.

She rolled over. "Nate?"

"Shh...go back to sleep."

"Is everything okay?"

He pulled her to his chest. "It is now." He kissed her on

the forehead, breathing in her scent and absorbing her warmth. "It is now."

Piper rested her head on him, and soon, her breathing deepened.

It took Nate a little longer, but eventually, slumber overtook him. As he fell asleep, he swore, he saw Jordan give him a thumbs-up. It only lasted a second, and then his friend was gone. Nate thankfully didn't dream again that night.

CHAPTER THIRTY-TWO

The next morning, Piper woke to Nate kissing her. She briefly recalled him sneaking into her room and slipping into bed with her in the middle of the night. Something must have been bothering him because he had never done that before.

The day before, they'd gotten a little bit of time alone, and Nate had told her about what his stepmom had said to him on Friday night when Piper was in the restroom and how he'd invited his dad to watch the game with him. But something told her this wasn't why Nate had come to her.

Last night, he had pulled her into his arms, and they'd both fallen asleep. But, now, Nate's hands were touching her all over. He caressed the back of her leg, her hips, her belly, and her breasts. His movements were slow and tender, yet there was an urgency behind them.

She instinctively knew that he needed her, and she wanted him to know that she was there for him.

She ran her hands over his head and down his back, and

when she was ready for him, she cupped his ass and nudged him toward her.

She opened her legs, and he pushed inside her. She bit her lip to hold back her moan. She still had guests in her house, and she didn't want to wake them.

Nate put his arms around her and one hand into her hair. As he drove inside, he watched her. His face was serious and intent, and his crystal-blue eyes flared with heat.

She brought her thighs up to his hips, encouraging him in further. He groaned as he sank in to the hilt. His thrusts increased in speed and intensity, and she clutched at his back.

It was as if the both of them needed him to go as deep as he could.

Nate's expression changed, and she knew he was close. Watching him like that, it was intimate, and her orgasm exploded out of nowhere. She hadn't even realized she was close.

Nate took her mouth again to stifle her cries, and she wrapped her legs around him, wanting him inside her when he came. Her climax gave way to his, and she felt his cock jerking inside her.

A warmth spread through her upon his release, and she was vaguely aware that it wasn't from her this time. But it didn't matter at that instant. She didn't want the moment to end.

But it had to end. It was Monday morning, and before she was ready, Nate slowly slipped himself from her arms. They both needed to go to work, and he needed to leave before her mom and Don awoke.

He kissed her good-bye and promised to call later. She watched him dress and leave as silently as he'd arrived.

It was only after she got out of bed and into the shower did she realize what she had felt when they made love. Nate had left a bit of himself behind in her.

She needed to talk to Nate about being more careful.

When it came to pregnancy, she wasn't worried. Her periods had always been predictable, and she'd just had her period the weekend Nate was out of town. Besides, she and Jordan had been having unprotected sex for years without any pregnancies.

Piper was more worried about Nate and his numerous partners. She had been checked at her yearly gynecology appointment at the urging of her doctor. And she knew Nate took care of himself and got tested regularly, but she had no idea when the last time was. Nor did she know when he'd last had sex with someone else. They'd never talked about exclusivity, and she'd told him more than once that they weren't dating.

Both of them really needed to be more responsible in the future.

After she got dressed, her mom and Don were ready to go. Their bags were packed, and their car was loaded up, so Piper sent them back to Nebraska with hugs and plans to see them at the wedding.

Piper finished getting ready for work, now in a hurry, completely forgetting about their unprotected sex.

That was, until Saturday.

It was Saturday night, and Piper and Nate were on the dance floor at a local establishment. They had met Ty and Ethan for drinks, and Kayla was supposed to show up after dinner with her family.

The place they'd chosen was almost a cross between a bar and a nightclub. It was smaller than a nightclub, and there were a lot of people standing around toward the front with tables full of customers. But in the back was a good-sized dance floor.

Nate pulled her toward him as they swayed to Rag'n'Bone Man's "Human." He danced like he made love. With his whole body and one hundred percent skill. She saw women watching him.

That's right. Eat your hearts out, ladies. He's fucking me tonight.

Piper turned her back to Nate's front and rubbed her ass against his hard-on. She rested her head on his chest and swung an arm around his neck. They continued to move to the beat of the music as his hand crept lower. She did nothing to stop him, and when he made a fleeting brush against her clit through her skirt, she sighed.

She wanted him to continue, but this wasn't the time or the place.

The song ended, and "Can't Hold Us" by Macklemore and Ryan Lewis started to play. Its faster tempo made it hard to grind with Nate, and they broke apart. While she liked the song, her drinks were starting to catch up to her bladder.

"I'm going to use the restroom," she shouted in his ear.

"Okay, I'll meet you back at the table."

The restrooms were in the very back of the bar, and there

was the usual line to get into the ladies'. By the time she walked out, at least fifteen minutes had passed. She hoped that Kayla showed up soon, so she'd have someone to keep her company when she went the next time.

Piper had eyes for the table at the front of the establishment, so she almost didn't see them. But something off to the side caught her eye. She was about to turn her gaze back forward, but she did a double take.

It was Nate, standing against the wall, practically in the corner, with a woman. They were talking, but despite the loud music, they didn't need to be that close to hear each other.

Piper felt like she'd been punched in the gut. A sick feeling came over her, and she feared she might have to go back to the ladies' room to throw up.

The woman was gorgeous. Long, straight, thick blonde hair and beautiful, pale skin. Not like Piper's where it showed every flaw or like back in high school where she couldn't hide a zit to save her life. No, this woman had probably never had a pimple in her life. Her skin was like porcelain even if she did have a little too much makeup on.

Someone ran into Piper, and she took her eyes off Nate and his companion.

"Sorry," the guy yelled over his shoulder as he rushed past her.

Her shoulder hurt, but she welcomed the ache. Jealousy was a horrible beast, and she hated that it had roared its ugly head.

She quickly moved on toward the table before Nate saw her watching him.

She hated herself for feeling this way. She had no romantic claim on Nate. They were friends, and that was it. He had never kept it a secret that he had sexual partners. Her head knew this.

Unfortunately, somewhere along the way, her heart had begun to do its own thing and have its own thoughts.

Well, it would just have to stop. Nate was her friend. She had known, going into this, they wouldn't have a sexual relationship forever, and she'd known Nate would never commit to her.

She rubbed her hand between her breasts. *Stupid heart.*

She was almost to the table, and she shook off her unwanted feelings. She was not going to be the jealous girl. She was not going to call Nate out on anything. This was a reminder that they needed to discuss the whole no-condom thing, but she would make no demands of him. She just needed to play it cool.

She could totally do that.

"Hey, Piper," Ty said as he reached the table.

Piper beamed at him, hoping her smile didn't look fake.

"Where's Nate?" Ty asked.

She shrugged. "I left him on the dance floor when I went to use the restroom." It was the truth. She certainly wasn't going to tell Ty and Ethan what she had seen. They'd know right away how envious she'd been.

Ethan jerked his chin in the direction behind Piper. "There he is now."

Piper turned to look, putting the phony grin on her face, prepared to act as if everything were normal.

Except he wasn't alone.

The blonde was with him, and anyone could see by the look on her face that she liked Nate.

"I can't do this," she muttered. Not if she wanted to keep her dignity.

"What?" Ty asked.

She turned to Nate's friend. "I'm sorry. I have to go." She looked at Ethan. "Tell Kayla to call me, okay?"

Ethan looked confused, but he nodded.

"I'll see you two later. Tell Nate bye for me."

She didn't wait for an answer. She bolted for the front door and got the hell out of there.

CHAPTER THIRTY-THREE

N ate approached the table where his two friends
stood with Vanessa at his heels. He hadn't
expected to see one of his regular lays there
tonight.

He'd run into her after leaving the dance floor, and she'd
made it very clear that she was more than willing to leave the
bar. With him.

He'd had to politely turn her down and explain that he
was there with someone. To say Vanessa had been shocked
would be an understatement. However, Nate didn't know if
it was because he was out with a female or because someone
had turned her down. She'd never hidden the fact that she
was beautiful and knew it. Not many guys would turn her
down.

But not many guys got to go home with someone like
Piper.

The good thing about his relationship, or lack thereof,
with Vanessa was that she wasn't hurt or upset. She'd asked

him to introduce her to his friends since hers had already left for the night.

Nate had figured, *Why not?* Ethan was dating Kayla, but Ty was single.

"Hey, guys, this is Vanessa. Vanessa, this is Ethan—he has a girl—and this is Ty. Ty is single."

Ethan nodded hello. Ty, in normal Ty fashion, took Vanessa's hand, kissed her knuckles, and said something to her in French.

Vanessa giggled.

"Hey, where's Piper?"

Ty lost his flirty smile, and Ethan looked away, shifting his feet.

"What?" Nate asked.

"She bolted, man," Ty said.

Nate was confused. "What?"

"Yeah, she said she had to go and left."

Nate looked at Ethan for confirmation that this was true.

Ethan's eyes were sympathetic. "She said to tell Kayla that she was sorry she left and that she'd call her later."

Nate looked around as if he'd see Piper, but of course, she was gone. "When did she leave?"

"Right before you walked up. Not more than two minutes ago."

Nate spun around and took off for the door.

Piper walked briskly toward her car, cursing her high heels and the number of drinks she'd had. There was no way she would be able to drive home, but she only had her car key and a little money on her. She'd had to wear a skirt tonight with tiny pockets, so now, she needed to snag her purse from under the seat in her car to order an Uber from her phone. She hadn't brought it into the bar because she hadn't wanted to lose it.

She was almost to her vehicle when she heard someone running up behind her. Her female senses went on high alert, and she scanned the parking lot. It wasn't secluded, but she was the only person out there.

Besides the person coming up behind her.

Freaked out, Piper started to run. She didn't get very far before her heel got caught on the asphalt, and she tripped.

"Ah!" she yelled as the ground came up to meet her face.

She closed her eyes and braced for impact, but strong arms wrapped themselves around her.

She froze for a second, realizing she hadn't fallen, but then reality set in that the stranger had caught her. She tried to kick him just as he set her on her feet, and she tripped again.

"Damn. Piper, are you okay?" Nate said as he righted her once more.

Piper turned around and smacked him on the arm.

"*Ow*. What was that for?"

"For scaring the ever-lovin' shit out of me."

"Huh?"

"Pro tip: don't ever come up, running silently, behind a woman in a dark parking lot."

He looked sheepish. "Oh. Ah...sorry."

"You about gave me a heart attack."

"Sorry," he said again.

Piper shook her head, and suddenly, she remembered why she had left the bar in the first place. She almost asked Nate where his friend was—emphasis on *friend*—but that would be snarky.

She looked behind Nate. "Are you alone?"

His brows furrowed. "Yeah. Why wouldn't I be?"

Okay, Piper, play it cool. Casual.

She pushed her hair over her shoulder. "Oh, I saw you with someone. I thought she might have come with you."

Nate grinned, his eyes dancing in the lights of the parking lot.

"Why are you so happy?"

He took a step closer to her, and she backed up, her legs hitting a car. She glanced over her shoulder, relieved to see it was her car behind her.

When she turned back to Nate, he still had that goofy smile on his face, and for some reason, this bugged her.

"There is nothing funny about this situation."

Nate tilted his head and tapped his chin. "Correct me if I'm wrong, but I think someone is jealous."

If she denied it, he'd know right away, so she played dumb. "Who is?" She looked around as if she were trying to find whom Nate was talking about. The second she did it, she knew it was over the top.

Nate laughed. "Remember when I told you never to go to Vegas?"

She crossed her arms over her chest. "Yeah. So?"

"You're a horrible liar." He stepped closer, put his hands on her hips, picked her up, and set her on the hood of her car.

235

She raised her chin. "Isn't that a good thing? Nobody likes a liar."

Nate kissed her neck. "You're right. I'd take jealousy over lying." He sucked on the spot where her neck met her shoulder.

She moaned. "I'm not jealous."

Nate straightened and pulled her butt to the edge of the hood. "That's good because I told Vanessa that I'm not available anymore." He slid his hand up her thigh, not stopping when he reached the hem of her skirt.

"Oh. Why is that?" she asked as casually as she could manage.

He pulled on her thong until it snapped and pushed two fingers into her.

Piper squeaked.

"Oops."

She grabbed on to his shoulders as he massaged her G-spot.

"So wet."

"Oh God," she sighed, and her eyes fluttered closed.

"Sorry, I got distracted. To answer your question, I told her I was with you."

"Huh?"

Nate chuckled. "I told Vanessa I wasn't available"—he leaned closer until his mouth was next to her ear—"because I'm with you. You're the only one I want."

"Oh God, I'm going to come."

He kissed her neck again. "Not without me."

Piper opened her eyes and dived for his fly. She yanked it open and grabbed on to his cock. "Now," she told him.

Nate pushed her skirt up and drove inside her.

"Holy shit." Piper circled him with her arms and legs, pulling him close. He felt amazing. "Don't stop. Please, don't stop."

"Never," he said as he thrust into her.

Piper grabbed his face and brought his mouth to hers. His tongue swept inside her mouth, and she moaned around him. He tasted so good, and he'd chosen her over the beautiful blonde.

She separated their lips but spoke against his mouth, "I'm going to come all over you."

Nate grinned. "I can't wait. I want you to do it. Now. Come."

And Piper did. She came so hard, her legs dropped from his waist, and she fell back against the car. Thankfully, Nate broke her fall, and she didn't have to worry about a concussion mid-orgasm.

Nate grabbed her hips and pulled her toward him. Their bodies slammed against each other, and then he came, pouring himself inside her. He kept their bodies connected as he finished, but he was forced to pull out when they heard the sound of voices coming closer.

He pulled down her skirt, shoved his cock inside his jeans, and zipped up. He offered her his hand and helped her off the hood. As soon as she stood, gravity took over.

Piper looked down. "Damn it, Nate."

He looked her over but was oblivious to her dilemma.

"You came inside me again."

So much for having a talk about safe sex.

CHAPTER THIRTY-FOUR

The sound of a horn honking woke Piper from her nap. She brushed the hair from her eyes and the drool from her lips, hoping Nate hadn't noticed.

She grabbed the lever on the side of her seat and set the back of her chair up. "How long was I out?"

"A little less than an hour."

"Ugh. That means we have three hours left."

It was the Wednesday before her mom's wedding, and Nate and she were on their way to Nebraska. She'd taken a page out of her mom and Don's book and left at five in the morning.

Too damn early.

"Do you want me to drive?"

"Nah, I'm good."

"Good, because I don't want to drive."

Nate laughed.

"How are you not tired?"

"*I* didn't stay up until after eleven last night."

She scrunched up her nose. "Yeah, in hindsight, that wasn't my smartest decision." She held up a finger. "However, you could have let me sleep another half hour instead of having sex with me."

Nate smiled at her. "No regrets."

"Yeah, me either. We'll have to sleep in separate beds at my mom's, so we're going to have to sneak in some private time."

Since the night of parking lot sex three weeks ago, Piper and Nate had come to an understanding. They were only doing the nasty with each other, and for now, there was no sex without a condom. Nate had shown her his latest test results, which showed him in the clear, and promised to get tested again. Piper had made an appointment with her OB/GYN to go on birth control, but she wasn't able to get in until the week after the wedding. It kind of sucked, but she and Nate would make do.

Nate laced his fingers with hers. "That's no fun."

She squeezed his hand. "I know."

They'd been spending almost every night together, and she was going to miss sleeping by him.

The next three hours crawled, but they finally pulled up to her mom's house. Piper went to open the front door, only to discover it was locked. She rang the bell but no answer, and she had to fish out her key.

She'd warned her mom that they were leaving early in the morning, and she'd even texted her a couple of times on the drive.

They carried their luggage in and found a note by the

front door. Despite her mom embracing technology, she sometimes did things old school.

"My mom and Don had to meet the cake lady at eleven." Piper looked at her watch. "Which is about now. They won't be home until about twelve thirty, and then we can go to lunch." She sighed. "So much for getting up early. They're not even here."

"I guess we can unpack a little, and then I'm raiding the fridge. I can't wait until almost one to eat."

"Me either."

They went down the hall, and Piper went to drop her stuff off in the bedroom she'd grown up in while Nate went to the guest room. It was where he'd slept when they came for Jordan's funeral, so he didn't need a tour of the house or anything.

Piper held her breath as she entered her old room. When she'd come for her husband's funeral, she had hated being in there every single second. It held way too many memories.

This bed was where Jordan had made love to her for the first time. Her bedroom was where he'd asked her to move in with him. It was the place she'd known they were going to spend the rest of their lives together.

The rest of his life anyway.

Piper braced herself and pushed the door open. She was prepared for grief to overtake her, but it didn't come. Of course, she was still sad and still missed Jordan, but when she looked around, the memories she had there didn't strike her down. She actually smiled when she saw the stain next to her desk were Jordan had spilled red Gatorade. Her mother had been furious, but since Jordan had been a guest, she had gritted her teeth and told him it was okay.

"Hey, you ready to find some food?"

Piper turned and smiled at Nate in the doorway. "Give me a minute. I'll meet you there."

She unpacked her toiletries, setting them on the desk, and then went to meet Nate in the kitchen. He was taking a bite out of a sandwich and had a piece of paper stuck to his chest.

"What's this?" she asked, and she grabbed it.

"It's another note from your mom," he said, his mouth full of food.

"Don't eat too much. We're going to lunch at twelve thirty," Piper read. She raised her brow at Nate. "So, naturally, you're eating a whole sandwich."

He swallowed. "I'm a growing boy."

"Right," she said doubtfully.

"Don't worry; I'll still eat lunch."

Piper grabbed a bag of chips from the pantry to munch on. If she ate like Nate was, she wouldn't be hungry for lunch.

Nate finished his sandwich and yawned. She'd forgotten that she was the only one who'd slept on the drive to her mom's.

"Let's go lie down. We can watch TV in my room."

Nate wiggled his eyebrows. "Ooh. You're going to sneak me into your room while your mom's away? You're a naughty girl."

"If you consider napping naughty, then I'm your woman."

Nate laughed and followed her to the bedroom.

They lay down together, and Piper thought about all the times she had lain there with Jordan. She looked over at Nate. One arm was behind his head, and the other hand held the remote. He wasn't paying attention, so she took the opportunity to study him.

"I can feel you looking at me," he said, keeping his eyes on the television.

Piper laughed. "I can't help it. You're so handsome."

He rotated his head to look at her. "Well, I could have told you that."

She rolled her eyes. "You're so modest."

His smile faded somewhat. "What are you really thinking about?"

"How glad I am that you're here. Thank you for coming."

"Come here," he told her.

She scooted closer, and he cupped the back of her head.

"Thank you for asking. There's nowhere I'd rather be."

Piper grinned and kissed him. She rested her head on his chest and basked in Nate's embrace. She tried to pay attention to the show he'd turned on, but her eyes began to droop.

She woke up later to the sound of the door to the garage slamming closed and voices talking. Her mom and Don were home.

She looked up at Nate and saw he'd fallen asleep, too. She tried to gently get up to go say hi to her mom, but she didn't get far when he awoke.

She winced. "Sorry I woke you."

He rubbed a hand down his face. "That's okay." He cocked his head toward the door. "Sounds like just in time, huh?"

"Yeah. I'm sure they'll come looking for us soon."

"We'd better get up then."

Piper swung her legs off the bed. She couldn't believe she'd taken two naps that day, and it wasn't even one in the afternoon. "We're never traveling that early again."

"Deal."

Piper picked up the remote, turned off the television, and grabbed the chips she hadn't even eaten. When they got to the door, she looked behind her and discovered her first thought was about how she'd taken a nap with Nate rather than thinking of Jordan this time.

"Did you forget something?" he asked her.

She turned to him. "Nah. I have everything I need right here."

"Let's go say hi then." He smoothed a hand down his bald head. "Does my hair look okay?"

"Perfect," she told him.

"That's good because you have a nasty case of bedhead."

She gasped and ran to the vanity. In the mirror, she saw her dark hair needed a quick finger-comb, but that was it. She stood and pivoted.

"Made you look."

"And, to think, I was going to smuggle you into my room tonight," she said as she marched past him, out the door.

"Ooh, I can't wait," he said from behind her as they walked down the hall.

"Not going to happen now, bud."

"Yes, it will."

"Oh, yeah? How can you be so sure?"

He leaned down next to her ear. "Because I know where

your sweet spot is." He straightened and moved past her. "Hi, Karen. Hi, Don. Thanks for inviting me." Nate turned and winked at Piper as her mom opened her arms to him.

What am I going to do with that man? she thought.

Love him, a voice inside her said.

She could have sworn, it'd sounded like Jordan.

CHAPTER THIRTY-FIVE

The next morning, Piper got up early. She had something she needed to do that day. She showered, got dressed, and went to the kitchen to make some coffee and grab breakfast.

Her mom was already awake, still in her robe, and she handed Piper a to-go mug.

"Thank you." She took a sip of her coffee. "What's on the agenda today? When do you need me home by?"

"Can you be back by ten?"

It was eight now. "Sure." Piper grabbed a banana and a protein bar. "I'd better go right away then."

Her mom hugged her and said, "Tell Dad hi for me."

Piper smiled. "I will. Tell Nate when he gets up that I'll be home by ten."

"Will do."

Piper's first stop was to the floral shop to buy two bouquets. Then, it was onto her morning destination.

The cemetery was large and thankfully quiet with only a

few cars around. Piper headed for the first grave. When she reached it, she sat down in front of it and traced her fingers over the letters.

Wyatt Donovan. Beloved husband, father, and son.

"Hi, Daddy."

She set the flowers down next to the other bouquet that was there. Her mom must have been there recently.

"So, you probably heard that Mom is getting married again." She laughed. "I was as surprised as you must have been. But you should know that he's really good to Mom. I met up with his two kids yesterday, and they are also very nice to Mom. I know she misses you, but I think Don makes her very happy."

She pulled at the grass underneath her.

"Also, I met someone, Daddy. Kind of. I actually already knew him. But I think I could really fall for him." She sighed. "I don't know what to think though. He's never really had a girlfriend, and he's the first guy I've dated since Jordan passed away. I'm trying not to overthink anything and just enjoy our time together."

Piper took out a tissue from the pile in her pocket.

"I wish you were here, so you could tell me not to worry. You were always so good at stepping back and letting things be. I could really use one of your hugs right now." She sniffled and wiped her eyes. "But please don't worry about me. I know that things will work out the way they're supposed to." She hoped anyway.

"I hope you're taking care of Jordan and that he's taking care of you. I really miss you both."

She stood up, grabbing the remaining set of flowers, and walked to another part of the cemetery.

"Hey, baby," she said and sat down. "I know you're not big on flowers, but I brought you some anyway." She leaned closer and whispered, "Next time, I'll bring you your favorite Five Guys burger."

She set the flowers next to the others that were there. They were most likely from Jordan's parents, who were invited to the wedding, but her mom might have said hi while she was here, too.

"So, I'm sure you heard me tell my dad that I met someone. But you probably already know that person is Nate." She laughed. "Can you believe it? I think you once told me that, back in college, Nate went on a date with a different girl every night one whole week." Piper shook her head at the thought.

"But you should know that he's been treating me very well. He actually told me that he wasn't seeing anyone else. Go figure."

She looked at the name staring back at her.

Jordan Stevens. Son, brother, husband, forever in our hearts.

"I don't know what to do, Jordan. Is it too soon for me to date someone else? Am I dishonoring you by moving on? I can't lie. Nate makes me happy. But, sometimes, I feel guilty."

She pulled out another tissue.

"I wish you were here to tell me what to do." She laughed. "But that's stupid. Because, if you were here, then I wouldn't be with Nate." A sob escaped her. "God, I miss you so much."

Piper dropped her head in her hands and wept. She let herself cry as long as she needed to.

When she calmed down, she wiped her eyes and blew her nose.

"Look at me. I'm a blubbering mess." She laughed at herself. She joked because she didn't want Jordan to feel guilty for dying. It wasn't his fault that the car had slammed into him.

She took a couple of deep breaths and touched his tombstone. "I love you, you know. And I'd really appreciate it if you could send me a sign or something about what I should do." She was teasing, but a message from Jordan would sure help her out. "No matter what, I will always love you. Take care of my daddy for me, okay?" She leaned closer and whispered again, "His wife's getting remarried. He might need you to hold his hand."

She kissed her fingers and set them on top of his name. "Good-bye, baby."

When Piper got back to her mom's, her mom was gone. Nate was just coming out of the shower, towel wrapped around his waist.

"Hey. How did it go?" he asked.

She wrapped her arms around him and rested her cheek on his chest. He was so warm and alive. "Can you just hold me for a moment?"

He enveloped her in his strong arms. "Of course." He kissed the top of her head. "Whatever you need."

The second Nate saw her, he knew Piper had been crying. It was far from the first time, but he still hated it just the same. His chest hurt to know she was in pain.

She lifted her head and set her chin on his chest.

He cupped her face and brushed his thumbs over her cheeks. "You've been crying. Are you okay?"

"Yes. It was a therapeutic cry. I think I needed it."

"Did you tell Jordan hi for me?"

She smiled. "No. But I did talk about you."

He wanted to ask her what she had said, but that was her private conversation with her deceased husband.

He made a joke instead. "Did you tell him about my dashing good looks?"

She pretended to think about it. "I don't think that came up."

"That's too bad."

She laughed and placed her cheek on his chest again. "I suppose I should let you get dressed for the day."

"Yeah, your mom might be home soon."

Piper stepped back. "Where did she go anyway?"

Nate shrugged. "She was gone when I got up."

"I'll text her. Did you get any coffee?"

"Not yet."

"You go get dressed. I'll get you some."

"Thanks."

Nate went into the guest bedroom and pulled out clothes from his suitcase. He had just slipped on his boxer briefs when Piper came back with two mugs. She handed him one.

"Thanks, babe."

She smiled. "You're welcome." She took a drink out of her own cup and sat on the bed.

He raised an eyebrow. "Are you going to watch me get dressed?"

"As long as you don't mind."

"Never." He liked having her watch him.

She put her mug on the nightstand and lay down on the bed. She was quiet as Nate put on his shorts and shirt. She looked content, lying there, and he liked that she liked being with him, even when doing such mundane things as putting on clothes.

When he was finished, he sat on the edge of the bed, and she grabbed his hand and played with his fingers.

He didn't say anything. He just let her have her thoughts without him intruding and asking questions.

He took a drink with his other hand and simply enjoyed being with her. After a minute, he realized her hand was lying limp on his. He looked over.

She'd fallen asleep, which made sense since she'd had an emotionally draining morning.

Nate set his cup down, stood, and tucked her under the covers. He kissed her on the forehead, picked up his coffee, and quietly left the room.

CHAPTER THIRTY-SIX

 ate took a seat in the pew as everyone took their places for the wedding rehearsal. He turned, resting his leg on the bench, so he could watch Piper. She was at the end of the aisle with her mom, Don, and Don's son and best man, Greg, as the pastor gave out instructions.

She laughed at something someone had said, and Nate smiled. He didn't know when it had happened, but his feelings for Piper had long left Friendshipville behind. He'd been debating on how and when to tell her.

He'd wanted to tell her this weekend, but he felt like it might be stealing her mother's thunder. He also wasn't sure how she'd take it after visiting Jordan's grave yesterday.

Yes, she'd come to him for comfort, but going to see her deceased husband had obviously stirred up her feelings. What if she wasn't ready to truly be with Nate?

Nate swung around as he heard someone moving along

the pew to him. It was Don's daughter, Christie, and her two children.

Nate and Piper had met Christie, Christie's husband, and Greg the other day at lunch, and while Christie's kids hadn't been there, she'd talked about them.

"Did I miss anything?"

"Nope. They're just getting started."

"Oh, good. Michael couldn't find his shoes." She rolled her eyes. "What else is new?" She leaned back in her seat, so he could get a better view of her kids. "Nate, this is Michael and Olivia."

Nate smiled and waved. "Hello."

"Hi," Olivia said.

"How old are you?" Nate asked.

"I'm seven, and Michael's five."

"Wow. You're so old."

Olivia put her hand over her mouth and laughed.

Christie leaned closer. "Michael doesn't say much to strangers. He's shy."

Nate smiled. "Are you two in the wedding?" he asked the kids.

Christie shook her head. "We all decided it would be easier and things would go smoother if there were no flower girls or ring bearers. It was enough work for me to be in the wedding."

Nate laughed.

Karen and Don had decided to only have a matron of honor and a best man, so Christie was playing the piano.

Nate turned back around to watch Piper. She put her

arm in Greg's, and they walked to the front of the church, splitting off when they got there.

Karen and Don followed and took their places at the front.

Nate tried to picture Piper at her wedding to Jordan. He hadn't known her well then, and he didn't have a good recollection of the wedding. He remembered drinking too much at the reception, but his memories of Piper were vague.

Next, he pictured her walking up the aisle to meet him there. She'd look beautiful in a white dress with her dark hair spilling down her shoulders. And, when she reached him, she would smile, and he'd take her hand in—

"Nate."

He looked at Christie.

"Can you watch my kids for a few minutes?"

"What?" Nate hadn't heard her question.

She pointed to the front of the church. "The pastor wants to do it again, this time with the music. My husband's not here yet. Can you watch Michael and Olivia? I'd ask someone else, but—"

He put up his hand. "No, no, it's fine. Go ahead."

She turned to her children. "You two listen to Mr. Nate now, okay? Daddy will be here soon, but until then, Mr. Nate is in charge."

"Okay, Mommy," Olivia said.

"Thank you so much," Christie told Nate.

"No problem." He was just sitting there anyway.

But, about ten minutes later, it was apparent that the rehearsal wasn't going to finish soon, and Olivia and

Michael's dad hadn't shown up yet. Michael was obviously getting bored, based on the amount of fidgeting he was doing in his seat.

He needed to get the kids out of there.

"You guys want to go outside?"

"Yes!" Olivia said.

Michael vigorously nodded his head, his blond curls bouncing.

"Okay," Nate said with a smile.

He ushered the kids out of the pew and approached the piano while Christie was in mid-play. "Is it okay if I take them outside? I saw the playground across the street. They're getting bored."

Christie sighed and glanced at her phone. "That would be wonderful," she told Nate. "James is stuck at work. I thought he was on his way a long time ago."

"It's no trouble," Nate told her and turned back to the kids.

"Thank you. Again," Christie called from behind him.

"You're welcome," he said over his shoulder. "Okay, you two, let's go outside," he told the children.

They were finally—*finally*—done with the wedding rehearsal, and Piper breathed a sigh of relief. Her mom and Don had to have picked the most anal-retentive, control-freak pastor in all of Nebraska because that rehearsal shouldn't have taken that long. At least her mom and future stepfather would have a perfect wedding.

Piper looked around. "Where's Nate?"

Her mother shrugged. "Sorry, honey, I haven't seen him for a while."

"He's outside with my kids at the park across the street," Christie, Don's daughter, said from the piano. "Bless his heart. He's probably going insane right about now. I was just going to relieve him."

Piper and Christie walked outside and made their way across the street. Before they even got there, they could hear laughter and screaming. The kind of screaming you did when you were having fun.

Nate was running, and the kids were chasing him. He was obviously going slow, so they were right on his heels.

Christie breathed a sigh of relief. "They look like they're having fun."

Piper smiled. "Yeah, they do."

"Those two can be a handful sometimes, and I felt bad for leaving them with Nate. I just met the man, and here I was, pawning my kids off on him."

Piper laughed. "I think he's having just as much fun as they are. I'm sure he was bored, watching the rehearsal, too. He was probably grateful to have an excuse to come out here."

Nate slowed, and the two kids tackled his legs. He made a big production of being caught. Christie's little girl jumped up and down with her arms in the air, and her little boy jumped on top of Nate's chest. Piper heard his *oomph* from way over here.

"Mr. Nate, Mr. Nate, we beat you," the little boy said.

"Yeah, you did. I'm no match for you two," Nate told him.

"Your boyfriend is a natural," Christie said.

"I'm sorry, what? I was watching those two," Piper said.

"I said, your boyfriend is a natural. Michael is very shy around strangers, and Nate has him hopping on his chest."

Piper realized that she had never really thought about Nate being or not being father material. The fact that it seemed like he would never settle down prevented the idea from even being brought up. But, apparently, he was good with kids. Watching him with Christie's children warmed Piper's heart, and for a fleeting second, she let herself imagine what it would be like if Nate were with their kids.

She quickly shook off the fantasy though. Now was not the time to daydream about things she couldn't have.

Christie's phone pinged, and she pulled it from her pocket. "Of course my husband shows up now. Just in time for the rehearsal dinner."

Piper laughed. "He came for the best part."

Christie clapped her hands. "Olivia, Michael, it's time to go eat. Daddy's here."

The two turned to their mother. "Mommy," they both shouted and ran toward her. They'd been having so much fun with Nate that they hadn't even noticed their mom's approach.

"Thanks again, Nate," she called to him.

"My pleasure."

"See you at dinner," Christie said to Piper.

After the three of them left, Piper walked over to Nate as he got up from the grass.

"You ready to eat?" she asked him.

"I'm ready for bed. Man, those two have a lot of energy."

"How about dinner and then an early bedtime for you?"

Nate put his arm around her. "Only if you're going to tuck me in."

Piper looked up at him and laughed. "I'll see what I can do."

CHAPTER THIRTY-SEVEN

Nate held Piper in his arms as they danced in the banquet room in the basement of the church. All the tables had been pushed aside after everyone was finished eating.

The rehearsal was done, the wedding was done, and the reception was done. Now, it was time for the dance, and Nate was glad that Piper finally had some free time.

She'd been running around, helping her mother, the last few days. He'd tried to help as much as possible, but he didn't know much about centerpieces or party favors. But, even though they'd been busy with doing a list of jobs for the wedding, Nate wouldn't have wanted to be anywhere else.

And, while watching Piper walk down the aisle this afternoon, looking beautiful, he'd realized that he wanted her to be walking down for a different wedding.

He wanted her to be walking toward him.

Now, he just needed to find the right time to tell her.

He knew there was a strong chance that she wouldn't feel

the way he did, or it would take her some time to get to the same place he was. He'd give her as much time as she needed.

Someone cleared their throat next to them, and Nate swung them around to see who it was.

Piper immediately pulled away from him. "Mr. Stevens, Mrs. Stevens, I'm so glad you could make it." She tried to sound sincere, but he heard the tension in her voice.

"Piper." Mr. Stevens looked at Nate. "Nate."

"Hello, Mr. Stevens. Mrs. Stevens."

Jordan's father turned his attention back to Piper. "It was kind of your mother to invite us."

Nate had been dismissed. Jordan had always talked about how stiff and cold his parents were, but Nate had always thought it was an exaggeration until he'd met them.

The first time Jordan's parents had come to visit him at college, they had insisted Jordan meet them in front of the dorm. They'd taken him to dinner and dropped him off after. They'd made no effort to see Jordan's dorm room, to meet his roommate and dormmates, or to see what Jordan was involved in.

When Nate had mentioned it, Jordan had shrugged it off. That was how they had always been. It was probably the reason Jordan was so outgoing and nice to everyone. And it was definitely the reason Jordan's younger brother had become a tattoo artist. Jordan's parents didn't even talk to Liam anymore. But Nate had to wonder if they had reached out to their only remaining child after losing Jordan.

Mr. Stevens looked around, obviously finding the place lacking. Mrs. Stevens was clutching her purse like someone was going to steal it. They were in the reception hall of a church, for heaven's sake. They didn't allow liquor, so all the guests were sober, yet it wasn't good enough for the Stevens.

Yeah, Nate doubted they'd invited Liam back into their lives. At the funeral, they'd barely even acknowledged their younger son.

Mr. Stevens cleared his throat. "Nate, would you mind if we spoke to Piper alone?"

Nate looked at Piper. She had never liked being around her in-laws, always feeling like they were judging her. They probably were. And he wasn't going to leave her alone if she didn't want him to.

She put her hand on Nate's arm. "It's okay."

Piper watched Nate walk away, desperately wanting to call him back. She could tell by the expressions on her in-laws' faces that they had something on their minds that she wasn't going to like.

They had never been warm people, but she could practically feel the chill coming off of them tonight.

She followed them off to the side where it was quieter and less crowded.

Paul cleared his throat. Again. It was an annoying habit of his. "We have something unpleasant we need to discuss with you."

No shit, Sherlock.

"Okay. I'm ready." She wasn't sure what exactly they wanted her to say.

"We've heard some unpleasant news tonight."

Paul paused, as if he was waiting for her to volunteer information, but she didn't have a clue as to what they were talking about.

"I'm sorry to hear that."

Cheryl, her mother-in-law, made a tsking sound with her tongue, like Piper was a child who had disappointed her. "Piper, we know that you are involved with Nate."

"Oh?"

"We saw you...close to him in the hall earlier," Paul said, like he'd caught Piper having sex with Nate or something when it had been a few stolen kisses. They had been more sweet than hot and heavy.

"*How could you?*" Cheryl said through a clenched jaw.

Piper was so shocked that she took a step back.

"He's barely been dead a year, and you're already off with *his friend*. Have you no respect for our son?"

Piper held up her hand. "I loved your son very much. I still love your son. My relationship with Nate has nothing to do with my feelings for Jordan."

"Apparently not," Cheryl said.

Paul cleared his throat. "What my wife is trying to say is that it is disrespectful to Jordan and his memory. You should not be flaunting off your new beau so soon. You shouldn't even have a new beau so soon."

Wow.

Piper had never been a big fan of her in-laws, and they had never been big fans of her, but this was crossing the line. "I'm sorry, but my relationship with Nate is none of your business."

"When it affects our son and his legacy, it sure as hell is," Cheryl said.

Piper's eyes widened. She had never heard Cheryl say *hell* before. She clasped her hands together. "Look, Paul, Cheryl, I'm not going to discuss this with you any further. I understand you are still grieving over the loss of your son. I can hardly begin to imagine how that feels. But I lost a husband. I loved him—still love him—very much. What goes on between Nate and me has nothing to do with Jordan. Now, if you'll please excuse me, my mother needs my help. Thank you both for coming. I'm sure you can show yourselves out." Piper spun on her heel and walked away.

"Piper." Cheryl's voice had lost its scorn, and only sadness remained.

Piper stopped but didn't turn back around.

"I know you went to visit his grave. I know you mean it when you say you still love him. Please, think of Jordan. Think of how sad he is in heaven, watching his wife with another man. His friend. Someone he trusted. I admit, we're worried about what others think when they see you with someone else, but mostly, I worry about my baby, up in heaven, feeling like his heart has been ripped out."

Piper didn't know what to say, but she felt like she'd been punched in the gut.

"Please, just think about it."

Piper sensed, more than heard, them walk away. Her first instinct was to find Nate, but her second instinct was that she needed to get out of that room. It suddenly felt like the walls were closing in on her.

She quickly went out into the hall and slipped out the

back door. She didn't want to run into her in-laws by going out the front.

There were a few people smoking outside, so Piper quickly walked past them to find some seclusion. She ended up across the street at the park where Nate had just played with Christie's kids.

She took a seat on the swing and rested her head against the chain.

Am I really a horrible wife?

The thought of Jordan up in heaven, looking down on her, watching her with Nate, while his heart broke, brought tears to her eyes and made her feel incredibly guilty. She'd always assumed that Jordan would want her to move on with her life, but what if it was too soon? And what if seeing her with his friend was like a stab in the back?

She had asked Jordan for a sign when she went to visit him, and Cheryl had mentioned her visit. Was this her beloved husband's way of saying he didn't want her with Nate? She couldn't have gotten a more direct message.

And, now, Piper's heart was breaking. She didn't want to hurt Jordan, and she didn't want to give up Nate. She'd finally felt happy again. She'd actually gone weeks, rather than days, without bursting into tears.

Could she really give that all up? Could she really go on being with Nate, knowing it wasn't what her husband wanted?

One thing was for sure.

She had no idea what she was going to do.

CHAPTER THIRTY-EIGHT

Nate looked around for Piper but didn't see her anywhere. It had been a while since the Stevens asked to speak to her alone, and Nate had gotten caught up in a conversation with Don and his son.

But, now, he was beginning to worry.

"Excuse me," he told Don and Greg.

Nate walked around the room but still no Piper. He pulled out his phone. No missing texts or phone calls. He tried calling her, but he didn't get an answer. He sent her a text and asked her where she was, but he didn't wait around for a response.

Five minutes later, he found her outside, across the street, sitting on one of the swings.

She looked up when she heard him approach, and it was apparent that something was wrong. He wasn't sure, but she might have been crying, and she looked miserable. And he strongly suspected it had to do with her in-laws.

Nate got down on one knee in front of her. "Hey, are you okay?"

"No," she admitted.

He put his hands on her knees and rubbed them in an attempt to comfort her. "What happened?"

"Do you think I'm a bad wife?"

Nate was taken aback. "No." Then, he got angry. "Why? What did they say to you?"

She shrugged.

"Come on, Piper. You know you can tell me."

"They told me that I'm dishonoring Jordan and his memory by being with you."

"Excuse me?"

"They said it's too soon and that dating his friend is cruel. They think I'm moving on too fast."

Nate clenched his jaw. He wanted to find Jordan's parents and shake them. They hadn't been there when Piper cried in his arms every night. They hadn't been there while she basically stopped having a social life. How dare they make her feel guilty.

"Piper." Nate sighed. He needed to think about how to word this. She was obviously feeling guilty. "You know that Jordan was their son, and they love him, right?"

"Yes."

"It's hard for them to see you with someone else because it's a reminder to them that he's gone."

"I suppose you're right." She sighed. "But what if it is too soon? What if Jordan's up there, watching us, thinking we betrayed him?"

"Piper, you know that Jordan asked me to take care of you."

Her green eyes widened. "Exactly. He wanted you to take care of me. Now, you're sleeping with me. I need time to think about this."

Shit.

This was not going well, and he was losing her. He had reminded her of Jordan's dying wish to show her that her husband had asked Nate to be with her, but she took it as an opposite sign. That they were to remain platonic.

He hadn't wanted to do this here and now, but she needed to know that their relationship was special.

He grabbed her hands. "Piper."

She looked into his eyes.

"I love you. I want to be with you as more than friends. I want you to be with me." *Forever.*

She jumped up from the swing, pulling her hands from him and storming around him. "Did you not hear what I just said? I need time to think."

Nate slowly stood and tried to reach for her.

She yanked herself out of the way. "Here I am, feeling guilty, and you think that telling me you love me will just make it all go away."

Nate took a deep breath. He knew she was upset, and he needed to remain calm. "No. That's not it at all. I wanted you to know that you're special to me."

She put her hands up in the air and shook them. "I can't deal with this right now. Now, I have to feel guilty about you, too."

Nate took a step back. "I see. Guilty because you don't

feel the same way."

"I didn't say that."

"But you didn't *not* say that." This was not how he had imagined it going when he pictured telling her that he loved her. "You know, I never took you for a coward. Who cares what your in-laws think? If you want to be with me, then you should be with me."

She huffed. "I can't believe you just said that to me. You, Mr. I Don't Do Relationships Because My Mommy Died."

"Whoa." He couldn't believe she'd just said that. That was a low blow.

She pointed to her chest. "I lost my husband. I'd put myself out there and fallen in love, and I lost." She pointed to him. "You. You won't even consider giving a relationship a chance. You lost your mom. Yes, it was sad. But she wasn't your wife."

"Well, Piper, I guess you're right. The only women I've loved left me. First, my mother and then my grandmother. Even though they didn't leave on purpose, it still cut deep. So, maybe I did close myself off from relationships. Easier not to get hurt that way. But you're also wrong, Piper. Because I did give a relationship a chance. I opened my heart to the one person I thought wouldn't hurt me, and she did. Thanks for reminding me why it's better to stay single."

And, with that, Nate spun on his heel and walked away.

As Nate walked away, Piper collapsed onto the grass and sobbed.

She let herself cry for a solid ten minutes. She cried for Jordan. She cried for herself. And she cried for Nate.

She was a horrible person. If she hadn't felt guilty before, she sure did now.

The look on his face when she'd said that about his mom. She couldn't believe those words had come out of her mouth. Ten minutes ago, she'd thought the night couldn't get any worse. Boy, was she wrong.

She already regretted what she'd said to him. He'd just kept pushing her, and she'd exploded. Not that it was an excuse to attack him like that.

She owed him the biggest apology in the history of apologies.

She was exhausted and felt like shit, and she just wanted to go home, hide under the covers, and forget tonight ever happened. She wanted to wake up and have it be fourteen months ago when Jordan was alive.

But that would be taking the easy way out. Because, if Jordan were still alive, then she wouldn't have to deal with grief and her guilt. Nothing she did would bring her husband back, and did she really want to erase everything she now had with Nate?

The answer was no. Nate had taught her that life wasn't over.

But did she love him, too? More importantly, was she willing to let herself love him? Could she let go of Jordan and move on?

Piper stood. She brushed the grass off her bridesmaid dress and did her best to straighten it.

First things first, she had to go inside and finish her mother's wedding. She didn't need another thing to feel guilty about, and she needed to give Nate some time to cool off. He didn't get mad very often, but when he did, it was best to give him some room.

She did send him a quick text though.

Piper: I'm sorry. Can we talk later?

She waited a minute, but there was no response.

She sucked up her emotions and went back to the church. She snuck into the restroom and tried to get rid of the tearstains on her face. It was hard when her purse with her makeup was sitting at the table in the banquet room, but she managed. Thankfully, the lights were turned down for the dance.

Piper finished up in the restroom, put on her best fake smile, and went back to join the crowd. She made small talk with her relatives and helped her mom and Don pack up all the leftover food and centerpieces.

She hadn't seen Nate since he left her outside.

Her mom and Don had decided to get a hotel room for their wedding night, so Piper went home alone. When she got there, the guest bedroom was closed. She thought about knocking on the door, but if Nate was sleeping, she didn't want to wake him.

They had made plans to spend the night together since it would be just the two of them in the house, but instead, Piper climbed into her bed alone.

It was a long time before she fell asleep.

CHAPTER THIRTY-NINE

Nate woke to his four a.m. alarm and got on his phone to order an Uber to pick him up in twenty minutes. In the meantime, he dressed and packed up his belongings. His flight was at seven a.m., but before Nate left Nebraska, he needed to make one more stop.

His phone alerted him to his ride being there, and Nate left the guest room. He paused at Piper's door but didn't knock. It was ridiculously early, and he wasn't ready to talk to her. He didn't want her to think he was ignoring her, but he couldn't face her yet. And he couldn't spend another day there with the tension between them. He didn't want to ruin the rest of her trip with her mother. And he didn't want a six-hour car ride filled with awkward silence. It wasn't healthy for either of them.

He was still hurt, and he didn't want to say anything he'd regret. Although he doubted things would ever be the same between them.

Nate stopped in the kitchen and grabbed a notepad and

pen. He wrote Karen a note to thank her for everything and apologized for leaving. Then, he hopped in the Uber.

When they arrived at the cemetery, Nate asked the driver to stay and promised him a big tip. Then, he had to do a bit of hunting before he found Jordan's grave.

"Hey, buddy." He knelt in front of Jordan's headstone. "So...you probably know everything that's going on, but I figure I owe you an explanation. I have no idea what you meant when you told me to take care of Piper, but I've tried my best. As I'm sure you witnessed, I told her I loved her last night, but, buddy, I don't think there's any competing with you." Nate was joking, but it was partly true.

"I had this strange conversation with my stepmom a few weeks back. Yeah, yeah, I know what you're thinking. Really? Really, dude. She basically told me that just because Piper loved you didn't mean she couldn't love me." Nate laughed, but it wasn't really funny. "But you, man, you are irreplaceable. But I already knew that. I think I was fooling myself, thinking that Piper would ever love me."

Nate paused and collected his thoughts. "Your wife sure knows how to cut to the heart of things. She told me I didn't date because of my mother. She's probably right. And maybe that's why I fell in love with her. Because I could never really have her, and I could prove to myself that I'd been right all these years. Relationships aren't worth it."

Nate sighed and shook his head. "I'm sorry. I didn't mean to dump all that on you. But I needed someone to talk to, and I guess you're perfect. You can't tell anyone else what a lovesick sap I am."

He looked down at the ground. "Anyway, I came here to

apologize. I'm sorry I didn't do as you'd asked. I'm sorry I'm the reason you're in the ground in the first place. I'm sorry I didn't take care of Piper the way I should have. I am really failing at the friend thing, aren't I?" Sigh. "But please don't worry. I will let Piper know I'll be there for her if she really needs me. I know we can't be friends like we were before, but that's probably for the best."

Nate stood. "I hope you can forgive me for everything. I'm sorry I took you away from Piper. I'm sorry I thought I could ever fill your shoes. I'm sorry I ever tried. I miss you, buddy. I'm sorry we don't get to spend any more time together either."

Nate looked toward the car waiting for him. "I'd better go. Love ya, man."

He took his time walking back to the Uber. There was a feeling of finality as he made his way back, and he tried to stretch it out. But that only lasted a minute.

Nate opened the car door and got inside. "Airport, please."

Piper woke up to noises coming from the rest of the house and her stomach growling. She rolled over and looked at the clock. It was after ten in the morning.

It had taken her forever to fall asleep, but once she had, she had been out. She hadn't woken up once last night.

Piper's stomach grumbled again.

"Okay, okay, I'm getting up," she told her empty belly.

She pushed off the covers and did a quick hair and face

check in the mirror before leaving the bedroom. After their fight last night, Piper didn't want to see Nate while she looked horrible.

The newlyweds were in the kitchen, making goo-goo eyes at each other.

"Good morning," Piper called out.

Piper's mom jumped and blushed. "Good morning, Piper."

Piper went to the cupboard to grab some cereal and to the fridge to get the milk. "So, where are you two going to live now that you're married?"

"We were actually just talking about that." Her mom looked to her new husband. "We think we're going to put both of our houses on the market and buy a new one together."

Piper spun around from where she was pouring her cereal in a bowl. "What?" But she'd grown up here. Her mom couldn't move.

"Yes. I lived here with your father, and he lived in his house with his first wife." Her mom pointed to herself and Don. "We want something that's ours together."

Piper's heartache must have been written all over her face because her mother stepped forward and pulled Piper into her arms.

"Don, can you give us a minute?"

"Of course. I'll be in the other room if you need me."

Her mom let go of her and met her eyes. "I'm sorry, honey. This probably comes as a surprise to you."

Piper felt a tingle in the backs of her eyes. She couldn't believe she was going to cry over this. "More like shock." She didn't understand why this was upsetting her so much. She hadn't lived here for years.

Her mother gave her a sympathetic smile. "Does this have to do with Nate leaving?"

"*What?*"

Her mom winced. "Yes, honey. He left Don and me a note, thanking us for everything and apologizing for leaving."

Her mom grabbed the note off the counter, and Piper snatched it from her mother's grasp.

It was true.

Piper dropped the note and ran to her room. Her phone wasn't next to the bed, where she usually kept it, so she practically ransacked her room, looking for it. She finally found it in her purse. She unlocked the screen as quickly as she could with shaking fingers and went to her messages.

> Nate: I decided it was best for me to head home. I don't want to ruin the rest of your trip with your mom. We will talk soon. Right now, I need some time.

She read the words over and over as her mom stood in her doorway.

Piper crumbled onto the bed. "He really left."

Her mom came in the room and sat next to Piper. "What happened, honey?"

"We had a fight."

"You really care about him, don't you?"

"I do," Piper said. She hadn't really understood how much until this moment.

"So, what happened?"

"I saw Jordan's parents."

"Ah."

"Ah? What does *ah* mean?"

Her mother smiled. "Just that they've never been the nicest people. What did they say?"

Piper replayed the conversation with her in-laws, and then she had to confess about the horrible things she'd said to Nate. "I know it's not an excuse, but I felt so confused, and at the time, I felt like he was pushing me to make a decision."

"Do you feel that way now?"

She shrugged. "I don't know."

"I have a question for you."

"Okay."

"Let's say that you and Jordan had never met. You're not a widow. There isn't a certain amount of time required to grieve. Everyone is different. With all that said, how do you feel about Nate? Do you want to be with him?"

Easy answer. "Yes."

"Do you love him?"

Easier answer. "Yes."

Her mom put her arm around her. "Then, you need to cut yourself some slack. If Nate makes you happy and treats you right, then it doesn't matter what anyone else thinks."

Piper laid her head on her mother's shoulder. "Thank you."

"Ah, honey, you know I'm always here for you."

Piper took a deep breath. "I don't know how I'm going to fix this."

Her mom gave her a reassuring squeeze. "I'm sure you'll figure it out."

CHAPTER FORTY

Piper did not figure it out.

It was the Thursday after her mother's wedding, and she still hadn't talked to Nate. Sure, she'd gotten home late on Monday evening and had to work all week, but there was still extra time in the day. Had she met up with Nate though? No. And he'd canceled on their usual Wednesday night dinner last night.

They'd texted some. He wasn't ignoring her. But he wasn't his usual self, and it seemed like all their conversations were short, polite, and initiated by her. She felt like she was messaging with a stranger.

"Hey, aren't you leaving early today?" Simone asked Piper.

She looked at the time on her computer. "Crap. Yeah, I'd better get going."

Lainey peeked her head around the corner. "Make sure the doctor gives you the strongest birth control there is because Nate could knock a girl up just by making eye contact with her."

Piper forced a laugh. "I'll make sure and tell my OB/GYN that."

She hadn't said anything to her friends yet about what had happened over the weekend. If she told them, it would be like admitting things might really be over with Nate.

Maybe she wasn't so different from her in-laws after all.

The only reason she kept her doctor appointment was so she could leave work early, and she felt like she was breaking the rules if she left and didn't go to the clinic. Because she had a feeling that she wouldn't need birth control now that she probably wasn't going to have sex again for a very long time.

She told her coworkers good-bye and made it to her appointment with five minutes to spare. After waiting twenty minutes, she was called back to see the doctor.

They asked all the normal questions. Blah, blah, blah, but when they got to her last period, she realized she was late.

"Not again."

"I'm sorry?" the nurse who was taking the initial notes and vitals asked.

Piper pulled out her calendar and gave the nurse the date of her last period. "I'm late. This isn't the first time this has happened." She didn't want to tell the nurse when it'd happened before because she really didn't feel like getting sympathy about her deceased husband. The focus right now needed to be on if something was wrong with her and if she'd ever be able to have children. "I'm ninety-nine percent sure it's stress-related," was all she said.

The nurse smiled. "Okay, I'll put it in your chart, and you can discuss it with the doctor."

"Thank you."

Five minutes later, Dr. Palmer walked in.

"Hi, Piper." The doctor sat next to her. "You're here for the pill, but I hear you've been under some stress, and you're missing your periods again."

Her OB/GYN already knew her history with her husband passing away and how she hadn't menstruated for a couple of months. Dr. Palmer had long brown curls and brown eyes, and she was about Piper's age, which made it easier to talk to her.

"Yes. I started seeing someone."

"Oh, that's great."

"But I think we're over."

"Ooh. I'm so sorry to hear that."

"And it was kind of messy. I haven't talked to him since my mom's wedding."

The doctor started typing on the computer. "So, your mom just got remarried, *and* you broke up with your boyfriend?"

"Yep." She held up a finger. "And my mom is selling the house I grew up in."

The doctor winced. "Have you been experiencing anything else that's different?"

Piper shrugged. "I've been a little tired lately."

The doctor typed a few more words and then turned to Piper. "You know, your husband has only been gone a year. And then a new relationship, your mom's new marriage, and your breakup...that can be a lot on the body. Are you still seeing the psychologist I recommended?"

Piper looked away. "No," she admitted. Piper wasn't opposed to therapy; she was just opposed to therapy with that particular person. "I went a few times, but we just didn't click."

"That's okay, Piper. I can give you a couple of more names. But I really think you need to talk to someone." She held up a hand. "Now, I'm not saying there can't be a physical reason for your symptoms, but the mind is powerful, especially when you're under stress. I'll run some tests today, but I would really like it if you gave therapy another try."

"Okay," she reluctantly agreed.

"Great. I'm going to send you off to the lab, and then you can come back here and wait in this room."

"No pap smear?"

The doctor smiled. "Nope, you just had one five months ago. So, we'll run some other tests, and if those come back okay, you can start the pill after your next period."

Piper went to the lab, had her blood drawn, and came back to the room to wait. She thought about what the doctor had said, and she picked up her phone. But, instead of texting, this time, she hit Call.

Nate picked up on the third ring. She didn't know if that was a good or bad sign. But she knew that, until she talked to Nate, she wouldn't feel better.

"Hello?"

"Hi, Nate."

"Piper?"

"Yeah, it's me."

Nate didn't say anything, so she plowed through.

"Say, would you be willing to meet me for dinner tomorrow, so we can talk?"

"Uh..."

"Please. I know you're mad at me, and you have every right to be. Please let me at least apologize to you."

First step: apologize to Nate. Second step: earn his forgiveness. Third step: tell him I love him, too.

She heard him sigh, which wasn't a good sign.

"I'll meet you for lunch."

"Lunch?"

"Yes. I already have dinner plans."

Piper literally bit her lip to keep herself from asking with whom. "Okay, lunch it is." It was better than nothing.

"Eleven thirty okay?"

"Eleven thirty it is."

"Okay. Later."

"Bye," she said, but he'd already hung up the phone.

He hadn't even said where they were going to meet.

She didn't feel much better, but she did feel like it was a start.

A few minutes later, the doctor came back.

"Well, Piper, it looks like your iron is low."

She perked up. Low iron. That was fixable.

"It is?"

"Yes. That probably explains why you're feeling tired."

"What about everything else? Will this affect reproduction in the future?"

"I'm still waiting for some results." The doctor lifted her arm and looked at her watch. "And I will have to get those to you tomorrow because I need to be somewhere in twenty minutes. But the good thing about stress and low iron is that there are ways to manage them. So far, I haven't seen anything that would affect you getting pregnant in the future."

Piper breathed a sigh of relief. "Thank you."

The doctor held out a piece of paper. "Here is your prescription for the pill. But I don't want you taking it until we get all your labs back. And you need to go buy some iron tablets and start taking them every day. Also, try to eat food with iron, like spinach."

Piper nodded, but when she went to grab the paper, the doctor pulled it out of her reach.

"But that doesn't mean you don't call and talk to someone. Okay?" She gave Piper a pointed look.

Piper chuckled. "Okay."

The doctor handed her the prescription and pulled out another slip of paper from her jacket. "And here is the list of psychologists. I'm going to follow up with you to make sure you do it. And you just ask my kids, Piper; you don't want to get on my bad side."

Piper laughed. "I will start calling them tomorrow."

The doctor lifted her eyebrow.

"I promise."

"Okay. Then, I suppose you can leave."

Piper laughed again and left, feeling a little lighter. She was going to meet Nate for lunch tomorrow. She was already on her way to the pharmacy to pick up an iron supplement, and she would eat something healthy for dinner. Then, tomorrow, she'd start calling around to see which therapist was available.

She didn't have everything figured out, but she was on her way.

CHAPTER FORTY-ONE

Nate drummed his fingers against the table while he waited for Piper to show. He hadn't felt this nervous about seeing a girl since high school.

He had been avoiding Piper since the wedding. But that was because he knew it was going to be hard to be with her like they had been before. Except, this time, there would be even more rules. No cuddling, no hugging, no touching, and absolutely no sex.

It was going to be torture.

But Nate had made two promises to Jordan. He'd promised to take care of Piper, and he'd promised he would fix their friendship. Piper didn't want to be with him, and while it hurt, he understood. She still loved her husband, and she didn't have room for Nate in her life like that.

And, while he'd been fine with partial relationships in the past, he wouldn't settle for being a consolation prize with Piper. He didn't want her love scraps. He wanted everything.

Marriage, kids...a family. Something she didn't want. At least, not with him.

And that was why they needed to go back to being nothing more than friends. She could continue to love Jordan, and Nate would go back to meaningless sex. It was a lose-lose situation all around. But, hey, that was life, right?

A minute later, Piper breezed through the door, and his heart squeezed in his chest. This was going to be harder than he'd thought.

The real punch to the gut was seeing the smile on her face and the light in her eyes. She obviously was just fine with their breakup.

Ouch.

He stood when she approached.

"Hey, Nate."

She leaned into him, so he quickly grabbed her hand and shook it.

No hugs.

"Hi, Piper," he said as nonchalantly as possible. "Do you want to sit?"

She looked at him weird but said, "Yes."

Nate pulled out her chair, helped her get situated, and then sat back in his own seat.

She cleared her throat. "First, I want to apologize to you. I said some horrible things to you."

He had known an apology was coming because Piper had never been purposely cruel to anyone. This he had prepared for. "Thank you. And I understand you were upset. You were overwhelmed."

"Does this mean you accept my apology?"

"Yes."

Her shoulders sagged. "Oh, thank heavens."

"Piper, I could never stay mad at you."

Roll back the sap, Hall.

"That's a relief."

The server came over at that moment to take their drink orders. Perfect timing because it helped Nate reel in his feelings. He needed to stay strong.

He really wanted alcohol, but he had to go back to work. "Just water for me."

"Water for me, too," Piper said.

The server left, and she looked at Nate.

"I think we need to talk about us."

"I agree," Nate said. "I think it's best that we go back to being just friends."

♡

Piper sat back in her chair in shock. "You do?"

"Yes. I think it's for the best, don't you?"

This was not how today was supposed to go. Not at all.

"So, you're just going to go back to acting like you've never been inside me?"

Nate flinched, and she thought maybe she'd reached him, but then he shrugged. "I can if you can."

Ouch.

She'd come here, so optimistic that she'd been unable to keep the grin off her face today. And, now, Nate was taking her heart and stomping on it. If he hadn't made the statement about never staying mad at her, she would think he was being very aloof.

The server came back over at that point and asked them if they were ready to order.

"We need a couple more minutes," she told him. She'd suddenly lost her appetite.

"Good idea," Nate said. "I need to use the restroom real quick."

He didn't even wait for her response. He just got up and left. It was like he couldn't wait to get away from her.

He'd been gone only twenty seconds when his phone buzzed. She told herself not to look at it, but it was sitting right there, face up, and she was only so strong.

It was a text.

> Vanessa: Hey, Nate, now that you're back on the market, what time are we meeting up tonight? I miss that big dick of yours.
> Call me.

Piper felt like she was going to puke.

Nate had already told his old fling he was single again. It hadn't even been a week. All that talk about being in love with her hadn't meant a thing.

Piper was staring at the table when Nate came back from the restroom.

"Piper?"

"Huh?"

"You okay?"

No.

"Sure."

"Anyway, as I was saying, I think it's best that we go back to being friends. Is that cool with you?"

She looked up from the table. "No."

His brows furrowed. "No?"

Piper pushed back her chair. "No. I can't go back to being friends with you. I'm sorry." And, with her last ounce of strength, she got up and left the table.

Nate watched Piper walk out of the restaurant in a daze. He couldn't believe that she didn't even want to be his friend. Within a week, everything had gone to hell. He'd had the greatest girl in his bed, and now, she didn't even want to be his friend.

He'd never felt more unloved in his life. Not even after he'd lost his mom.

His phone buzzed, and out of instinct, he picked it up.

> Ty: So, I might have let it slip to Vanessa
> that you and Piper were on the outs.

Nate checked his other messages.

> Vanessa: Hey, Nate, now that you're back
> on the market, what time are we meeting up
> tonight? I miss that big dick of yours.
> Call me.

He groaned. He really didn't want to deal with her right now. He should have never introduced Vanessa to Ty, and he should have never told Ty about his fight with Piper.

Nate: I told you not to tell anyone.

Ty: I thought you meant not to say anything
to Ethan. Sorry, man.

Nate had meant that, too, because Ethan was dating Kayla, and Kayla was friends with Piper. But he hadn't meant only that.

Nate took out his wallet and threw a five on the table.

He no longer felt like eating.

Piper could barely see the road through her tears. She swiped the back of her hand over her eyes as her phone rang. She took a sniffle to try to clear her nose.

Then, she picked up her cell without even looking, hoping it was Nate.

"Hello?"

"Piper?" It definitely wasn't Nate.

"This is she."

"Oh, good. It's Dr. Palmer. I apologize for not getting back to you until now. I had a conference all morning."

"That's okay." Piper hadn't gone to pick up her prescription yet. And, now, with Nate screwing someone else, it wasn't like she needed birth control anyway.

"It looks like the only thing I'm concerned about is your low iron."

"That's good." At this point, she'd take any good news, no matter how minimal.

The doctor said something else, and Piper had to swerve

not to hit a car. Dr. Palmer continued to speak, oblivious to Piper's near-death experience. She quickly pulled over to the side of the road and barely managed to say good-bye before the doctor hung up.

Piper's heart was racing from the adrenaline spike, and this time, she knew she was going to vomit.

She barely got her car door open before she threw up.

CHAPTER FORTY-TWO

Two weeks later, on Saturday afternoon, Nate was having lunch at his parents' house. He was sitting outside with his dad, enjoying the first day of September and the beautiful weather. His dad had steaks on the grill, and Nate's mouth was watering. His dad had many faults, but grilling steaks was not one of them.

Nate took a sip of his beer and rested his head back against the Adirondack chair.

His dad checked the steaks and sat down next to Nate. "So, how are things going with that backyard you've been working on? Piper's backyard?"

Nate picked up his head. While he and his dad were putting in an effort toward a better father-son relationship, he still held things back. It wasn't necessarily on purpose; it was just from years of doing it.

"Oh, um...we aren't together anymore, so I never got to finish the project."

"Oh," his dad said, surprised. "I'm sorry to hear that."

"Me, too."

His dad's surprise turned to shock. He probably hadn't been prepared to hear Nate open up like that.

His dad cleared his throat. "What—can I ask what happened?"

Nate shrugged. *Why not?* "Piper wasn't ready to move on from her husband. I told her I loved her. She didn't feel the same. We fought. I tried to stay friends. She didn't want to."

"I'm sorry, Nate."

Nate took a drink of his beer. "Me, too, Dad. But what can I do?"

His dad rubbed his chin. "Can I offer a different perspective?"

"Sure."

"I don't like to talk about this much, but you know I've been in Piper's position before."

Oh, yes, Nate knew that well.

"When Sofia—your mother—passed away, I was devastated. I didn't know what to do without her. I had no idea how to take care of a five-year-old by myself. Your mother had always done everything because I worked while she stayed home. I was very fortunate that Nathan and Maria—your grandparents—stepped in to help. My parents were too far away, and I would have been lost without Sofia's mom and dad."

Nate shifted in his seat but didn't say a word, for fear his father would stop.

"Looking back, I know that you felt neglected. I never meant for that to happen, Nate. I never meant to make you feel alone or like I didn't care about you. I ignorantly thought you would be fine because Nathan and Maria took such good care of you." His father turned to Nate. "I'm so sorry, son. I know I can never make up for what I did, but I want you to know that I have regrets. If I could do it over differently, I would."

Nate swallowed. He actually felt a tingling behind his eyes. Besides Jordan's death, he hadn't cried since elementary school.

His father continued on, "I know this has nothing to do with Piper, but it's something that I've needed to say to you for a long time. Tricia has been urging me to talk to you for some time, and I've been putting it off because I didn't want you to push me away."

"She has? You have?" Nate asked, surprised.

"Believe it or not, yes."

"I don't know what to say."

"You don't have to say much. Tricia told me she talked to you at the restaurant and tried to make her own peace. She knows she did you wrong, too. I'm sorry I didn't pick a better stepmother at the time for you, and I'm sorry I didn't stick up for you more."

"Thank you," Nate said with a choked-up voice.

"No, son. Thank you for giving me a second chance." His father looked away, and Nate thought he might have glimpsed tears in his dad's eyes. "Anyway, I felt like all that needed to be said before I gave you my advice."

Nate smiled. "Okay," he said with a nod.

His father took a deep breath, maybe to keep his voice from shaking. Maybe not. "As I said, when I lost Sofia, I was heartbroken. But, when I finally started to move on from my grief and met Tricia, I felt incredibly guilty."

"Funny you should say that. That's the very word Piper used."

"She probably didn't use it lightly. We're taught from an early age that, when you get married to someone you love, you are faithful. So, when your mom died, it was very hard to think of myself as a widower. I was married, yet I wasn't. I still loved my wife, but she wasn't with me anymore. And it's so different from a breakup because you didn't leave this person, and this person didn't leave you. Not willingly anyway. So, when I first started opening myself up to another relationship, I felt like I was cheating on her. Even when I told myself she was gone, I felt like what I was doing was wrong."

Nate was starting to understand how hard it had been for Piper to be with him.

"To help compensate for this guilt, at first, I told myself that Tricia and I would just be friends. Of course, then I started to have feelings for her, so then I told myself it was just sex."

Nate wrinkled his nose.

His dad laughed. "I told myself, as long as it was just friendship and sex and that I wouldn't fall in love with Tricia, I could justify the relationship. Because falling in love would be the ultimate betrayal. See, when you're young and you lose a spouse, you already feel guilty for being alive when your wife or husband is dead. It took me a little bit of time to forgive myself and allow myself to love again."

Could his dad be saying what he thought? He was almost afraid to ask.

"So, are you saying that Piper loves me, and that's why she pushed me away?"

His father shrugged. "I don't know for sure. I wasn't there. But I do know how she looked at you at the restaurant. And I suspect that you telling her you loved her freaked her out. Not because she doesn't love you, but because she does."

Nate took a long drink of his beer and sat back in his chair. "Whoa. I don't know what to do with all this information." He looked at his dad. "What made you finally forgive yourself?"

"Maria." His father took a sip of his own beer.

"*Abuelita*? Really?"

Nate's dad laughed. "Don't sound so shocked. That woman missed nothing. She knew I was struggling."

"How do I lead Piper to her own version of *Abuelita*?"

"That is something I can't answer for you, son. But she went to see her mother, right? And her mother just got married?"

Nate frowned.

"She talked about it at dinner that night."

"Oh...yeah."

"Well, maybe her mother is her *abuelita*." His father lifted his bottle to his lips again. "As long as she likes you. The mother does like you, right?"

Nate laughed. "I'm pretty sure she does."

"Then, I'd say you're golden, son."

"So, why haven't I heard from her in two weeks?"

"Maybe she's waiting for you."

Nate finished off his beer and thought about what his dad had said. "Maybe." Maybe she was.

"I'd better check the steaks."

And, with that, the conversation was over. But Nate felt lighter than he had in two weeks.

Because, now, he was filled with hope.

"Oh, and, Nate," his father said from in front of the grill.

Nate put a hand over his eyes to shield the sun. "Yeah?"

"You ever decide to finish Piper's backyard, you give me a call. We don't have much time until the first snow falls if we're going to finish."

Nate smiled. "Will do."

CHAPTER FORTY-THREE

"I think I'm going to move."

The table around Piper exploded.

"What? You can't do that."

"No."

"He's not worth it, girl."

"But I'll miss you."

"Men suck."

Piper laughed. "Whoa, whoa." She held up her hand to get her friends to stop. "I said, I think I'm going to move. I didn't say move away. I've been toying with the idea of selling my house."

Everyone quieted.

Piper was out to eat with Simone, Kayla, Lainey, Elise, and Rachel. She had decided the best way to get over Nate was to surround herself with friends. She was getting to know Rachel through Elise, and she had introduced those two to her work friends.

"Why?"

Piper pushed her food around on her plate. "Just because."

She got five *you're not fooling anyone* looks.

"Has anyone ever told you that you're a bad liar?" Lainey asked.

Piper stuck out her tongue. "Maybe. Fine, it's because of Nate."

"What happened now?" Simone asked.

"Nothing. That's the problem. Everywhere I look, I see him. And let's not forget my backyard. Even if I hire someone to finish it, I'll think of him every single time I'm outside." She shook her head. "No, thank you."

How ironic her life had turned out to be. One of the reasons she'd stayed in that house was because, after Jordan died, she didn't have very many memories of him there. And, now, she didn't want to live there because there were too many memories of Nate. She was already going to remember him for the rest of her life.

Speaking of which, she really needed to figure out what she was going to say to him. She'd been putting off that conversation for two weeks now.

"I can set you up with a good realtor," Rachel said, pulling Piper from her thoughts.

Elise smacked her in the arm.

"Ow. What was that for?" Rachel asked, rubbing her arm.

"Don't help her. She and Nate are meant to be together."

Rachel looked at Piper and shrugged, as if to say, *Sorry, I tried.*

"I just said I'm thinking about it. It's not set in stone. Let's talk about something clse."

The conversation moved on, and there was no more mention of Nate. The rest of the evening was fun, although Elise and Kayla did make a weird trip to the restroom together. Piper hadn't even realized they were that good of friends.

They all said good night at the restaurant. Elise was going home to Luke, Kayla had plans with Ethan, Rachel was going home to Sean, and Simone and Lainey were going out drinking. Meanwhile, Piper was going home alone.

Lainey and Simone tried to convince her to go with them, but she declined. Not only could she not go, but she also didn't want to. She'd rather go home and go to bed.

Once she got to her house, she noted how dark it was. The days were getting shorter, and the lack of lights on looked so uninviting. She missed having Nate around. Hell, she even missed Fred. It was undeniably time to make an appointment with a therapist if she was missing Nate's cat.

Piper walked into her home and turned on the lights. But rather than going to bed right away, she got on her computer. The great thing about the internet was a person could waste a lot of time on there. Before she knew it, over an hour had passed.

Her phone pinged.

Rachel: Did you order the chicken Alfredo?

Piper frowned.

Piper: Yeah. Why?

Rachel: I think I have food poisoning.

Piper: How do you know?

Rachel: Because my toilet is now my new
best friend.

Shit. They'd eaten the same thing for dinner.
A new text came in as Piper was replying to Rachel.

Kayla: I think eating out was a mistake.

Piper: Did you have the chicken Alfredo,
too?

Kayla: How did you know?

Piper: Rachel's sick, too.

Kayla: You're doomed.

Piper did a quick mental assessment. She didn't feel bad.
Her stomach didn't hurt. And thinking of food didn't make
her queasy.

Piper to Kayla: I feel okay now. I'll let you
know if that changes.

Piper to Rachel: Kayla's sick, too. So far, I
feel okay. I'll keep you updated.

Rachel: Good luck!

Piper shut down her computer and put her hand on her
abdomen. She really hoped she didn't get sick.

Piper went to the master bath and brushed her teeth. She was still doing okay...until she lay down for bed.

It came out of nowhere.

One minute, she'd felt fine. The next, her body was busy trying to get rid of everything in her stomach.

When she was between waves of puking, she texted her friends to let them know it was definitely the chicken Alfredo.

Piper was never eating Italian again.

At one point, she fell asleep on her bathroom floor, only to wake up and make a rush for the bowl. She did this over and over all night until the sun started to rise in the sky.

She'd never had food poisoning before, but now, she'd choose death over being this sick. She was sweaty and nauseated, her abdomen hurt from cramping, and she was thirsty as hell. But, every time she tried to drink water, she'd throw it right back up.

It was when she started to cry that she knew she was in a little bit of trouble. Tears were not a good sign, and she really couldn't afford to be dehydrated.

Kayla was right. Piper was doomed.

Nate knocked on Piper's door and then unlocked it. He didn't even realize that he had come in like old times until he shut the door behind him. But he wasn't going back now. He was already in the house.

"Piper," he called out.

It was eight in the morning, and light was streaming

through the windows, but she wasn't in the kitchen or the living room.

He knew she might still be sleeping, but the two of them needed to talk. He'd woken up that morning with texts from Luke and Ethan, telling him that Piper was going to move.

He couldn't let that happen. Not without them talking first.

"Piper," he yelled again, and he walked toward her bedroom. He didn't want to burst into the room and scare the crap out of her.

"Nate?" It was a weak-sounding call coming from her room, and he knew something was wrong.

He burst into the room. "Piper?"

"In here," she croaked from the bathroom.

He rounded the corner and stopped in his tracks. She looked like death. She was lying on her back on the floor of her bathroom. She was as white as the wall next to her, and her hair was matted to her head.

He got down on his knees beside her. "What's wrong?"

"I'm dying."

He felt like he couldn't breathe. "What?"

She tried to smile. "Not really. I just feel like I am."

Her revelation calmed him some.

"What's wrong?" he asked again.

"Food poisoning."

"Oh, babe." He'd been there. It sucked.

"Can you take me to the hospital?"

And he was back in panic mode. "Shit. Why?"

"I can't explain now. I'm dehydrated, and I need fluids. I

throw up every time I try to drink water. Can you take me? Please?"

He pushed her sweaty hair out of her face. "Of course, Piper."

"Thank you." She held up her hand. "Can you help me up?"

"Fuck that." He put his arms underneath her back and under her legs. "I'm not letting you walk."

He knew it was because she didn't feel well, but his heart warmed when she put her arms around his neck and her head on his shoulder.

She still trusted him.

Maybe his dad was right.

CHAPTER FORTY-FOUR

N ate helped Piper walk into the emergency room. She'd refused to let him carry her. While she appreciated him carrying her to his truck, apparently, she had too much pride to let him do the same once they got to the hospital.

Since it was Sunday morning, the ER wasn't terribly busy, but they still had to wait. They sat down in the waiting room, and Nate encouraged her to rest her head in his lap. On the other side of him, he set the bucket she had grabbed from her house in case she didn't make it to the bathroom.

She had no idea why he'd shown up at her house, but she was incredibly grateful he had. He hadn't hesitated when she said she needed help. It was almost as if their fight had never happened. Unfortunately, it had.

She'd worry about that later. Right now, she was going to appreciate his caring and warmth. She appreciated it so much that she dozed off.

"Piper?" a male voice called out in the room.

She slowly sat up. "Right here."

Nate helped her stand, and they walked back behind the double doors.

"We're going to head to the third door on the right," the man said.

Once in the room, she immediately lay down on the bed and clutched her bucket.

"I'm Henry, and I'm your nurse today. And I'm just going to ask you a few questions."

Piper was a little disappointed her nurse was a male. She needed to tell him something, and it would have been easier had he been a woman.

As the nurse asked her questions, she glanced at Nate several times. She really needed to find a way to get him to leave the room for a minute or two. Yet she didn't have a good excuse to get rid of him.

Henry was in the middle of his questions when the door opened.

"Piper, if you wanted to see me, you could have done it for free. You didn't have to pay for an ER visit."

Piper groaned into her pillow. Of course her doctor was going to be Luke. She should have insisted Nate drive her to another hospital.

"Nate," Luke said, shocked. "I didn't expect you to be here." He looked at Piper. "I'm glad you are though." He grabbed on to both ends of his stethoscope around his neck. "So, you're here because you think you have food poisoning."

"Yes."

"Yeah, I heard Rachel got sick."

"Another girl we went out to eat with did, too."

"That means we can pretty much rule out the stomach flu. Not that it matters much. We treat them both the same."

Henry walked back into the room, carrying an IV bag. Piper hadn't even seen him leave.

While the nurse started the IV, Luke continued to ask questions, "So, you've been throwing up?"

"Like you wouldn't believe."

Luke chuckled. "That's how it works, unfortunately. And you're worried about being dehydrated?"

"Yes." Piper looked at Nate. She wanted to tell Luke why she was so concerned, but she couldn't with Nate right there.

Luke went over to the computer and clicked on a couple of things. He didn't say anything while he read whatever was on the screen.

The nurse finished up Piper's IV and left the room.

"Have you had any diarrhea?" Luke asked her.

She felt her eyes get big. She didn't want to answer that. Not in front of Nate and not to Elise's husband.

Luke looked at her face and then at Nate.

"Hey, man, can you give me a couple of minutes alone with my patient?"

Nate didn't answer, but she could see he didn't want to.

"I just need to ask her a few questions, and then you can come back in," Luke reassured Nate.

"Okay." Nate stood. "I'll be in the waiting room if you need me," he told Piper.

"Thank you."

Nate left the room, and Luke pulled up the stool from under the counter and sat next to her.

"He's gone. You can tell me."

"No, I can't."

Luke laughed. "Piper, I'm a doctor. I've heard things way worse than diarrhea."

"Fine. Yes, I've had some. But it's mostly been throwing up. And I haven't...gone to the bathroom for a couple of hours now."

"Have you urinated at all?"

"Not since last night."

"It's a good thing you came in. Dehydration's nothing to mess with."

"Thank you. I felt silly for coming in, but I was worried." She looked down and put a hand on her stomach.

"Does Nate know about the baby?"

Piper whipped her head up. "How did you know?"

Luke raised his brow. "Because I can read."

She was confused.

"It's in your chart."

"Oh." *Duh.* "Um...no, I haven't told Nate yet." She met Luke's eyes. "You can't tell him either."

When she'd found out she was pregnant on the drive home from her lunch with Nate, who said he didn't want to be friends, her first thought was how she was ever going to tell him. She hadn't figured that part out yet.

He held up his hands. "I wouldn't dream of it. Besides, you're my patient. I can't say anything to anyone without your permission."

That was a relief.

"But you are going to tell him, right? I'm sure he's bound to notice sooner or later."

"No kidding. Yes, I'm going to tell him. I just haven't

figured out how. Things haven't been great between us lately, as I'm sure you know."

"Oh, I know. Nate's been miserable."

She didn't want Nate to feel bad, but hearing Luke say that flooded her with hope, even with Vanessa in the picture again. "He has?"

Luke looked at her like she was foolish. "Of course, Piper. You have to know he's crazy about you."

"Well, he did say he loved me. But then he turned around and told me he just wanted to be friends."

Luke looked at her with sympathy. "That's because that's what he thought you wanted."

"I really screwed up." She wished she had never yelled at him and said those mean things to him at the wedding.

Luke grabbed her hand. "The good news is, it's fixable. Nate might act tough and pretend like he doesn't care about relationships and such, but deep down, he just wants to be loved."

"Yeah, I know." And she had used that information against him in their fight.

"Now, if you tell him I said any of this, I will call you a liar and tell him I gave you drugs and you were delusional."

Piper laughed. "I have no idea what you're talking about."

Luke let go of her hand and winked. "That's what I'm talking about." He stood. "Oh, did my wife know that you were pregnant?"

Piper shook her head. "I haven't told anyone. Just you and my OB/GYN know. I thought Nate deserved to find out before anyone."

He nodded his head. "That explains it."

"Explains what?"

"Why she didn't say anything to me. I can't imagine her keeping something that big a secret."

"Didn't you two date behind everyone's backs?"

"Yeah. But that didn't involve a baby."

Luke had a point.

"I suppose."

"I'm going to tell Nate he can come back in. We're going to give you two bags of saline because we want you nice and hydrated for that baby and some antinausea meds, and then we'll let you go home. Sound good?"

"Yes."

"I'll come back and check on you in a while."

"Thanks, Luke."

"You're welcome."

Nate came back in a minute later. "Are you doing okay?"

"Yes."

"What did Luke want to talk to you about?" He waved his hands in front of him. "Never mind. None of my business."

Piper laughed. "Just some medical questions. Some embarrassing questions."

Nate looked relieved. "Good. I was worried."

She held out her hand, and he took it. "Thank you for caring."

"Always."

CHAPTER FORTY-FIVE

Nate decided to take Piper to his house. He would have gone to her house to take care of her, but he had stuff he had to do at home. Thankfully, she didn't protest.

He helped her inside and insisted she sleep in his bedroom. It seemed a little weird since they weren't together anymore, but he felt better with her being there, and she didn't object once.

He pulled the covers over her, tucking her in, when Fred walked into the room.

"Fred!" She pulled her hand out from under the comforter and patted the bed. "Come here, buddy."

Fred meowed and jumped onto the bed. He made a circle next to Piper and lay down.

She rolled onto her side and petted him. "I missed you, Fred."

Fred meowed his appreciation.

"You missed Fred? You must really be sick."

Piper laughed. "I missed you more." She scratched Fred's ears. "But who wouldn't miss the two of you, right, Fred?"

A little in shock from her admission, he cleared his throat. "I'm going to let you sleep. Your phone is on the nightstand. If you need anything, call me. I'll be here all day, but I might be outside or in the basement."

"Okay." She pulled the covers back up.

Nate quietly left the room and silently shut the door, leaving it open just a crack for Fred.

Several hours later, Piper woke up, feeling much better. She wasn't back to being one hundred percent, but sleeping in a bed versus the bathroom floor, uninterrupted, had done her body some good.

Funny how she'd managed to avoid morning sickness, only to get food poisoning.

Piper got out of bed, taking her time and going slow, afraid her stomach would notice she was up and moving and revolt.

She went to use the bathroom, relieved that she was peeing again, but then did a double take when she looked in the mirror.

Yikes.

She looked awful. She needed a shower.

The thought of being clean after last night was almost orgasmic.

She went to Nate's room and approached his dresser. Before their breakup, she'd had a drawer at his house.

Would her stuff still be in there, or would he have put everything in a box in the basement? Or worse, the garbage?

She pulled the drawer open, and there her clothes were.

She breathed a sigh of relief.

He hadn't gotten rid of her stuff.

She grabbed a T-shirt and yoga pants and headed for the shower. Once she was out, she opened her drawer in the bathroom. Her detangler, pick, extra makeup, and other stuff were in there, too. Another good sign.

She got dressed, combed out her hair, and went in search of Nate. She found him cleaning out his garage, a broom in his hand.

"Hey." He stopped sweeping. "Are you doing okay?"

"Yeah. I'm better now. Not all better. But better."

He moved the broom back and forth, almost playing with it. "That's good." He looked so forlorn.

"Are you sure?"

He shrugged. "I admit, I don't want you to leave."

She didn't want to leave either.

She pointed her thumb behind her. "Do you mind if we sit and talk for a minute?"

"Sure." He set the broom against the wall. "Let's go in the backyard."

She followed Nate outside, and they sat in his lounge chairs. His backyard faced the west, so it was nice and cool back there.

"So, what do you want to talk about?"

"I want to be completely honest with you."

He looked confused. "You haven't been in the past?"

She shook her head. "Wrong choice of words. I want to lay it all out for you and hold nothing back."

"Okay."

"And I'm hoping you will do the same with me. Although I won't hold it against you if you don't."

He nodded. "Okay."

It wasn't a no, but it wasn't a yes. But she suspected that Nate was waiting to see what she had to say.

She took a deep breath. *Here goes nothing.*

"I know I already apologized to you about what I'd said at my mom's wedding, but, Nate, you have no idea how horrible I feel. Immediately after I said it, I regretted it. I was just so confused, and my in-laws made me feel so guilty." She blushed at her next confession. "And this is probably going to sound silly, but sometimes, I ask Jordan to give me signs about what I should do. I had just been to visit him at his grave, and I'd asked him to help me out. When his parents came to talk to me, I thought that was his sign, and he was telling me not to be with you."

"I kind of understand. My dad talked to me about what it was like for him when my mother died."

"Wow. Really?"

Nate chuckled. "Really."

She was so happy Nate was connecting with his father.

"I don't know if this helps, but if I didn't care about you or want to be with you, it would have been easy to walk away." She looked Nate in the eyes. "But I realized I loved you, and that was what made me so distraught that night. I wanted to be with you, but a part of me felt like it was wrong."

"Because you felt like you were being unfaithful."

She was surprised by his statement. "Yes. That is a simple way of putting it. But, after I calmed down, two things occurred to me."

Nate swallowed. "What would those be?"

"I realized Jordan would *never* send his parents to deliver a message. And I know that there wasn't—*isn't* anything wrong with being with you because I love you. Some people only find love once in their lives. Do you know how lucky I am to find it twice?" It was a rhetorical question, so she kept talking, "I might be wrong, but that day we met for lunch, you told me that we would just be friends, and I'm guessing that's because you thought it was what I wanted. Or you were protecting yourself. Or both."

Nate nodded.

"But it's not what I want, Nate. I want to be with you. I love you." She looked away from him. "I don't expect you to tell me you love me, too. I know you've already moved on to someone else."

"No, I haven't."

Piper swung her head up. "You haven't?"

"No. I don't even know who you're talking about."

"Vanessa."

"Vanessa? What about her?"

"Um..." She'd told him she'd be honest. "I might have seen the text she sent you at the restaurant. It sounded like you had plans that night. She said she missed a certain part of your anatomy."

Nate laughed.

Piper didn't see the humor.

"I haven't even seen Vanessa for over a month. She heard from Ty that we were having trouble, and she thought she could hook up with me again. I immediately shut her down."

Piper couldn't stop the grin from forming on her face. "Really?"

"Yes. I told her my heart belonged to you."

"It does?"

"Yes, Piper, it does." He grabbed her hand and linked their fingers. "You were right about our lunch. I was trying to give you what I thought you wanted from me. I never wanted to be just friends. And I'm sorry about our fight, too. I knew something had happened, or you would have never gone outside to think. I shouldn't have pushed you. Instead, I should have listened to you when you needed someone to talk to."

Piper got up from her seat and went to sit on Nate's lap.

"I smell," he warned her. "I've been working all afternoon."

"I don't care," she said as she cuddled into him and breathed him in. "I love the way you smell."

He rubbed his hand along her leg. "So, about that Jordan thing. The signs. Did you ever get one?"

"Oh, *yeah.*"

"You did. What was it?"

She lifted her head and looked at him. "I'm pregnant."

CHAPTER FORTY-SIX

There was noise coming from Nate's house, and seconds later, Luke and Elise walked through the sliding glass doors.

"Hey, guys," Elise said. "We brought food." She set the paper bags on the patio table and opened them. "Chinese food and chicken noodle soup for you, Piper."

Piper stood from Nate's lap. "Thank you."

"Don't thank me. It's what the doctor ordered." She pointed to her husband. She looked behind Piper. "What's up with him?"

Piper looked behind her. Nate was still sitting in his chair, staring off into space.

"Nate?"

Nate seemed to come back to reality. He looked at the three of them, got up from his seat, grabbed Piper by the hand, and said, "I need to talk to Piper alone. Give us a minute."

He pulled her inside and locked the sliding glass door

before leading her into the living room where Luke and Elise couldn't see them.

"You're pregnant?"

She gave him a big, fake, cheesy grin and held out her hands. "Surprise."

"When did you find out?"

"After our lunch."

"Oh, Piper," he said and pulled her into his arms. "I'm sorry."

She leaned back and looked at him. "It was a shock to the system, but I had actually gone to the doctor because I was worried something was wrong. When I hadn't gotten my period, like after Jordan died, I'd thought something would stop me from having kids."

He stared down at her belly. "I can't believe it."

"Me either. Are you mad?"

He looked up at her face. "Hell no." He smiled and kissed her. "In fact, if those two weren't in the backyard, I would show you just how *not* mad I am."

Piper kissed him again and put her hand on his thick erection. She squeezed him and said, "I don't care if they're out there. I want you inside me."

Nate took her mouth again and walked her backward until her butt hit the couch. He broke the kiss and asked, "You sure?"

"Oh, yeah."

He grinned and spun her around. "Bend over."

She did, so he pulled down her pants to mid-thigh.

"God, I want to touch you, but that will have to wait until later." He paused. "Shit, I don't have a condom."

"You don't need one."

"Oh, yeah."

She heard his clothes rustle, and then, with one hard push, he was inside her.

She clutched the back of his neck. "Oh God, that feels so good." She hadn't had an orgasm in over three weeks. She was overdue.

Nate groaned and thrust into her. Because her pants kept her legs together, he felt even bigger inside her than normal. He hit her G-spot over and over again, and she knew she wasn't going to last long. And she knew it was going to be messy.

With the last of her stable senses, she asked, "That pile of laundry in front of me, is it clean?"

"Yes."

"Oh, thank God." She let go of his neck and grabbed a towel. She shoved it between her legs just in time because she exploded. Everywhere. She dug her nails into the couch cushion and rode the wave of her climax.

Nate grabbed her hips and slammed into her a couple of more times. He held her ass to his pelvis.

"Damn, I can feel you throbbing around me. That must have been one hell of an orgasm." He slowly pulled out of her.

She used the towel to clean herself up and turned around. "That's what happens when you don't orgasm for three weeks."

"I suppose."

She studied his face. "So, you're telling me that you haven't gone three weeks without coming?"

"Give me the towel. I'll put it in the laundry."

She handed it over.

"I'm a guy. Of course, I haven't gone three weeks without coming," he said like she was crazy.

He went to the basement where the washing machine was and came back a minute later.

"So, you're telling me you jerked off?" she asked out of curiosity.

"Yep." When he reached her, he cupped her cheeks. "If it helps, I thought of you every time."

She grinned. "I suppose it does. Not that I would ever deny you self-gratification."

Nate laughed. "Thanks. I think." He moved down her body, kneeling in front of her, and put his ear to her belly. "I can't believe our baby is in there."

She ran her hand over his bald head. "Me either. Most days, I don't feel like I am even pregnant."

There was a rattle as someone tried to open the door.

"We'd better go back out there." Nate unlocked and opened it. "We're coming; we're coming."

Piper walked past him and said in a low voice, "Technically, we already did."

Nate laughed at her lame joke.

The four of them sat around the table, and Piper slowly ate her soup. She didn't want her stomach to rebel by eating too fast.

"Is everything okay between you two?" Elise asked.

"Yes. We made up," Piper answered.

"Woohoo!"

"And, right before you got here, I told Nate he was going to be a father."

Elise set her fork down. "Shut up." She looked at Luke. "Can you believe it?"

Luke shoved some food in his mouth with his chopsticks. "Yep."

Elise's shoulders dropped. "You already knew, didn't you?"

That caught Nate's attention, and he looked at his friend.

"I can't say anything," Luke said.

Piper helped him out. "Yes, Luke knew. He was my doctor this morning, so it was kind of hard for him not to know."

"I can't believe you didn't tell me."

"Elise, you know I can't. I could get fired. Or sued."

"I wouldn't have told anyone."

Luke just looked at her.

"I wouldn't have," she insisted. "We did date for over a month without anyone knowing, except Nate because you couldn't keep a secret."

Piper lightly smacked Elise in the arm. "That's what I told Luke this morning."

"Thanks for sticking up for me."

Luke rolled his eyes. "Elise, when it comes to one-half of our livelihood, I'm not risking anything." He nodded toward her abdomen. "That baby isn't going to pay for itself."

"Fine, you're right," she reluctantly agreed.

"I'm just glad Nate came over this morning. I don't know if I would have made it to the ER on my own." That

319

reminded her. She looked at Nate. "Why did you come over this morning out of the blue?"

Nate swallowed a bite of food. "To talk to you. Luke and Ethan both sent me texts that you were going to move, and I panicked."

Luke's brows furrowed. "I didn't text you."

Nate looked at his friend. "Yeah, you did."

Luke pulled up his phone while Piper noticed Elise was being very quiet. He started reading from the screen. "*You need to go talk to Piper.* Three exclamation points? *She is planning to move.* Four exclamation points?" He put the phone down and looked at his wife. "When have I ever used an excessive amount of exclamation points?"

Elise shrugged. "I don't know how you two talk to each other."

"If you had scrolled up and read a few messages, you would have known that guys don't talk like that."

Elise balked. "I can't violate your privacy like that."

Luke raised his brow. "Yet you can sneak into my phone and message Nate, pretending to be me."

Elise raised her chin. "It was an emergency. They needed to get back together."

Luke shook his head. "Elise, what am I going to do with you?"

Elise grinned. "Love me."

Piper suddenly remembered something from the night before. "Is that why you and Kayla were whispering in the corner?" she asked Elise.

Elise shrugged. "I figured, if all of us had misunderstood your moving houses to moving away, then Nate would, too."

"Sneaky," Piper said with a grin.

"I thought so."

"So, you weren't planning to move away?" Nate asked.

Piper shook her head. "No. I was just thinking of selling the house."

Nate looked crushed. "Why?"

"Because it reminded me too much of you."

Nate smiled sweetly at her.

"Plus, my backyard is a mess."

"Don't worry, babe; I've got that handled."

CHAPTER FORTY-SEVEN

Piper carried two cups of coffee outside to where Nate was sitting in her finished backyard.

He'd been working overtime to get the project done, and with the help of his dad and some volunteers, they'd finished.

It was beautiful and more than she could have ever imagined. Last night, they'd had a deck-warming party instead of a housewarming party. It had been a great time, and they'd stayed up late, so she had been surprised to wake up in bed alone.

She found him sitting outside. He hadn't even made coffee, and she had to wonder how long he'd been sitting out there.

She knew he'd had fun last night, yet something was off with him.

"Hey," she said as she came up behind him.

He looked over his shoulder. "Oh. Hey."

"Here." She held out one of the mugs.

"Thank you," he said as he took it from her and drank.

She sat next to him. "Whatcha doing out here?"

"Thinking, I guess." Nate looked down at his hand, and Piper's gaze followed.

Is that a...

"Is that a ring?"

He flipped the top open, and a beautiful solitaire diamond lay inside. "Yes."

"Is that—is that for me?"

"Yes. I wanted to give it to you last night in front of everyone, but..."

"But what?" It was obvious something was bothering him.

"I need to tell you something first."

Piper put a hand on Nate's arm. "You know you can talk to me about anything."

He smiled ruefully at her. "Thank you."

"Now, tell me what is bothering you."

Nate set the ring box on the arm of his chair and stared at it. "It's my fault that Jordan died."

"What? That's ridiculous."

He met her eyes. "It's not ridiculous. It's true. I was the reason that Jordan didn't come home after work. It was my idea to go have a beer. I was the one who let him drive. If I had never asked him to go out after work, he would have been home, safe. With you." He rubbed his hands against his jeans. He hadn't realized they were so sweaty.

"What do you remember about the accident?"

What does she mean by that?

"We were driving home when we hit someone, knocking Jordan's car into the middle of the intersection. That was when someone else hit us." He still didn't understand how the third car hadn't seen the accident ahead and hadn't slowed down before coming upon them.

"When did you learn all this?"

"When I was in the hospital. Although, to be honest, I don't remember much about the conversation. I was on pain meds, and I had a concussion."

"And no one talked to you about it later?"

"No. I think everyone was afraid to bring it up much." He looked at Piper. "How are you not mad at me?"

She cupped his cheek. "Oh, Nate. You are too hard on yourself."

"I don't know about that."

"Well, as someone who loves you, I do."

He smiled at her despite everything they were talking about.

She dropped her hand and took a sip of her coffee. She was allowed only one a day, and she made sure to get the cup every day.

"How often do you think you and Jordan went for drinks after work?"

He shrugged. He honestly didn't know the number.

"At least several times a month. There was nothing special about that day. You didn't force Jordan to do anything he didn't want to do. He was a big boy. He could have told you no. He wanted to go with you that day. And Jordan was responsible for his own drinking. You were not his father."

Her words made him feel a little better.

"Also, you have been misinformed about the accident, and I feel bad that we never talked about it. I suppose it was a topic that made us both uncomfortable."

"Misinformed?"

"The accident was not your fault. The accident was not Jordan's fault. The person who hit you was a guy who was speeding and trying to get away from his girlfriend. The second person who hit you was the girlfriend."

"How did I not know this?"

Piper tilted her head. "You knew she got sentenced with reckless driving, right?"

Nate nodded. "Yeah, I was kept updated about that. I knew she was charged and sentenced in court. But no one ever talked about the specifics of the case with me."

"It's probably because they already knew."

"Although hearing the boyfriend died makes much more sense now. I always thought he was in the car with her." He shook his head. "I feel so stupid."

Piper grabbed his hand. "Hey, no, don't feel stupid. You were in a major accident. You were injured. It's not your fault that you don't remember everything."

"I feel like I've been in the dark for so long." He looked at Piper. "What about Jordan? He had a few beers."

She shook her head and smiled. "He was under the legal limit. He did nothing illegal. It was simply *the wrong place, wrong time* sort of thing."

He squeezed her hand. "I'll probably always feel a little responsible, you know."

"I know, baby. But that's why we need each other. To keep each other's guilt at bay."

"That, and because we love each other."

"Definitely because we love each other." She grinned. "So, does that mean I get the ring now?"

Nate laughed. "Nope. We have to wait for the next big party."

Her mouth dropped open. "But we don't have any parties." She narrowed her eyes. "You're just messing with me."

"Of course I am." Nate slid off his chair and got down on one knee. He grabbed the ring box and flipped it open to face her. "Piper Donovan Stevens, will you do me the honor of marrying me?"

She threw her arms around his neck. "Yes."

EPILOGUE

SEVERAL YEARS LATER

Piper stared at the stick in her hand and sighed. She looked up to the ceiling and said, "Okay, Jordan, you can stop sending signs. We get it already."

She walked out of the master bathroom, paused to pick up baby Luka from his bassinet, and went into the kitchen.

Nate was leaning over with an elbow on the counter, trying to convince their one-and-a-half-year-old to eat her vegetables. "Come on, Soph. Please eat for Daddy."

Sophia laughed and shook her head.

Nate glanced up at Piper and straightened. "What's wrong?" He could read her face too well.

She was about to tell him when she heard what sounded like a cat dying from the living room. *Not again.*

She quickly gave Nate the baby and the stick and marched into the living room.

"Wyatt Jordan, how many times has Mommy told you

not to climb on the kitty like that?" She leaned over and pried the three-year-old's thirty-five-pound body off the cat. "Fred doesn't like it when you smother him."

"But, Mommy, I love the kitty cat." Wyatt stuck out his lower lip.

"I know, honey. You just have to love the kitty gently."

Fred walked behind Wyatt and gave Piper the stink eye.

Piper pointed a finger at him. "You're the one who's always begging for love. Don't look at me because it's not exactly what you wanted. Be careful what you wish for, Fred."

Fred turned his back on her and walked out of the room, and Wyatt's crystal-blue eyes lit up as he ran after the cat.

Whatever. Piper didn't have the energy to chase after him.

She flopped back onto the carpet and closed her eyes. All she needed was five minutes.

"You're pregnant again?"

She opened her lids to see Nate standing over her with Luka on one hip and the positive test in his other hand.

"Yep."

"But-but-but I had a vasectomy."

After their third baby, they'd decided someone needed to get fixed, and Nate had volunteered.

"Yeah, well, remember our date night?"

Nate grinned at the memory of the two of them having sex in the back of their minivan. They didn't often get out of the house at the same time, and they'd gotten a little overly excited about being alone together.

Nate's grin fell when he realized what the backseat had led to. "Ah, hell."

"Yeah. I guess that's what happens when you don't wait the recommended time after a vasectomy before having unprotected sex." She sat up and held her arms out. "Give me the baby."

Nate set their six-month-old in her arms and went back to the kitchen.

Luka Nathaniel had come two weeks early while Elise and Luke were at their house. Not only had he been early, but he'd also come super fast. So fast, Luke had had to deliver him in their kitchen.

Piper was still embarrassed that her husband's best friend had seen her vajayjay. When Luke had tried to reassure her that hers wasn't special, it was just one vagina in a long list of vaginas he'd seen, he'd earned two punches to his arms. One was from his wife for saying he'd seen a long list of vaginas, for which he had to remind her he was a doctor. The other was from his best friend, for saying his wife's vagina wasn't special.

Poor Luke.

Despite that, Piper and Nate had decided to name that baby after Luke. To avoid confusion, they had decided on the name Luka.

"Luka, you were supposed to be the last baby. Why didn't you try to stop Mommy and Daddy?"

Luka laughed, his green eyes scrunching up, as he swung his chubby arms up and down. Piper ran her hand over his downy, dark hair. It was still soft, unlike Wyatt's, which was as coarse as a horse's mane but the same color as his brother's.

329

Nate returned with Sophia. She had brown hair, too, but not as dark as the boys, and she'd also gotten Nate's blue eyes. Blue eyes she used to manipulate her father into doing her bidding.

Nate had really wanted to name their daughter after his mom and grandmother. At first, Piper had hesitated at agreeing to the two names ending in A, but after a while, it had grown on her, and Sophia Maria was named.

Sophia clapped her hands and went after one of her favorite toys.

Luka squirmed in Piper's arms, so she set him down. He crawled over to his sister and sat next to her, but she pushed him away.

"Sophia, you need to be nice to Luka," Piper told her.

As usual, she ignored her mother.

A yowl came from down the hall, and Nate sighed. "I'll go get him." He came back, carrying Wyatt upside down over his shoulder.

Their oldest child was laughing. "Daddy, you're so funny."

Nate set Wyatt down. "At least someone thinks I'm funny in this house. Your mommy isn't laughing at me right now."

Wyatt came over and hugged Piper.

"Hey, buddy."

Wyatt stepped back. "Mommy, Daddy's funny."

"I know," Piper agreed because, if she didn't, he would just keep saying it until she gave in. "Why don't you go play with your sister?"

"Okay," Wyatt said and walked to the pile of toys that took up most of their living room.

Nate sat down next to her and pulled her close. "So, do you think it'll be a boy or a girl?"

"A girl. I've had morning sickness all week." Piper hadn't been sick with either of the boys, but Sophia had caused her to throw up all the way into her second trimester.

"Another girl. That's good for Sophia. We'd better start thinking of names."

"We don't have anyone left. You, your mom, your grandma, my dad, Jordan."

"There's you," Nate volunteered.

"Me?"

"Yeah. We can name the baby something Piper."

"Hmm." She hadn't thought about naming any of her kids after herself. "That's not a bad idea. But we still need a first name. And, despite my mother's suggestion on every kid we have, I'm not naming the baby Karen."

"Yeah, I understand. I really hope it's a girl, so my dad won't get his expectations up."

While Nate and his dad had come a long way, becoming closer and spending more time together, the little boy in Nate would probably never fully forgive his father. She urged him to go to counseling to talk about his dad—it'd helped her deal with Jordan's death and her new relationship with Nate—but he hadn't done so yet.

"Yeah, he looked crushed when we announced Luka's name."

"What were your grandma's names?" Nate asked.

"My dad's mom was Ida."

Nate wrinkled his nose.

"Yeah, I don't like it either. Plus, I didn't know her well. She died when I was about Wyatt's age. My mom's mom was Elizabeth though."

"Elizabeth Piper." Nate nodded. "It has a nice ring to it."

"It does." Piper looked down and rubbed her stomach. "Elizabeth Piper."

"I'm kind of excited."

Piper questioningly looked up at Nate.

"We're going to have another baby."

She smiled. "I was in shock, but I'm kind of excited now, too. But four kids under five...we're going to be so busy."

Nate kissed the top of her head. "Yeah, we will. Did you tell Jordan to stop sending us messages already?"

Piper laughed. "I *did*."

"Good. But, just in case, you're getting your tubes tied, right?"

"Oh, yeah."

IT'S COMPLICATED SAMPLE
PROLOGUE

Tiana Hall hadn't planned on flirting with her brother's groomsman. After all, it was a bit cliché for a bridesmaid to hook up with another member of the wedding party.

But there was something about Ty that was hard to resist. Maybe it was because she had a thing for older men. Maybe it was because she hadn't had sex in a long time. Maybe it was because she would end up having too much to drink at the reception. Or maybe it was because, sometimes, a woman simply needed a long fuck after a long night. Either way, Tiana had a feeling that before the evening ended, she was going to be coming all over Ty Morgan's dick.

Tiana, the groom's sister, moved into place at the end of the processional next to Ty, her brother's friend.

Her soon-to-be sister-in-law, Piper, was in the front with her mom. Piper's father had passed away, so her mother was giving her away. Then, it was Piper's cousin, Cindy, the maid of honor, who was walking down the aisle with Luke, the groom's best man and best friend.

"Are you ready for this?" Tiana asked Ty.

He sardonically scratched his dark chin. "I don't know. We only walked down the aisle three times last night. What if I accidentally steer right or left?" His deep brown eyes glistened with humor, and Tiana smiled.

She wouldn't have been able to resist returning his grin if she'd wanted to. Ty Morgan was one fine black man. Fine *older* black man. At twenty-four, Tiana always found men in their thirties sexier than guys her own age. Ty was around her brother, Nate's, age, maybe a little older, and Nate was nine years older than her.

"It's a good thing I'll be holding on to your arm," she told him. "I'll make sure you walk in a straight line," she teased him.

"Good." He looked into her eyes. "Maybe you can help me walk in a straight line after the wedding reception, too. I have a feeling your brother's going to fill me with drinks."

Tiana played it cool. "Does this mean you're not going to ditch me at the reception?" she asked casually.

"Of course not."

The music started playing in the chapel and the words, "All rise," could be heard through the double doors.

Ty leaned down closer to her ear. "You are my date after all, right? That's what walking down the aisle together means."

Tiana turned her head, and their faces were inches apart. She sucked in a breath and swallowed. "I don't think that's an official rule." She pointed to the couple in front of them. "Luke is married to someone else."

The corner of Ty's mouth lifted. "Then, let's make it our

rule. You're my date tonight." He held out his arm as the doors to the chapel opened.

She slipped her hand in the crook of his elbow. "You've got yourself a deal."

The wedding was short and beautiful. Her brother looked especially handsome in his tux, and her new sister-in-law looked stunning in her wedding gown. No one could tell that she was five months pregnant even though the two of them weren't keeping it a secret.

They had just finished dinner, and the tables were being cleared away to make room for the dance. Tiana excused herself from the rest of the wedding party and headed for the bar. Piper was sweet, but Tiana didn't know her very well.

"White wine, please," Tiana told the bartender.

"You weren't trying to ditch me, were you?" a deep voice said from behind her.

She looked over her shoulder and tilted her head. "I thought you'd ditched me. You left the table and didn't come back."

"Never," Ty said. "I was waiting for you to finish."

"Waiting for me to finish, huh?" She met his dark eyes and licked her bottom lip. "What a gentleman."

Tiana heard the clink of her glass hitting the bar, so she turned her back to Ty to grab it.

"Whiskey, neat," he said to the bartender. Then, she felt him move closer, and his breath fanned over her ear. "If you play your cards right, you'll find out how many times I let you finish before me."

Tiana's breath got stuck in her throat as the area between her legs practically caught on fire. She composed herself and turned around.

"If *you* play *your* cards right, maybe, just maybe, I'll be the one letting *you* find out if you can get me to finish before you." She took a sip of her wine, gave him a wink, and walked away.

"Challenge accepted," she heard him say behind her.

Tiana grinned all the way to the dance floor.

MEANT TO BE PLAYLIST

1. Aurora – Running With the Wolves
2. Bad Wolves - Zombie
3. Beyoncé - Halo
4. Celine Dion – Ashes
5. Christina Perri – A Thousand Years
6. Clean Bandit (feat. Julia Michaels) – I Miss You
7. Five Finger Death Punch – Gone Away
8. John Legend – All of Me
9. Lacuna Coil – End of Time
10. Lissie – Everywhere I Go
11. Macklemore & Ryan Lewis – Can't Hold us feat. Ray Dalton
12. Nilu – Are You With Me
13. Rag'n'Bone Man - Human
14. Rhianna – S&M
15. Seether w/ Amy Lee - Broken
16. Snow Patrol – Life On Earth
17. The Cranberries – Zombie
18. The Weekend - Call Out My Name
19. will.i.am – This is Love feat. Eva Simons
20. ZAYN feat. Sia – Dusk Till Dawn

Click here to listen to the Meant to Be Playlist on YouTube!

ACKNOWLEDGMENTS

First, we'd like to fellow author Angelina Kerner and her husband, Franklin. He translated Ty's greeting to Piper into proper French.

Thank you to our beta readers. You've been with us a few years now, it's nice to know we have such a great group to go through our books and make them better!

Thank you to our ARC readers, old and new, and all the bloggers who helped spread Nate and Piper's story. You guys are great, and we appreciate everything you do!

Thank you to our editor, Jovana Shirley, for putting in the hard work to make *Meant to Be* the final piece of work it is. You've been with us since the beginning and we don't know what we'd do without you!

Lastly, thank you to all our family members who put up with us when we are hard at work. We are lucky to have such supportive people in our lives. We love you!

ABOUT THE AUTHOR

R.L. Kenderson is two best friends writing under one name.

Renae has always loved reading, and in third grade, she wrote her first poem where she learned she might have a knack for this writing thing. Lara remembers sneaking her grandmother's Harlequin novels when she was probably too young to be reading them, and since then, she knew she wanted to write her own.

When they met in college, they bonded over their love of reading and the TV show *Charmed*. What really spiced up their friendship was when Lara introduced Renae to romance novels. When they discovered their first vampire romance, they knew there would always be a special place in their hearts for paranormal romance. After being unable to find certain storylines and characteristics they wanted to read about in the hundreds of books they consumed, they decided to write their own.

One lives in the Minneapolis-St. Paul area and the other in the Kansas City area where they're a sonographer/stay-at-home mom/wife and pharmacist/mother by day, and together they're a sexy author by night. They communicate through phone, email, and whole lot of messaging.

You can find them at http://www.rlkenderson.com, Facebook, Instagram, TikTok, Twitter, and Goodreads. Join their reader group! Or you can email them at rlkenderson@rlkenderson.com, or sign up for their newsletter. They always love hearing from their readers.